ALSO BY ROBYN HARDING

The Swap
The Party
Her Pretty Face

ROBYN HARDING

the
arrangement

POCKET BOOKS

New York   London   Toronto   Sydney   New Delhi

Pocket Books
An Imprint of Simon & Schuster, Inc.
1230 Avenue of the Americas
New York, NY 10020

This book is a work of fiction. Any references to historical events, real people, or real places are used fictitiously. Other names, characters, places, and events are products of the author's imagination, and any resemblance to actual events or places or persons, living or dead, is entirely coincidental.

This Pocket Books paperback edition November 2021

POCKET and colophon are registered trademarks of Simon & Schuster, Inc.

For information about special discounts for bulk purchases, please contact Simon & Schuster Special Sales at 1-866-506-1949 or business@simonandschuster.com.

The Simon & Schuster Speakers Bureau can bring authors to your live event. For more information or to book an event, contact the Simon & Schuster Speakers Bureau at 1-866-248-3049 or visit our website at www.simonspeakers.com.

Interior design by Jill Putorti

Manufactured in the United States of America

10 9 8 7 6 5 4 3 2 1

ISBN 978-1-9821-7905-2
ISBN 978-1-9821-1051-2 (ebook)

For Ethan

the
arrangement

Prologue

"Daddy?"

Nat's voice on the phone was small and tremulous. She hadn't called her father *daddy* since she was a little girl. Hadn't called him at all since she'd graduated from high school, since she'd moved to New York, since she'd started her new life. Their estrangement was not Nat's fault; her dad had made his indifference clear when he'd abandoned his wife and ten-year-old daughter to start over in Nevada. Their relationship had dwindled to a few irregular e-mails, the occasional Christmas gift, an infrequent fifty-dollar bill tucked into a birthday card. There was a vast distance between Natalie and Andrew Murphy—emotionally and geographically—but she had nowhere else to turn.

"Natalie?" At least he knew it was her. Nat was his only child, as far as she was aware. Of course, her father could have built another family during their years apart, but those children would be babies. Or toddlers, maybe. They would not be calling him, in tears, from a police station. "Hold on a sec," he said.

Her dad was in a bar, or a restaurant, possibly a casino. Through the phone, she could hear jovial voices, the clinking of glasses. Was that the dinging of a slot machine? Andrew Murphy had been living in Vegas for almost twelve years now. She wondered how often he'd thought about the little girl he'd left behind, so bruised and damaged, so shaped by her father's desertion. Nat had refused to be defined by this one incident, to allow it to haunt her. But a psychologist would have a field day with her back-story, especially now. A mental-health professional might even blame Andrew for what his daughter had done. For the crime she had committed.

On her father's end of the phone, a door slammed and the background noise ceased. Her dad was in a bathroom, or a storage closet, or a soundproof office. All she could hear now was the thudding of her own heart.

"It's been a long time," he said, sounding awk-ward, formal. "How are you?"

There was no time for small talk. "I'm in trouble."

"What kind of trouble?"

"I'm at the Chelsea police precinct. In New York. I—I've been arrested."

"Jesus Christ, Nat. For what?"

She opened her mouth, but the words wouldn't come. How could she tell him what she had done? He was a stranger to her, and she to him. But she needed his help, needed his money . . . *if* he had any. Her mom could not afford to help her—that she knew. Her distant father was her only option. And he *had* to rescue her because, in a way, this was all his fault. If her dad had loved her, cared for her, been there for her, Nat would have made different choices.

She pressed her mouth to the phone, kept her voice low in the crowded, frenetic room. The words, when they came, sounded surprisingly calm. Flat even. Oddly devoid of emotion.

"I killed someone," she said.

Four Months Earlier

1
· · · · · ·

The Roommates

The first thing Nat noticed when she awoke was the taste in her mouth: metallic, burnt, chemical. Jesus . . . What had she drunk last night? The pounding in her head answered: too much. She reached for the glass of water sitting on the floor next to her mattress. The tepid liquid soothed her parched throat but made her stomach churn and roll. She flopped back down, willing the nausea to abate. She didn't want to vomit into her overflowing wastebasket. And she didn't want to stumble through the apartment to the tiny bathroom she shared with her two roommates. Her insides were just starting to settle when she noticed Miguel, sprawled on his back, snoring softly beside her.

Shit.

Nat must have been really wasted to have brought

her coworker home. *Again.* She had made a vow not to hook up with Miguel anymore. Not because he wasn't sweet, and funny, and hot—he was. But he was also a little in love with her, and she didn't want that to turn into *a lot* in love with her. They were just twenty-one, both students who worked at the same bar. A relationship with Miguel would be complicated, was bound to get messy. Nat had already been involved in one toxic, twisted, ultimately catastrophic relationship. She wasn't going to do complicated and messy again.

She lay there, for a moment, observing her sleeping partner. Next to Miguel's warm, brown back, Nat's naked body looked fish-belly pale. Her father's Gaelic genes, the dismal winter weather, and her poor diet were to blame. When Nat was properly nourished and getting adequate sunshine, her skin was peaches and cream, in pleasing contrast to her thick dark hair. When she was perpetually bundled in a winter coat, hat, and scarf, subsisting on packaged ramen and frozen pierogies, her pallor became ghostly, her hair a flat, mousy brown. She needed sunshine, citrus fruit, and protein. But Mother Nature, and her bank account, were conspiring against her.

The third thing she noticed that morning—after the toxic taste in her mouth, the pounding in her head, and the bartender in her bed—was the noise from the kitchen. A cupboard door banged aggressively. Pots and pans crashed together as they were dropped into the sink. Her roommates were pissed about something and were relaying it in their usual passive-aggressive manner.

"I'm so fucking over this."

The muffled voice belonged to Mara, an angular, ginger-haired NYU student. She was getting her master's in economics. Or was it political science? Something dry, dull, cerebral—at least to an art student like Nat. Mara was intense and easily irritated and borderline OCD. What normal college student organized her canned goods by expiration date? Cleaned the fridge and sink twice a week with a bleach solution? Carried her toiletries back and forth from her bedroom to the bathroom, because, if left there, they'd be contaminated, with . . . what? Mildew? Urine? Feces?

"You were right," Toni grumbled, loud enough for Nat to hear, "we shouldn't have let an artist move in with us." The jab smarted. Toni and Nat had been friendly when Nat first rented the spare room in the Bushwick apartment, a couple years ago. Unlike Mara, Toni was funny, messy, *normal*. Nat had felt an instant affinity for the girl with the bright smile, dark skin, and thick mass of braided hair. The pair had stayed up late drinking wine on a few occasions, had bonded over their love of salacious reality television and their adulation of Mariah Carey. But they'd grown apart recently. Toni was a fourth-year nursing student now, who kept long and grueling hours. Apparently, she no longer had time for trash TV. Or a sense of humor.

There was another bang, a jar being slammed onto the countertop, and more cursing from one of the roomies. Nat knew she had to get up, had to apologize, had to make things right. The rent for her tiny bedroom in the rundown apartment was

straining her budget, and she was already on unof-
ficial *probation* after breaking Mara's Crock-Pot. A
note had been slipped under her door after she'd
attempted to cook a frozen pot roast and cracked
the ceramic vessel.

*If you can't respect my appliances and use them
as per instructions, I'm going to have to reconsider
your tenancy.*

Mara's name was on the lease, which gave her the
power to choose her roommates. It was obvious she
wanted rid of the messy, hard-partying art student in
the third bedroom. Nat wasn't even sure what she
had done to anger them this time, but she hoped it
wouldn't constitute a second strike. Her Bushwick
home was affordable (just), safe (relatively), and
accessible (forty-two minutes by subway) to the
Manhattan campus of the School of Visual Arts. Nat
had to get out there and kiss some roommate ass.

Ignoring her throbbing head and roiling belly, she
dragged herself out of bed. Miguel didn't stir. How
could he sleep through the ruckus? Nat's yellowing
terry-cloth robe hung from a hook on the door, and
she grabbed it, wrapping the musty garment around
her. She noted then that she was still wearing panties.
Maybe she and Miguel hadn't had sex? She felt disgusted with herself for not remembering. The night's
events were hazy, blurry, jumbled. She'd gone to
her job at Donnelly's bar after her illustration class.
Her lover had slipped her a few shots of vodka to
get her through her waitressing shift. After closing,
they'd shared a bottle of wine, and maybe a few

Paralyzers. Or had they been White Russians? She definitely had to cut back on her drinking.

She stumbled into the kitchen and spotted the offending mess. A couple of pots were stacked in the sink. An open jar of tomato sauce, its contents dripping down the side, sat in a red ring on the table. It came to her in a flash of remembrance: pasta. She and Miguel had been hungry when they got home. Nat had made them rigatoni with jarred marinara. They'd sat at the tiny kitchen table and ate. And then Miguel was touching her, and kissing her, and they'd ended up in bed. Clearly, they had not halted their foreplay to wash the dishes.

"Sorry, guys. I'll clean this up."

Mara whirled around, her ubiquitous bleach spray in hand. "You should have cleaned up last night."

"I know. I screwed up."

Toni, pouring coffee from a French press into a chipped mug, didn't look up. "If you're hungry at four A.M., go to a diner."

Nat remembered Miguel's suggestion to that effect. But she barely had enough money to cover her next tuition installment, and it wasn't looking good for her rent. Even a burger would have broken the budget. Miguel would have paid, she knew, but his finances had to be tight, too. She hadn't wanted to feel beholden to him, so she had offered to cook. And then, they'd ended up in bed.

"Toni and I aren't comfortable with all the guys you've been bringing home," Mara said, attacking the tomato sauce on the table as if she were cleaning up a chemical spill.

Nat felt her cheeks flush, a combination of humiliation and anger. *All* the guys? She could count on one hand the number of men she'd brought home since she'd been living there. Nat was not promiscuous; she was *twenty-one*. And her roommates weren't exactly virgins. Mara had had a fling with one of her TAs just last year. And Toni used to have noisy sex with a hot computer science student, back when she drank wine and watched *The Bachelor*, and laughed, on occasion. Both her roommates needed to lighten up, probably needed to get laid.

Nat kept her voice calm. "I don't bring home many guys."

Toni smirked. "Really? Isn't there a guy in your bed right now?"

"No," Nat lied.

"We heard his voice last night," Mara sniped.

"It's not what you think," Nat retorted. "A friend from work walked me home. Friday nights are crazy at the bar, and we were hungry and exhausted, I made us some pasta and invited him to crash."

It might have been true. She was still wearing her panties, after all.

She watched the other women exchange a look. Was it doubt? Skepticism? Or guilt? Yes, that's what it was. They felt bad for accusing her when they didn't have all the facts. Nat hammered the nail in.

"I'd appreciate not being slut-shamed when I was only helping out a colleague."

"Sorry," mumbled Toni, dunking her lips into her coffee.

Mara kept scrubbing, probably formulating an articulate apology.

That's when Miguel walked into the kitchen—

rumpled from sleep, hungover, handsome. And stark naked.

"Is everything okay out here?" he said, hands inadequately covering his crotch. "I heard banging. . . ."

Nat observed the expression on her roommates' faces. This time, it could not be misconstrued.

Validation. And disapproval.

2

. . . . . .

The Commute

On Monday, Nat took the subway into Manhattan. Outside, it was a brisk February morning, but the press of bodies in the car precipitated a drastic rise in temperature. She unfurled the fuzzy gray scarf from around her neck and lowered the zipper on her thrift-store wool coat. She kept her knitted gloves on. Public transit was crawling with germs.

The L train from Jefferson Street station took her directly into Manhattan, to Third Avenue and Fourteenth Street, just a ten-minute walk from the School of Visual Art's main campus. The train was packed, as was the norm when she had morning classes. Nat was lucky to get a seat, even if she was wedged between an overweight guy who smelled like salami and a kid whose music was so loud she could hear every word of the rap song he was listening to through his headphones.

She kept her eyes on the floor—the big guy next to her precluded her digging her phone out of her coat pocket—her gaze blank. Locals didn't gawk at the colorful cast of characters sharing their morning commute. More than two years in the city, and it still gave her a little thrill to think of herself that way. As a local. A New Yorker. Not many kids from Blaine, Washington, made it all the way to New York City. To Seattle, sure. Some adventurous types might get as far as San Francisco. But Nat had outdone them all.

She was ten the first time she realized she was destined to outgrow her hometown. The community of roughly five thousand people abutting the Canadian border on a briny stretch of the Pacific was quaint, picturesque, comfortable. . . . It had a seedy side, too, a kind of darkness, a toughness peculiar to the region. But it was too provincial, too constricting for an artistic soul; she knew it even then. Her father must have had a similar revelation, because that's when he walked out on Nat and her mom. It had been a difficult marriage, and Andrew Murphy was a hard man to love. He was prone to angry outbursts, long silences, critical diatribes (he would later blame his undiagnosed depression). Nat and her mother had wept when he stormed out, never to return. But it was his rejection, more than his absence, that hurt. It didn't take long for them to realize they were better off without him.

While Nat resented her father's desertion, she also envied it. Her dad had been restless, bored, and unhappy, so he had packed up and left his wife and only child. He'd gone to work as a pit boss in a big flashy casino. Did the glitz of Las Vegas provide the stimulation he'd missed in Blaine? The excitement his wife and young daughter couldn't provide? Nat was angry at him; she hated him. But this didn't stop her fantasizing about a life with him in Sin City.

They would live in a small apartment just off the strip. At night, when her dad worked, she'd wander the neon city, a girl alone under the lights. She'd meet blackjack dealers and showgirls, acrobats and mafiosos. In her fantasies, her dad was a peripheral character. Natalie was effectively an orphan; a debauched Pippi Longstocking.

But Nat was not as selfish as her father. She could not abandon her mom . . . though she needn't have worried about Allana Murphy. The woman was blond and beautiful, only thirty-five when her husband left her. The suitors were at the door as soon as word got out. (The dating pool was small but active in a town that size.) Her mom had a handful of boyfriends over the next couple of years, no one to whom Nat had gotten attached. And then, when Natalie was thirteen, her mom married Derek Heppner. He was a big man, a builder, with a reddish-blond beard that made him look like a Viking. He adored her mother, and had seemed fond of Natalie, at first. But then everything changed, and Nat knew she could leave. Knew she *had* to leave.

Salami-guy got off at Bedford Avenue, his vacated seat quickly taken by a hipster who emanated a distinctly foresty fragrance. Nat was grateful her new neighbor didn't smell like cold cuts, but she may have been allergic to his beard oil. She wrinkled her nose in an effort to stave off a sneeze.

No matter how uncomfortable her commute, how tight her budget, or how lonely she sometimes felt in the giant, anonymous city, Nat never regretted her cross-country move. Living in New York wasn't supposed to be easy. It was hard, but it was worth it. Especially for an artist, like Natalie. She fed off the creativity running rampant through these hallowed streets, drawing inspiration from the artists who came before her. The city nourished her soul, stimulated her mind, filled her entire body with a humming, vibrating, energy.

New York meant *possibility*.

Her life, had she stayed in Blaine, was easy to imagine. She would have gone to a nearby college and studied something practical: accounting, or marketing, maybe. She'd have gotten a job at a bank, or in an office, or at the duty-free store. Her sketching would have been relegated to a hobby until life got too busy and she gave it up all together. She would have married Cole, her handsome high school boyfriend, and had a couple of kids before she was thirty. They would have settled into a small but comfortable home, purchased with a down payment provided by Cole's parents, who owned several fishing boats and a mail company servicing Canadians who wanted to avoid cross-border shipping fees. And then . . . and then what?

Would Cole Doberinsky have been a domineering husband, dictating her clothes, her hobbies, her friends? He was the only child of wealthy parents; he was used to having things his way. When they'd dated, Nat had seen glimmers of a controlling nature. He texted her constantly, required instant responses. He needed to know where she was and who she was with. What she was doing, thinking, feeling . . . But she had never considered him obsessive, had not considered him dangerous.

Until he broke into her house.

She suddenly felt queasy, but it was not motion sickness, not a reaction to the abundance of fragrances wafting around her. It was the memory of Cole and that night, shortly after she'd articulated her plans to leave Blaine, that turned her stomach. He'd been hurt and angry when she ended it. She'd regret this, he'd said. After all, he came from money, a stable home, had been accepted into a nearby business school. Nat was the product of a messy divorce, a low-income upbringing, was heading down a dead-end career path. He'd been mean and condescending. But she could never have predicted what he had done.

Cole had broken a basement window and squeezed himself inside her family's darkened home. He had crept toward Nat's upstairs bedroom (across the hall from her toddler brother and sister; her mom and Derek slept on the main floor). What would have happened if her stepfather hadn't woken up, hadn't intercepted the younger man, hadn't beaten him until he was barely conscious before realizing he knew the culprit? Would Cole have harmed her? Her young half siblings? Himself?

"I just wanted to be close to her. I just wanted to watch her sleep, one last time."

That's what Cole told the cops who arrived that night. Like it was totally harmless, totally *normal*. He was drunk and maudlin and sloppy. The officers seemed to pity him, brushed his actions off as puppy love gone awry. But they hadn't seen the way Cole looked at her as he was placed in the back of the squad car. He hated her. She could see it in his eyes, feel it emanating from him in palpable waves of animosity. Would Cole have placidly watched her slumber? Or would he have grabbed a pillow and held it over her face?

As always, the memory elicited a muddle of emotions in Nat: guilt (she'd endangered her family, her mother's new *perfect* children); fear (was Cole still obsessed? Would he harass her again if only he could find her?); anger. At Cole Doberinsky. And at herself. How had she not seen how needy he was? How unstable? Cole had told her he loved her, that he couldn't live without her, but he'd only wanted to possess her. To keep her down. To hold her back.

They didn't press charges. It would have been scandalous in their small town. Cole's family was wealthy, influential, well-liked. Nat's family could not take them on. And Cole was now "back to his old self," her mother had informed in one of her e-mails. She and her mom didn't talk about the incident; didn't talk much at all, come to that. For a few years, Nat had been the only child of a single mother; more than just a daughter then. She'd been a friend, a confidante, a shoulder to cry on . . . But Derek filled those roles now. Her mom was too busy being a part-time real estate agent, a devoted wife, and mother of two adorable towheaded children, to focus on the daughter from her disastrous first union. Nat had been resentful, at first, but no longer. At twenty-one, she was fine with the long silences punctuated by newsy e-mails (Astrid scored a goal in soccer! Oliver will play a squirrel in the school play!), the obligatory birthday cards containing professional photos of her half siblings frolicking in a hayfield. Her mom's missives were just reminders of the life she'd gladly left behind.

The train eased into the Third Avenue station, and Nat and several fellow passengers moved toward the exit. This was her life now: one small drop in an ocean of people carving out a life in the world's greatest city. Anything could happen in New York. Sure, that anything might be a mugging or a terrorist attack (thanks for pointing that out, *Derek*, moments before she boarded the plane). But the scariest thing that had ever happened to her was as she lay in her own bed, under her parents' roof, in sleepy Blaine, Washington. Nat would take her chances.

It was her high school art teacher who had urged her to apply to the School of Visual Arts. Ms. Nguyen had confidence in Nat's artistic talent. The teacher had helped with her portfolio, had pressured her to fill out a multitude of scholarship applications. (Tuition was *outrageous*, Derek had said. They would not/could not pay.) To Nat's delight, she'd been accepted into the faculty of illustration. (She and Ms. Nguyen considered it the most practical of the streams. Still, *highly impractical*, according to her stepfather.) She'd received a school bursary and a partial scholarship that would cover a significant chunk of her tuition. She'd deferred acceptance for a year to work full-time at a Greek restaurant to pay the rest. In New York, her part-time bar job covered rent with a little (not enough) left over for food. She didn't need anyone to support her. Financially or emotionally. She was on her own. Completely independent. It was how she wanted it, she told herself. But the truth was . . . she had no choice.

Emerging onto the street, the wind greeted her with an icy slap to the face. She had a short walk straight up Third to the Twenty-Third Street campus. Huddling into her wool coat, she hurried along the avenue, head lowered against the chill blast. With her gloved hands tucked into her pockets, she felt her phone vibrate. Extricating it, she read the text from Miguel.

Hang out tonight?

She removed her gloves then paused, her thumbs hovering over the keyboard. *No thanks*, she should have texted. *This is casual. Friends with benefits. Nothing more.*

But she couldn't deny how nice it would be to go to Miguel's apartment, to curl up beside him on his ratty sofa, and study. Later, they might watch Netflix or a movie. They didn't have to make out, didn't have to end up in bed together. Miguel could be her buddy, her pal, her refuge from the toxicity permeating her apartment. She didn't *need* him, she just . . . enjoyed him. She typed:

kk

Shoving the phone back into her pocket, she hurried to campus.

The Penthouse

Nat had naively envisioned art school as full-time drawing classes, but apparently there was more to creating a marketable artist than studio time. The illustration faculty demanded several credits in the humanities, sciences, and art history. Nat understood that the study of past cultures was valuable in developing her artistic point of view, but that didn't mean she had to like it. As the Western civilization professor droned on about Voltaire, Nat slouched in the tiny desk, her mind fixated on her upcoming bills. She was forecasting her next week's salary and tips and applying them to her current bank balance, when the instructor's nasal voice, appropriate to his nebbish appearance, jarred her from her calculations.

"Don't forget the midterm on Thursday."

"Shit," Nat muttered, as she closed the neglected notebook on her desk. The impending test, combined with her financial shortfall, made her chest constrict. She struggled to take a breath.

"You okay?" It was Ava, a gifted artist, seated across the aisle. The two young women had several classes together and had been study partners on occasion. They were friendly but not friends. Nat had very little time to socialize. And Ava was . . . different. She lacked the edge that most art students had. Her clothes were sexy, designer, *new*—unlike the alternative, secondhand threads worn by most of their peers. Ava's blond hair was expensively cut and highlighted, her skin buffed and lightly tanned. She had long acrylic nails, mink lashes, and microbladed eyebrows. And, she had no visible tattoos or piercings, which made her an art-school anomaly. Nat, with the tiny gem in her nose and only two holes in each ear, was conservative by art-school standards.

Nat smiled at her classmate's concern. "I'm fine. Just a little stressed."

"Me, too." Ava stood, gathering her books and her big YSL satchel. "I consistently zone out in this class. I'm going to have to cram like crazy, if I'm going to pass the midterm."

"Same."

"We could study together," Ava proposed.

Nat had three hours until her next class. "Good idea."

The pair made their way to the library and found it packed. Clearly, they weren't the only students trying to cram more than a month's worth of information into their brains in a matter of days. The women moved to the student center and found it less crowded but exponentially louder. An improv club was holding a rambunctious meeting that made concentration impossible.

"We can go to my place," suggested Ava. "I live in Chelsea. I'll make tea."

As they scurried west across chilly Twenty-Third Street, Nat wondered about her companion's background. The beautiful clothes, the salon hair, the apartment in pricey Chelsea. They all added up to a rich girl. Nat's middle-class upbringing had imbued in her a mistrust and mild resentment toward the wealthy. When her dad lost his accounting job at the manufacturing plant, he'd blamed his boss. *That rich prick was out to get me from day one.* This attitude was subtly reinforced by her mom and Derek, who rarely failed to make a snide comment about anyone who appeared to be financially thriving. *Must be nice*, they'd sniff, whenever a neighbor got a new car or a boat or took a tropical vacation. But this was New York. It ran on money. Wealth was to be admired, not sneered at.

Ava led the way into a tall upmarket apartment building where they were greeted by a weathered doorman who looked more suited to captaining a fishing boat than opening doors in a posh co-op.

"Morning, ladies." His accent was familiar. Brooklyn.

"Hi, Pete," Ava said, as they breezed past.

Inside the mirrored elevator, Ava stabbed the

button marked PH. Nat refrained from gasping, but a penthouse in Chelsea? Even a tiny studio would have been way beyond Nat's budget. How rich was this girl?

Her query was answered the moment they entered Ava's apartment. It wasn't a huge space, except by New York standards, but it was undoubtedly high-end. The unit had an open-plan living room, a designated dining room, and a sleek, modern kitchen. It appeared to have been professionally decorated, but Ava was artistic, stylish, creative. She may have personally chosen the low, slate sofas; the leather-upholstered wing-back chair; the creamy wool carpet with its subtle geometric design. But who had paid for it?

Ava led Nat past the smoked-glass dining table into the kitchen with its modern, top-of-the-line appliances. "Tea?" she asked, reaching for the stainless-steel kettle.

"Yes, please."

As Nat watched her host fill the kettle and place it on the gas range, she thought of her own shabby kitchen and her own stove. It was scuffed and stained, two of the four burners inoperable. When she'd first moved into her run-down apartment in Bushwick, it had seemed quaint, charming, full of character. But now, in her classmate's upscale pad, she realized it was simply a dump.

"Nice place," Nat said, trying to sound casual, or, at least, not awestruck.

"Thanks. I love it here." Ava dropped tea bags into two mugs.

"Do you live here alone?"

"Yep."

"Want a roommate?" Nat was joking, obviously. She barely knew Ava. But if the girl had offered her a space, she would have jumped at it. Nat loved Bushwick—the galleries, the bars, the street art—but she would have said goodbye to her cramped bedroom, her crowded commute, her judgmental roommates, and never looked back.

Ava laughed. "Sorry. It's a one-bedroom."

"Does it have a closet? A bathtub? I can sleep anywhere."

The blonde laughed again in lieu of a response. "Want to see the best part of this place?"

"Let me guess . . . It has a roller coaster? A stable full of ponies?"

"Better."

Ava led her to double glass doors that opened onto a good-size patio. The furniture was stacked and covered for winter, but Nat could envision the enclave with plants, a patio sectional, glowing lanterns. Like the interior, it would be tasteful, classy, a calm oasis from the bustling city below. Ava pointed due east, to the prime view of the Empire State Building.

"It's amazing at night when it's all lit up," Ava said, eyes affixed to the iconic structure. "In the summer, I sit out here with a glass of wine, and I just stare at it. I can't believe I actually live here." She turned to face Nat. "I grew up working-class in the armpit of Ohio."

"Me, too. Except I'm from Washington State."

Their eyes met then and they shared a look of recognition. *There's friendship potential here*, Nat

realized. She had dismissed Ava as *different*, with
her fancy clothes, bags, and lashes. But they were
kindred spirits, in a way. The kettle whistled then,
and they hurried back into the warmth of the apartment.

With their steaming mugs of tea, the women
settled in the living room. The designer couch was
more comfortable than it looked, and Nat sank
into it, sipping her hot drink. Ava, in the leather
wing-back chair, dug her textbooks out of a sleek
backpack and placed them on the black marble coffee table. Nat was about to reach for her own books,
when her eyes fell on a framed etching on the wall.
It was the portrait of a man's long, ruddy face: ugly,
entrancing, powerful.

"Oh my god"—she leaned forward for a better
look—"is that a Lucian Freud?"

Ava glanced toward the artwork. "Yeah . . . It was
a birthday present."

From whom? Nat wanted to ask, but she couldn't.
It would be gauche. She'd taken enough art-history
classes to know that the etching would be worth at
least fifty grand. "It's intense," she said instead.

"I'm not a huge fan, but my friend said it was a
good investment."

Her *friend*?

Nat pasted on a pleasant smile even as her brain
scrambled to piece together the details of Ava's
situation. She came from a working-class family in
Ohio but lived in a pricey Chelsea penthouse. Despite her humble beginnings, Ava clearly had rich
friends. Nat had so many questions—how do you

afford this apartment? Your clothes and bags? Who bought you the Freud? But she couldn't interrogate this girl. She liked her.

"Okay," Ava said, opening her textbook. "Let's talk about Nietzsche."

4

· · · · · ·

Strike Two

Later that night, pressed against Miguel's warm, naked body in his twin bed (*Oops*), Nat's mind returned to Ava's luxurious apartment. Miguel lived in a walk-up studio with mice, crumbling walls, and plumbing that screamed when a neighbor took a shower—entirely appropriate to his student status. As she stared at a mushroom-shaped water stain on her lover's ceiling, she recounted her day's experience.

"I went to study at a friend's apartment in Chelsea today. She lives in an amazing penthouse." Nat described the view of the Empire State Building, the elegant furnishings, the original Freud as a birthday present.

"She must have rich parents."

"No, her parents are working-class."

"Rich boyfriend?"

"She never mentioned one."

"Maybe she's a hooker?"

Nat was defensive. "No way."

"Not like a streetwalker," Miguel clarified. "Like an escort. Or a sugar baby."

Nat propped herself up on an elbow. "Are you serious?"

"It's not uncommon here," Miguel said, sounding sage. He had grown up in the Bronx, had moved to Brooklyn when he started at St. Joseph's College. Unlike Nat, he was a true New Yorker. He'd seen it all and was unfazed.

Of course, Natalie had heard about high-end escorts, about sugar babies—she was from Blaine, not *Mars*. She'd seen reality shows, Instagram feeds, online clips of vapid girls with lip injections, breast implants, and closets full of shoes and bags. These girls were spoiled and materialistic, willing to trade sex for money and toys, trinkets and tropical holidays. They weren't talented art students who crammed for midterm exams. They weren't like Ava.

"She doesn't seem the type."

"I'm not sure there is a *type*, anymore," her worldly partner said. "You'd be surprised how many girls have a sponsor. Desperate times and all that."

Nat suddenly felt claustrophobic in the tiny bed. "I should go."

Miguel pressed himself against her. "Stay."

She should have felt warm and safe and desired, but instead she felt crowded, sweaty, itchy. She wouldn't sleep well in this single bed. And spending the night was too intimate, too much like a relation-

ship, which this wasn't. It was friendship. It was sex.
It was not a romance.

"I can't." She threw the blankets off her and
reached for her underpants on the floor.

"I'll walk you home. It's late."

"I'm fine. It's only a few blocks."

But Miguel was already getting dressed.

They strolled through the darkened streets, past
the row houses, their regal history defaced by paint,
stucco, or vinyl siding. Conversation was light, gos-
sipy, revolving around their colleagues at Donnelly's,
the bar where they both worked. By the time they
reached Nat's building, it was almost 1:00 A.M. They
faced each other at the bottom of the steps for an
awkward moment. The whole friends-with-benefits
scenario got a little confusing when it came time for
a good-night kiss. Leaning in, Nat gave him a quick
peck on the lips that Miguel tried to segue into an
open-mouth kiss. She turned her face away, but he
missed her cue.

"Maybe I could come in?" he tried.

Nat had a double futon. They could sleep comfortably side by side. But no. Way too *coupley* . . .

"Sorry," she said. "My roommates."

"I promise I won't flash them again."

Nat giggled, which Miguel seemed to take as
encouragement. His hands slid under her coat and
encircled her waist. She stepped back.

"Don't."

"Come on," he said, moving toward her. He
found her belt loops and tugged her closer. Something flared inside of her: anger, revulsion. Her mind
flashed back to Cole, his possessiveness, his needi-

ness. She remembered the barrage of texts he would send if she didn't respond to him instantly, the harassing phone calls if he didn't know where she was. She was not ready for another relationship.

"I said no." It came out harsh and angry.

Miguel stepped back, holding his hands up in surrender. "Sorry."

"Just . . . Back off, okay?"

"Jesus, Nat." He shook his head, exasperated. "One minute, you're into me, then the next minute, you want nothing to do with me."

"I told you when we first hooked up: this is casual."

"We've been seeing each other for three months, sleeping together a few times a week. That's not casual. That's a relationship."

A cruel laugh erupted from within her. "That's the *last* thing I want."

She saw the hurt in his warm brown eyes, but his voice was cold and hard. "Fine," he snapped. "I'll leave you alone."

"Perfect."

As she watched him walk away, her anger dissipated. Her rejection had wounded him; she could see it in his slumped posture, in his ambling gait. A twinge of guilt tickled her belly. Miguel was a decent guy, undeserving of her ire. She had enjoyed her time with him. Maybe they could have had something, if she'd wanted a relationship. But she didn't. Not after things with Cole had turned so sick and creepy. And she was not going to be pressured into a romance just because the guy was *nice*.

She entered her darkened apartment, tiptoeing

to her room. The environment was still tense after her roommates had freaked out over Nat's late-night pasta party, had accused her of promiscuity before a naked Miguel had strolled into the kitchen like exhibit A. Nat had kept a low profile since then, avoiding the apartment as much as possible. When she was home, she fastidiously cleaned up her messes, had lightning-fast showers, and ensured no overnight guests. Her roomies may have disliked her, may have looked down their noses at her, but that was not just cause for eviction. As long as Nat kept her head down, they were stuck with her.

The door to her bedroom was shut tight (hiding the chaos from obsessive Mara's judgment). She opened it and slipped inside, picking her way through the mess of clothes, canvases, books, and coffee cups, to the bedside lamp. Flicking it on, she allowed her eyes to adjust to the light. Her bed was unmade, the fitted sheet having popped off one corner, revealing the bare mattress (there was something so crack den about a bare mattress). Amid the tangle of sheets was a cereal bowl, an empty can of Coke, a scattering of pastel crayons. Her private space was an unequivocal disaster, but it was her *private* space. Toni and Mara would not dare to enter it, would never know the squalor in which she lived. That's when she spotted the folded piece of paper propped against her pillow.

No. No way.

Nat had been on her best behavior since the pasta incident. Surely, Mara couldn't write her up for leaving a few dirty dishes on the counter. Or was this about Miguel's naked, prebreakfast appearance? Were they really that offended by it? The guy was gorgeous, with his strong, lean body and smooth brown skin. They should be writing her a thank-you note! But, of course, she knew that this was not. With a sense of foreboding, she grabbed the ragged paper torn from a spiral notebook and opened it. She read the handwritten missive.

Natalie,
  Your share of the electric bill is late. AGAIN. You still owe Toni money for the last two bills, and I covered the internet bill for you last month, too. We are both sick and tired of supporting you. Please pay the money you owe us IMME-DIATELY.
  And consider this strike two.
Mara and Toni

Fuck.

The Test

Students trickled out of the classroom, chatting animatedly about the preceding midterm. The hum was generally positive. The exam had been easier than anticipated; multiple choice, with no trick questions. Even the negative comments were light-hearted.

"I totally blanked!" It was Nat's pal Keltie, her face full of metal rings and studs. "I was like, who is Descartes again?"

Ivan, who bore a striking resemblance to a young George Michael, quipped, "I think I mixed up Martin Luther with Martin Luther King."

Their complaints were expressed with a disingenuous giggle. But Nat stayed mute. She shuffled out behind them, a heavy black lump in the pit of her stomach.

She had studied hard: twice with Ava (once at the penthouse, once in the library); had pulled out her textbook whenever she found a seat on the subway; had reviewed her notes as she hid from her roommates in her mess of a bedroom. But her brain had been short-circuited by the written second warning, by the money she owed for the electric bill, by the rent that was due in a couple of weeks. She couldn't retain information about the fucking Reformation when the specter of homelessness loomed before her.

Ava was waiting for her outside the classroom. "How did it go?" Her cheerful expression relayed her confidence in her performance.

"I failed it," muttered Nat.

"No way. You knew everything at our last study session."

"A lot has happened since then." To her chagrin, Nat's voice shook and her chin crinkled. Damn it. She couldn't fall apart over a stupid exam. It would be weak, pathetic, melodramatic. But it wasn't just the exam. The life she had worked so hard to build was crumbling before her very eyes. (This was obviously the wrong internal monologue to have when trying not to cry.)

Ava reached out and squeezed Nat's upper arm. "It's okay. It's just one midterm."

The touch and sympathy undid her. Tears filled Nat's eyes, threatening to spill over. "It's not just the exam. It—it's everything."

Ava knew enough not to embrace her forlorn friend and risk a complete collapse. Her eyes darted around at their carefree peers. "Let's get out of here," she said. "We can get a drink somewhere."

"It's barely noon," Nat sniveled.

"It's five in Iceland."

Nat chuckled despite her angst. She followed Ava out of the building.

They found a hole-in-the-wall bar—long, narrow, dim, as if to deny the fact that it was daylight outside. Physically, it was not unlike the bar where Nat worked, but Nat's place of employment was fun, vibrant, catering largely to college students and Williamsburg hipsters. This establishment appeared to cater to gloomy, hard-core day-drinkers. As Ava ordered them two pints of beer at the bar, Nat briefly pondered the backstory of the other patrons. Divorce? Unemployment? But her mind quickly returned to her own problems. She was twenty-one years old and embroiled in a financial, academic, and residential crisis. Her self-absorption was only natural.

When Ava returned to their sticky table, Nat dunked her lips into her beer. It was bitter, hoppy, cheap. Ava watched her for a moment, her own beverage ignored.

"What's going on?" she asked.

Nat forced down two more sips of liquid courage before telling her classmate—now her friend, her confidante—everything.

"Shit," Ava murmured. "Can your parents help you out?"

"My mom and stepdad have two little kids and not a lot of money," Nat said, fiddling with a paper coaster. "My dad could be a millionaire, for all I know. But I wouldn't take a dime from him."

"You could take a semester off and work," Ava suggested.

"I'd lose my partial scholarship. And even working full-time I wouldn't make enough to save up tuition and cover my living expenses."

"What about a student loan?"

The concept of incurring a debt that would take years to pay off on an illustrator's salary made Nat's chest tighten. She tried to take a deep breath, but the pressure wouldn't allow it. She was suffocating. She was coming undone. Tears slipped from her eyes, streaking her cheeks. A guttural sob escaped from her throat.

Ava's hand landed lightly on Nat's. "We'll figure something out. There's always a way."

Nat turned her hand over, gripped her friend's fingers. "How do *you* do it?"

Ava gently extricated her hand and took a drink of beer. Her expression was unreadable as she set the heavy glass down on the damp coaster.

"I have friends who support me."

It was rude, invasive, too personal, but the question flew from Nat's lips. "Are you an escort?"

"No," Ava snapped, two spots of color appearing on her fair cheeks. "I'm a sugar baby. It's different."

"Different how?"

Ava leaned in. "Escorts get paid to have sex. I get paid for my *time*."

"Tell me more."

"I go on dates with rich, successful men," Ava said,

her voice low. "I look pretty. I flirt, listen to them talk about their work, their kids, their marathon training, whatever. . . . At the end of the night, they give me three, four, five hundred bucks."

"Just for dinner?"

"Just for a drink. Just for a coffee. It's called a pay-per-meet."

Nat's eyebrows lifted—at the sum, and at the brazenness of the transaction. Even without sex, it sounded tawdry, exploitive, uncomfortably close to prostitution.

Ava read the judgment on Nat's face. "As women, we're expected to give men our attention and our support . . . even our bodies for free. Getting paid for it is empowering."

Nat forced a slight smile, while her mind grappled with the concept.

"If there's chemistry with a daddy, we might set up an *arrangement*," Ava continued. "We discuss everything up front. How often we'll see each other, what we'll do together, how much money he'll give me each month . . ."

It may have been crude to ask, but Nat had to. "How much?"

"It depends." Ava's finger traced a dark, circular watermark on the table. "If I see a man four times a month, I usually get between twenty-five hundred and five grand."

"Wow."

"I won't undersell myself."

Sell myself. The prefix did not change the meaning. Nat leaned in. "And sex?"

"It's like any relationship. If I'm into the guy, I'll sleep with him. If I'm not, I don't."

Nat was almost afraid to ask. "How old are these men?"

"It varies"—Ava lifted her beer to her lips—"midthirties to seventies."

Seventies? Images of saggy butts, shriveled penises, droopy testicles flitted through Nat's mind. Ava was twenty-two! How could she go there? But these men were rich. They paid for Ava's beautiful apartment, bought her pricey art for her birthday. Maybe generosity compensated for gray pubic hair? An involuntary shiver of disgust rattled Nat's shoulders.

Ava clocked it, and her tone became defensive. "Success is an aphrodisiac. I enjoy being with powerful men. They're more mature and more caring than all the selfish, horny *boys* I was dating before."

Nat sipped her beer and thought about her own dating life. Cole had been selfish and horny. Not to mention insecure, cloying, unstable. . . . Miguel was sweeter, kinder, but also needy, clingy . . . and, yes, selfish and horny. And neither of them could take her to a Michelin-starred restaurant, buy her a Birkin bag, or even help pay back her roommates. But still . . . Nat simply could not fathom a romantic relationship with a man old enough to be her father.

"I've always liked older men," Ava continued, a suggestive twinkle in her eye. "There's a lot to be said for experience."

Nat suppressed more images of elderly genitals. "Are these guys married?"

"Sometimes. But sometimes they just work a lot.

Or travel a lot. Or they're socially awkward." Ava
toyed with her coaster. "I'm busy, too. I like my space.
When I'm with a daddy, we enjoy each other. When
we're apart, we're completely free."

She made it sound so mature, so reciprocal, almost liberating. Ava and her suitors were up front
with their needs, their wants, their parameters. It
sounded positively *evolved*.

"We're living in the best city in the world," Ava
said, "but you can't enjoy it without money. I eat at
the best restaurants. I shop at exclusive boutiques. I
live in a gorgeous apartment." She took a sip of beer.
"One of my blessers took me to Rome last year. He
bought me a Versace dress."

"Did you . . . *sleep* with him?"

"I gave him a couple of blow jobs," she said dismissively. "Well worth it."

"Right." But Nat's voice was thin, revealing her
ambivalence.

Ava seemed to intuit her companion's moral
quandary. "I'm not hurting anyone. I get what I want.
The daddies get what they want. Even the wives . . .
I'm sure half of them know and don't care."

They finished their beers, then meandered back
to school, both sluggish and bleary from the midday
alcohol. As they strolled, Ava continued proselytiz-
ing about the sugar lifestyle: the gifts, the meals, the
trips . . . the mutual respect, even affection. One of
her sponsors had proposed marriage. She had loved
him, in a way, but not *that* kind of way. When they
reached the school, they paused before parting.

"Like with any online dating, you have to be
careful. There are salty daddies out there. There are

creeps and weirdos. But it could be the answer to all your problems." Ava turned then and moved toward her class. "Think about it," she called breezily over her shoulder.

Nat headed to the studio, her mind replaying her friend's confession. Ava had presented a solution to all her problems. But could Nat cross that line? Could she sell herself? The beer buzz was clouding her thoughts, convoluting her views.

Think about it, Ava had said.

Nat was quite sure she would think of nothing else.

The Sugar Bowl

Donnelly's was a cramped, grimy, run-down bar, perpetually packed with a vibrant, eclectic crowd. Tips could be meager, especially when the students were out in force, but Nat related to her budget-conscious clientele. And though she was usually exhausted after school, she never resented her job. It was a respite from her grubby apartment, her condescending roommates, her art-history homework. Her colleagues were diverse, interesting, generally upbeat. And the sexual chemistry between her and Miguel always made her shifts fly by. But tonight, there would be no fun flirtation with her former lover. Miguel was pissed, his hostility rippling off him like heat.

Thursday was one of their busiest nights. Nat focused on her tables, smiling, chatting, flirting when

she thought it would help. Given her current financial straits, every penny counted. At a corner back
table, she served a group of middle-aged men, their
thinning hair touching their open collars, their leather
jackets smelling like money. She clocked their Rolex
watches, their Botoxed foreheads, their unseasonal
tans from sunny vacations. They would be in the
music industry. Or club owners, maybe. These men
would have money to tip, if she did her job right.
She turned on the charm—smiling, laughing at their
jokes—and felt their eyes on her ass as she walked
away. Punching in her drink orders, Nat wondered:
*Is this so different than what Ava does? Aren't we both
monetizing our sexuality?*

The service industry could be a hard and ugly
place. Women put up with insults, ogles, even
harassment because they needed the money. Nat
knew what her postfeminist classmates would think
of this acceptance, but it was easy to have principles
when you didn't have bills and rent to pay. Some
women even had mouths to feed. And Nat's femi-
nism was less fervent, less defined. Of course, she
believed in equal rights for women. She wanted the
patriarchy to get fucked as much as the next girl. So
how did she feel about Ava letting men use her that
way? Or . . . was Ava using *them*? Would Nat feel
empowered taking a rich man's money in exchange
for her time and attention? Or would she feel dirty,
sick, ashamed?

It soon became clear that she wouldn't be getting a good tip no matter how hard she flirted with
the men at the back table. Miguel's anger toward
her was manifesting itself behind the bar. He had

the power to ignore her drink orders, and he was exercising it. She waited patiently as he mixed a negroni for one of his customers seated at the wood.

"When you're done there," she said sweetly, masking her irritation, "I'm still waiting for four pints of IPA and a lager."

"I'll get to them when I can," Miguel said, painstakingly pouring bright red Campari into a shot glass.

She leaned in, her voice low, conciliatory. "I'm sorry if I hurt you. I was too harsh, and I feel badly."

"Who says I'm hurt?"

"If you're not, can I please get my drinks? I can't afford to piss off my tables tonight."

"I'm busy, Nat," he said, adding a shot of vermouth slowly, gingerly, as if he were mixing explosives. "Not everything's about you."

But this was about her. She'd punched in her drink orders way ahead of Tim, the other server, who had already delivered his beverages to his satisfied customers. Miguel's patrons seated at the bar all had drinks except for the woman waiting for the world's slowest negroni. Nat's table of club owners would be getting antsy, annoyed, her tips diminishing by the second. There was nothing she could do but wait, as Miguel languidly stirred the orangey-red cocktail.

Finally, he slid the drink to his patient customer, leaving him no option but to fill Nat's orders.

"Keg's empty." His smile was mocking as he turned and strolled toward the basement cellar.

Her cheeks burned with anger and frustration. Miguel knew her financial situation, and he was hitting her where it hurt. He was not unlike Cole, after all. Miguel was only sweet and caring when she did exactly what he wanted. When his ego was bruised, he was spiteful and malicious. Well, he didn't know who he was fucking with.

Donnelly's had a strict policy banning servers from behind the bar. The bartender was responsible for the till, would dole out change to the waitstaff, who were not allowed in that sacred space. But with Miguel in the basement, Nat would be able to slip through the swinging half door, open the cash register, and take out a hundred bucks. She'd tuck it into her pocket and be back on the other side of the bar before her former lover returned. Miguel's cash would be out at the end of the night, but he wouldn't get fired. Not for a one-off. He'd get a warning, probation at the most. And it wouldn't be stealing, she rationalized. She was simply replacing the tips lost to Miguel's sabotage.

Adrenaline and anger made her heart race as she moved toward the cash register. With her hand resting on the low gate, she scanned the area for Tim the server, for Wayne the manager, for any suspicious patrons. No one was paying her any attention. She moved forward, casually opened the till, and prepared to liberate the money that was rightfully hers.

But her hand would not move to take the cash. She was not a thief, had never stolen anything in her life. Besides, it would take the entire contents of the register to solve her financial problems, and obviously she couldn't clean Miguel out. She had thought herself capable of anything to ensure her survival in New York City, but she'd been wrong. There were lines she couldn't cross.

"What are you doing?" She recognized the voice— deep, masculine, suspicious—before she even turned around. Her manager, Wayne. Shit.

She slammed the drawer closed. "N-nothing."

Her boss's brown eyes narrowed beneath heavy black brows. "You're not allowed behind the bar. You're not allowed in Miguel's till."

"I know. I just . . . I needed change. Miguel was in the cellar. He said I could help myself."

With impeccable timing, the basement door banged opened and Miguel entered. He was wheeling an aluminum keg on a dolly. "What's *she* doing back here?"

"She was in your till," Wayne replied. "She said you gave her permission to make change."

For a fraction of a second, Nat thought Miguel might cover for her . . . a way to get back in her good graces, or a nod to what they'd once shared. But his expression was stony, his voice ice. "No. I didn't."

"So, you were going to steal from us?" Wayne asked, voice vibrating with suppressed anger.

"No. I wasn't. I—"

But Miguel cut her off.

"It wasn't enough to dump me. You thought you'd steal from my till and get me fired, too."

"You refused to make my drinks! You were trying to punish me!"

"I was busy, okay? You're so wrapped up in yourself that you forget that there are other people working here!"

Patrons were watching them now, alerted by the raised voices, the contention in the air. Nat could feel her face burning with humiliation, her pulse pounding with dread. Miguel's eyes were fiery— rage, disgust, loathing. Wayne clocked the concerned looks of his customers. He had to shut this down.

"I'm not having you two working out some romantic vendetta in my bar." His voice was low but firm. "Nat, you're gone."

"What?"

"You heard me. You're fired." He took a few steps, then stopped. "Miguel, get back to work or you're next."

Miguel had the decency to look shocked on her behalf. "Nat . . . ," he began, but she hurried away, toward the staff room where her coat and purse hung from a metal hook. Tears were stinging her eyes, but she blinked them back. She was not going to fall apart in here.

It was outside, in the cool night air, that she let the tears pour down her face. She was in serious financial straits now. She had debts, her rent and tuition bills were looming. She had no job, no source of income, no . . . whatever Miguel had been to her. A sense of panic, of desperation nearly overwhelmed her. And then, a moment of clarity, an epiphany of sorts. There was an answer to all her problems.

She would do it. Once, maybe twice. Unlike Ava, Nat didn't need expensive clothes, shoes, and bags; didn't need precious art hanging on her penthouse walls. She just needed to pay back her roommates, cover her bills, and buy some groceries. And then, when she was out of the red, she would stop. Before things got intimate. Before things got creepy.

She pulled out her phone and texted Ava.

I want in

The reply was almost instant.

Welcome to the sugar bowl

The Profile

Nat had taken no offense when Ava recommended a substantial makeover prior to taking a photo for Nat's dating profile. She'd been trimming her own hair with paper scissors for the past year; her coif was in desperate need of a cut, some shaping, and a few subtle highlights to "add dimension," Ava's gifted stylist explained. The salon was high-end, classy, expensive. As Ava paid the bill, Nat poured on the gratitude.

"It's my pleasure," Ava said, slipping a platinum card back into her wallet. "Take me for a facial when you have your finances sorted."

Nat had never had a facial. A pedicure at a Bellingham strip mall was the sum total of her pampering experience. She could scarcely imagine a life where one regularly paid to have one's toenails painted, one's blackheads squeezed, one's pubic hair ripped out. Nat could do all that herself. All she wanted was to be able to pay her own way and, maybe, buy some sort of protein for dinner, like the occasional chicken breast.

Before they took the photo, Ava did Nat's makeup. The blond girl was skilled with contouring and highlighting, giving Nat a tutorial as she transformed her into a woman worthy of a rich man's attentions. When she was finished, Natalie took in her reflection. With her smoky eyeliner, her nude glossy lips, her subtly glowing skin, she looked like a different person. All traces of the creative, messy, complicated girl she was were obliterated, glossed over by a sheen of perfection. Nat stared at the stranger in the mirror and nodded her approval.

Ava loaned her a short black dress. "You've got a great body. You'll get more interest if you show it off."

While it felt exploitive, it made sense. As Nat posed in the figure-hugging outfit, pushing out her breasts, arching her back, she shook off her qualms. This was no different than wearing tight jeans to work at a bar, letting customers ogle her butt to increase her tips. She had a great ass, that she knew. Angling it toward the camera, she looked over her shoulder, smiled coyly. She could play this part.

When a suitable photo had been selected, gently retouched and uploaded, they turned their attention to the write-up. "Keep it fun and flirty," advised Ava. "You can talk money when they message you." Together they crafted a blurb. Nat was honest, mostly, sharing that she was an art student from the

Pacific Northwest. Creative and cool, with a good sense of humor. She selected a *no-strings* relationship, which suited her perfectly. It was what she had wanted with Miguel, but he'd been too immature to handle it. An older, powerful, wealthy man would desire it, would *pay* for it, Ava assured her. But it would never get that far . . . Just a couple of dates would get her out of financial trouble.

When her profile was complete and submitted, Nat prepared to trek back to Brooklyn. As she stepped into her winter boots, Ava offered last-minute advice.

"You'll start getting messages as soon as your profile goes live. The men on this site have had background checks, but you have to be careful. You have to be smart."

Nat felt a chill run through her.

"Get the money up front. Always meet in a public place. Never go to their apartment."

"Of course."

"And never tell a man where you live."

"Right."

"I always ask for a daddy's real name and where he works. Then, I can google him and make sure he's not a Splenda daddy."

Nat chuckled nervously. "What's that?"

"Guys who want to be sugar daddies but don't have enough money. You're not going to give up your whole fucking evening for a fifty-dollar Sephora gift card."

"No, I'm not."

"Still . . . They're better than the salt daddies. Guys who *pretend* to have money, who offer you gifts and trips and allowances, just to get into your pants. Salt and sugar look the same. You have to be careful."

Oh God . . .

Nat was in the hallway when Ava had one last morsel of advice. "Read their profiles carefully. Some of these men are into kinky sex, but they're usually up front about it."

Nat's voice was weak. "What kind of kinky sex?"

"Bondage is pretty popular. Master-slave relationships. Role-playing. That kind of thing . . ."

"Jesus."

"It's not that big a deal, really." Ava's response was breezy. "You just have to be up front about what you're willing to do, sexually."

"Nothing," Nat said quickly. "I'm only going to go on a couple of pay-per-meets."

Ava smirked. "Everyone says that, at first. But this lifestyle is addictive."

On the train, Nat sat in a sort of trance, a true New Yorker in her ignorance of her carriage-mates. It was impossible to focus on anything but the knowledge that, at any moment, Nat could receive a message that would save her life. *Change* her life, if she wanted it to. But she didn't. She had done the math: fifteen hundred dollars would pay off her debts and provide a financial cushion. She had a partial scholarship, could get another part-time job. In the summer, she would work full-time at a bar and get a morning job at a shop, or a restaurant. Nat could sustain herself; she was not going to be a sugar baby.

She didn't judge Ava for her choice. Nat was

open-minded, a freethinker. She had not been raised in a religious home where morals and values were articulated. And she had loathed the judgment and gossip so prevalent in her small town, often directed at her parents for their failed marriage, for her dad's abandonment, her mom's subsequent dating life. But she knew the sugar bowl was not for her. Nat was not attracted to older men. In fact, the thought of sex with anyone over thirty made her skin crawl. (*Maybe* she could stomach Brad Pitt, but even he did not arouse her.) She was not overly romantic— she understood sex without love or commitment. But sex without *attraction*, without *chemistry*, was impossible for her. Unlike Ava, Nat could never blow a septuagenarian for a trip to Rome and a Versace dress. Her gag reflex would not allow it.

Lost in the fog of her thoughts, the Jefferson Street stop was suddenly upon her. She disembarked the train and walked toward home. It was early evening but already getting dark. Nat huddled into her thrift-store coat, buried her face in her scarf, the midmorning promise of spring forgotten in the wintry chill of night. Turning onto her street, she saw that her building was lit from within, its warm glow menacing instead of welcoming. It meant that at least one of her roommates was home. Since her written second warning, she'd become a master of avoidance. Her luck would run out eventually, but not now. Please . . .

As she let herself in, she heard banging from the kitchen, smelled frying onions. Someone was cooking. She closed the door softly and silently removed her shoes. Scurrying down the hallway in her sock feet, she planned to slip into her room, unnoticed. But before she could reach her door, Mara materialized before her.

"Hi, Nat." Her red hair was pulled back, her face pointed. Like her words.

"Hi."

"Toni and I have been wondering when you're going to pay us the money you owe us."

"Next week," Nat said, forcing a confident tone. "I get paid on Friday." Her final pay, she knew, would not come close to covering her debt. But if she could arrange a couple of pay-per-meet dates with sugar daddies, she would have the cash.

"We actually need the money by Tuesday," Mara said, and there was a wicked glint in her eye. She was enjoying her power, lauding it over Nat. "If you can't pay us back, you're going to have to find another place to live."

"Tuesday it is," Nat snapped. She marched into her bedroom, slamming the door behind her.

Her fingers trembled as she pulled her laptop out of her backpack and turned it on. What if none of these rich men were interested in her? What if only perverts or sickos had sent messages? Her roommates wanted her out, that much was obvious. This website, these men, were her only hope.

Settling onto her unmade bed, she logged into the website. Next to her in-box, there was a red number: 13. She had thirteen messages. Her profile had been up for less than an hour! Feeling slightly sick (fear? panic? excitement?), she scrolled through the missives. Some of the men had posted a profile photo, some had not. The lack of an image was not subterfuge, Ava had advised. Some of these men were high-profile, well-known in their industries. Some—probably many—were married. She opened the first message from YezPlz.

> I'm a very sucessfull business man looking for lovely lady to spoyl.

His spelling did not inspire confidence in his success, nor in his ability to spoil.

She moved through the messages. BKdaddy, a flabby-looking tech multimillionaire, would pay her four hundred dollars to wear lingerie and massage his feet. Will.I.Be would love to treat her lavishly, but only if her blood type was A positive or O. (According to Will, blood type was the greatest predictor of relationship success.) RealDeal invited her over to his East Village apartment, where he'd pay her six hundred dollars to take a bath with him. (The blank stare in his profile picture screamed serial killer.) Wes-Jen was looking for a playmate for him and his wife. And then, there was Profman, a retired professor who was seventy-five . . . but don't worry, his age wasn't a factor, *downstairs*.

There were more messages, ambiguous one-liners complimenting her looks, wanting to get to know her better, suggesting they exchange cell numbers. Nat didn't have time for niceties or banter. She was considering the foot-massage guy when she opened the final message from Angeldaddy.

> I love art and creative people. Would you like to meet for a drink tonight? $500.

She clicked on his profile. There was no photo, but she found out he was divorced, a nonsmoker, a social drinker. His occupation was listed as lawyer, his net worth at $10 million, his annual salary at over a million. Jesus . . .

Before she could stop herself, she replied.

I'd love to. I'm in Brooklyn. Where are you?

The response was almost instant.

I'm in the financial district. Meet in DUMBO?
I know a little wine bar.

He could be Splenda, or salty. He could be a murderer for all she knew. But Nat didn't have time to be picky, didn't have time to do her due diligence. She was desperate.

Sure. Send me the address.

And just like that, she had a date.

The Baby

Gabe Turnmill was committed to his marriage. The fact that he was currently in the back of a town car, on his way to meet a hot young art student for a drink, was not a contradiction of this fact. He remained devoted to his wife, Celeste, had been since they met during their first year of law school at Yale. She'd been seated across a vast lecture theater the first time he'd spotted her—so bright, so engaged, so ethereal. Gabe had openly watched her, gawking at her composed beauty. She hadn't even noticed him.

He'd inveigled an invitation to a party Celeste was attending—even then, he'd been unafraid to go after what he wanted. He'd approached her, a tepid beer in hand, and sparked up a conversation. He learned she was the daughter of a Haitian doctor and a French-Canadian folk singer. She had grown up in Montreal; spoke fluent, unaccented English and French; had done her undergrad at McGill University. Unlike most of his Yale alumni, she was impressed by Gabe's humble beginnings. With Celeste, he didn't have to hide the fact that his father was a taxi dispatcher, that his mother ran an eldercare facility. He could admit that he had attended Princeton on a lacrosse scholarship, that law school was funded by an enormous student loan. She thought his accomplishments were more impressive because he wasn't born with a silver spoon in his mouth.

Celeste had been a serious law student, top of the class, determined to have an impact on the world. She wanted to be a public defender, representing the disproportionate number of people of color who ended up in the justice system. Gabe's grades were decent, his goals less altruistic. He wanted a lucrative career in corporate law. He wanted to be a one-percenter, a big shot, the guy behind the tinted windows in the back of the town car. Even then, Gabe knew what it took to get to the top and stay there: a ruthlessness, a moral fluidity, an in-depth knowledge of loopholes and gray areas. After law school, his mercenary approach built his reputation in the upper echelons of the business world. His finesse and discretion had kept him, and his clients, out of trouble. Out of jail in some cases. Back then, he'd had to spin his avaricious plans for Celeste. He wanted to make a difference in the world, too, he said, but he'd do so via the economy. She'd bought it. She still did. Gabe had charmed her, wooed her, and, eventually, married her.

That was twenty-nine years ago, and Gabe still cared for his wife in a platonic, companionable way. The morphing of his affections was only natural, given the changes in his partner. He'd married a passionate public defender, vehemently advocating for the wrongly accused, the marginalized, the victims of a broken system. Now, Celeste was a stay-at-home mom, having left her job when she was first diagnosed with breast cancer six years ago. After a lumpectomy, radiation, an estrogen-suppressing prescription, she was in full remission. But she wouldn't go back to the law. Her illness had been a wake-up call. Celeste wanted to focus on her health, spend more time with their daughter, Violet. Of course, Gabe had been supportive. He'd just made partner at his Wall Street firm. Celeste's salary had been negligible in comparison.

His wife was still beautiful, in a mature, maternal way, but he was no longer sexually attracted to her. Her health struggles had taken a toll, etching lines into her luminous dark skin that could have been erased with injectables or fillers, but Celeste didn't want a frozen face full of poison, she said. The medication had made her gain weight that no amount of tennis or Pilates classes could budge. Parts of his wife's body were starting to sag, but Celeste eschewed plastic surgery. She'd moved out to the Hamptons four years ago, rarely came into the city anymore. Celeste said she liked the serenity of their country estate, but she felt out of place in New York now, inferior to all the smooth, svelte society wives.

In contrast, Gabe had only grown more handsome, more distinguished over the years. His thick silver hair, his expensive clothes, his cool confidence were like catnip to females. Women flirted with him regularly, coming onto him like bitches in heat. He ignored their overtures. Given the current climate, he wasn't going to get involved with a colleague or, God forbid, an underling. He'd been reckless in the past, but not anymore. He would not make that mistake again.

It was his third affair (fidelity was not the norm in his circles) that had gone wrong. Melody, an attractive paralegal at the firm, had been emotionally unstable. She'd grown needy and demanding, texting him constantly, calling him at all hours, professing her love. Once, she'd even shown up at the house in the Hamptons under the auspices of delivering a brief. Thankfully, Celeste hadn't cottoned on, but Gabe had promptly ended the relationship. Melody had cried, threatened to harm herself, to tell his wife. The girl couldn't have known how close she had come to disappearing. Gabe was capable of anything to protect his wife, his daughter, and his good name. He had people who took care of problems like Melody. In the end, he'd offered the paralegal a payoff and a new job at a Midtown firm. She had accepted. Lucky for her.

Sometimes, though, at the oddest times, Gabe felt like Melody was watching him. It was paranoia; it had been years since he'd dismissed the woman from his life. But occasionally, he'd feel a prickle at the back of his neck, a frisson running up his spine, and he would sense that Melody was nearby, observing. He had yet to clap eyes on her, but that didn't mean she wasn't out there, waiting for an opportunity to destroy him. Gabe knew how to take care of himself. He traveled with protection. But the Melody affair had taught him a powerful lesson.

The website was the answer. It was used by several of his colleagues who, like Gabe, lived alone in the city all week while their families resided in Southampton, Amagansett, or Montauk. These girls—these *sugar babies*—did not cause problems. He was up front about the parameters of the relationship; *no strings*, though he classified himself as divorced in his profile. It was cleaner, simpler, and he attracted more women that way. (He didn't wear a ring, never had, claiming it irritated his finger.) But this girl, Natalie, was not going to fall in love with him, threaten his marriage, or harm his impeccable reputation. Dating rich men was her *job*, a way to cover the rent, to eat in nice restaurants, to buy designer clothes. The girls he'd found on the site had given Gabe the attention, the adoration, the sex he needed. And then, when he grew tired of them, they conveniently disappeared.

The long black Lincoln pulled up in front of a brick warehouse converted into a row of bistros, shops, and bars. "We're here, sir." It was his driver, Oleg, a big man, square of shoulder and jaw. He was an immigrant from Moldova, providing service, discretion, and sometimes muscle, for a bargain price.

"Stay in the area. I'll text you when I'm wrapping things up."

"Of course, sir."

As Gabe climbed out of the back seat, he thought about the girl he was about to meet. Her photograph had grabbed him instantly. Her cascade of dark hair, her pale skin, the glossy bow of her mouth. And her body in that tight black dress . . . He felt a flicker of excitement as he entered the rustic wine bar, the manager snapping to attention, recognizing a powerful, wealthy customer on sight. Gabe demanded a quiet table near the back, and his host dutifully complied.

Following the portly maître d' through the buzzing establishment, Gabe felt the familiar weight of eyes on him. People were drawn to his confidence, his authority, his presence. He was a *somebody*, they could tell just by looking at him. Gabe was the kind of man who could walk into a crowded bar, insist on the best table, and somehow, it would materialize. And, when a beautiful woman, thirty years his junior joined him, no one would bat an eye.

He felt no guilt about his marital status as he handed the manager his coat and sent him off to fetch a drink. Both he and his wife were satisfied with their *paper* marriage. Celeste wanted for nothing; Gabe made sure of that. She had a beautiful home, a spacious property, domestic support. Her days were filled with yoga and pottery classes, massages and nutritional consults. Celeste took care of herself and their daughter. That's all she had the energy for; there was none left for Gabe. And yet, he stayed, even though she had abandoned him: emotionally, physically, sexually. He was an attractive, virile man, who had stood by his wife, in sickness and in health. He deserved a fucking medal. And he deserved the sexy young woman who was about to enter the bar.

He deserved Natalie.

9

The Drink

Natalie's gloved hand gripped the railing as she descended the front steps to her Uber. To calm her nerves, she'd had a coffee mug full of vodka and Sprite while she'd straightened her hair. Then, when she was applying her makeup, she'd had another one to steady her hand. The drinks, her nerves, and the pair of high-heeled boots she'd donned for the occasion, were a dangerous combination.

Thankfully, she made it to the idling Toyota Camry without incident and climbed into the back seat. She couldn't afford the Uber, but she couldn't afford to show up late for this meeting, either. What was the protocol for a sugar date gone wrong? Was money deducted for tardiness? For not laughing at his jokes? For showing up tipsy? God, she hoped not. As the youthful driver shuttled her to her destination, she opened the dating app on her phone and read up on Angeldaddy.

He had messaged her his real first name: Gabriel. Like the angel. His username was clever. Gabriel's age was fifty-five. How old was her dad? In his late forties, but he looked older. When she'd last seen Andrew Murphy, a life of depression, cigarettes, and booze was already taking its toll. Rich people could pay for private chefs, personal trainers, even plastic surgery. But Angeldaddy would not be handsome. If he was, he wouldn't have to pay five hundred bucks for a date. Nat was prepared for the worst in the looks department.

She hadn't asked Gabe to send a picture before their rendezvous because his appearance was not relevant. Neither was the fact that he enjoyed good Scotch, a good workout, and a good movie. This was a glass of wine. This was five hundred dollars. This was a means to an end.

The Uber pulled up in front of a brick warehouse conversion just as she was beginning to feel woozy from staring at her phone while in motion. The bar was very cool, very hip, very intimidating; a place she would never have set foot in under normal circumstances. Tumbling out of the car, Nat moved toward the wine bar, checking the time on her phone. She was a little late. She was a little carsick. And she was a little drunk. But she was here. With a fortifying breath, she pushed open the glass door.

The bar was warm and cozy, with wide plank floors, brick walls, heavy wood tables. As soon as she entered, the manager, a stocky guy in a starched white shirt and jeans, greeted her.

"Are you meeting a gentleman here?"

Did he know? Was he judging her? She felt compelled to explain: *I'm not a prostitute. I have debts and bills. It's just one drink.* Instead, she said, "Uh . . . yeah."

"Right this way."

Obediently, she followed him, ignoring the tiny voice in her head that told her to turn around, to leave, to not look back. It was her conscience, reminding her that she was about to sell herself. Ava and the website could spin it, make it sound like a business deal, a mutually beneficial transaction, but at her core, Nat knew this was glamorized prostitution. *You don't have to do this*, the little voice said, but she did. If she backed out of this date, she wouldn't be able to repay Mara and Toni. She'd be evicted. She wouldn't have the money for the deposit on a new apartment. She'd have to drop out of school, go back home, work at the Greek restaurant again. She'd be a failure, a laughingstock. She instructed her conscience to shut the fuck up.

They were headed toward the back, toward a man seated at a secluded table, an amber drink in his hand. This could not be Gabriel. Instead of the wizened ogre she'd been expecting, this man had a full head of gray hair, a strong jawline, a dashing dark suit. He looked up and smiled, his blue eyes crinkling at the corners, his lips revealing a glimpse of square white teeth. As he stood to greet her, there was no denying he was an attractive man. *Old,* but attractive.

"Hi, Natalie," he said, leaning in and kissing her

cheek. It would have been presumptuous in any situation but this one.

"Hi, Gabriel."

"Call me Gabe," he said. She didn't suggest the diminutive *Nat*. She liked the way he said her full name: Natalie. It sounded like music.

Their attentive host took Nat's ratty coat, revealing the black peasant top and tight black jeans she was wearing. If she'd had more time to prepare, she'd have borrowed a dress from Ava. But this was the best she could do on such short notice. Gabe didn't seem to mind. His eyes drifted over her appreciatively as the bar manager pulled out her chair and she sat.

"Something to drink?" the manager asked.

Nat was already drunk. She should order a water, a diet Coke, or a Shirley Temple. But instead, she gestured toward Gabriel's drink—Scotch? His profile said he liked a good Scotch. "I'll have what he's having."

With a nod, the server left them alone.

"You like a rusty nail?"

So that's what it was. She'd never had one, but she played along. "I do."

"Not too strong for you?"

"I can handle my liquor." She sounded flirtatious, even suggestive. Gabe smiled, his eyes crinkling again.

"Tell me about yourself, Natalie."

Ava had warned her to protect her privacy, not to reveal the details of her current life. Nat heeded the advice.

"I'm from Blaine. In Washington State. Have you been there?"

"Can't say I've had the pleasure."

"Of course not. Why would you? It's small. And boring. That's why I left."

He lifted his drink, and the ice cubes tinkled. "I've been to Seattle, though. And Vancouver."

"Close enough."

"It's a beautiful area. The ocean and the mountains . . ."

"Yeah."

"Do you ski?"

"No. I don't really like the cold."

God, small talk with an old guy was painful. How did Ava do it with so many men? Nat's eyes flitted around the bar, chock-full of sophisticated, attractive patrons: couples, friends, a promising first date, perhaps. She and Gabe were the only awkward, mismatched pair there. Nat felt a cold gaze on her, and she turned to see a woman a few tables over. She was in her thirties, an attractive brunette dining with her husband (evident by their matching wedding bands). The woman was sneering at Nat, her judgment and hostility overt. This stranger knew what was going on here, and it disgusted her. A shameful heat crept into Nat's cheeks.

Thankfully, her drink arrived then. She took a large swallow. *Oh, Jesus!* She coughed and spluttered, the whiskey burning her esophagus.

Gabe slid a glass of water toward her. "You okay?" His voice was concerned, but she could see the amusement dancing in his blue eyes.

"Fine," she croaked, guzzling the water.

"I thought you could handle your liquor," he teased.

"I can." Her voice was hoarse. "I just need to get warmed up."

He smiled at her. "You're cute."

She looked up and met his gaze. It was intense, searing . . . and not as creepy as she had anticipated. Something stirred in her . . . not quite attraction, but, perhaps, a slight infatuation. This powerful man, in his expensive suit, with his fancy watch, was looking at her with such interest, almost fascination. Nat forgot about that woman's disgusted stare and allowed herself to feel flattered. Her cheeks were pink again, but not from shame: from the Scotch and the attention.

"Where did you grow up?" she asked, taking another sip of her drink.

"I'm from a small town, too," Gabe said, surprising her. As he told her about his humble beginnings in Michigan, she felt an affinity for him. They were not so different after all, both small-town people with big dreams. Except Gabe was rich and old; Nat was poor and young.

As Gabe talked about the lacrosse career that got him to Princeton, she heard the muted ring of a cell phone. Of course, this man was a big deal. He was busy and important and would get phone calls at all hours. But Gabe wasn't moving to answer it; he was too polite, too charming. He halted his story.

"Do you want to get that?"

It was *her* phone ringing, deep in the belly of her oversize pleather purse.

"I'm so sorry," she muttered, grabbing her bag

and rummaging through it. "No one ever phones me." She extracted the device and looked at the call display: Mom.

"Just my mom," she said, powering off the appliance. "I'll call her later."

"Are you sure? It could be important."

"It won't be." She sipped her strong drink. "My little brother probably got offered an internship at NASA. Or my sister made the Olympic swim team . . . even though they're only five and seven."

He chuckled. "I take it your siblings are over-achievers."

"*Half* siblings," she corrected him. "My mom remarried. Oliver and Astrid are the perfect, smart, blond kids she always wanted."

"You're not close to your family?"

"I don't really fit with them." She drank some more. "My mom and her new family look like one of those TV commercials where everyone is gorgeous and happy and playing Frisbee at a picnic. And then you find out it's an ad for herpes medication or something."

His chuckle egged her on.

"So obviously they're relieved I live on the other side of the country," she quipped. "You know, because I'm not a savant, or an elite athlete. And I have brown hair."

Gabe was laughing now, and she felt a little thrill. This rich, distinguished lawyer thought she was cute. And funny. And maybe she kind of was?

"Surely, that's not true," he said, amusement dancing in his eyes. "They must miss you."

Nat thought about the night Cole had broken

into their home. The fear, the panic, the anger. Her mother had forgiven her, but Derek hadn't. While he never articulated his resentment, he blamed her, it was clear. He'd nearly beaten an innocent kid to death. He was distant, cold, aloof. They were all better off without her.

"They don't," she said.

The restaurant manager reappeared then. (Apparently, Gabe was a VIP and could not be served by a mere waiter.) "Another drink?" the man suggested.

Gabe smiled at her. Those teeth. Those crinkly eyes. "What do you think, Natalie?"

She looked down at her glass, surprisingly close to empty. She was drunk, but pleasantly so. The booze made her feel warm and confident. Her date made her feel special. She'd planned to spend an hour with this man, get the money, and go home. But there was no rule against enjoying herself just a little. Glancing toward her sneering, judgmental neighbor, Nat found the dark-haired woman engrossed in her meal, the debauchery a few tables over, forgotten. Nat turned back to her date.

"Why not?"

10

. . . . . .

The Morning After

As soon as Nat opened her eyes, a swell of regret engulfed her. Through the pounding in her temples, the date came back to her in snippets. Gabe's white teeth. His intense blue eyes on her. She'd been telling him stories, making him laugh. Stories about what? Blaine. Perfect little Oliver and Astrid. But the end of the night was blank. How had she gotten home? Had she called an Uber? Hopped in a cab? If she couldn't remember that, what else was she forgetting?

A wave of nausea washed over her—from the alcohol, from shame, from self-loathing. How had she fucked this up? It was supposed to be one drink, one hour, five hundred dollars. Instead, she'd gotten blackout drunk and ruined everything. A slip of a memory flashed through her mind. She was stumbling out of the bar, strong hands on her elbow, on the small of her back. Did those hands belong to Gabe? Or the bar manager? One of them must have dumped her into a taxi.

Rolling over, she was able to reach her purse, nestled among the clutter of clothes, books, and pencils on her floor. Dragging it toward her, she fished for her phone, found it. She checked the time: 12:14 P.M. Opening her e-mail, she found no Uber receipt. So a taxi must have brought her home. Had Gabe paid for it? Or had she paid for it out of the money he'd given her? *If* he'd given her any money. She'd been drunk, messy, babbling . . . Even *she* didn't think she deserved remuneration.

As she dug for her wallet, she heard a knock at the front door. Nat didn't get up. It was a Saturday, so Mara and Toni were likely home, studying, cleaning, alphabetizing the cereal cupboard. And it wouldn't be for her, anyway. Nat's friends from school didn't live in the area. Miguel hated her and would not be dropping by. She recognized the quick, thumping footsteps of Toni, hurrying to answer the insistent knock.

Retrieving her battered canvas wallet, she opened it and peered inside. Three ones and a five. Disappointment crushed her chest. Why hadn't she gotten the money up front, like Ava had suggested? A successful date would have paid off her debt to her roommates. A couple more dates would have lined her bank account. But she didn't even have enough class to be a fucking sugar baby. She flopped back down on the bed. Tears of self-recrimination slipped from her eyes, ran down her temples, wet her hair.

"Natalie!" It was Mara's voice, shrill, irritated. As usual.

She dried her eyes with the bottom of her T-shirt and got up. She was too tired, too hungover to feel anything but resignation as she wrapped her robe around her and stumbled to the kitchen.

Her roommates were standing by the counter, arms folded, faces stern. Toni was in scrubs—either coming from or going to a practicum shift; Mara was in workout gear, her red hair piled on top of her head, making her resemble a woodpecker. Nat smelled spices, lemon grass, coconut, before she even spotted the brown paper bags full of Thai food.

"Ummm . . ." It was Toni, her hands migrating to her hips, "we're just wondering how you can afford to order a feast of Thai food when you owe us money?"

"I didn't order any Thai food."

"Really?" Mara said. "I'm not quite finished with my master's, but I *think* I can read your name right here on the bag."

"I didn't fucking order it, okay?"

Toni sniped, "Did your fairy godmother order it for you?"

No . . . But someone had. Without a word, Nat turned and hurried back to her bedroom. She grabbed her phone and opened the sugar-dating app. There were more messages—thirty-two more, to be precise, but she went directly to her conversation with Angeldaddy. With Gabe.

One new message. She opened it.

Thai food is the best hangover cure.

It came flooding back to her then. The driver, the big black car. Gabe helping her up the steps of her building. Her fumbling with the key, him taking it, opening the door. Had she kissed him? Invited him in? No, no, she hadn't; she wouldn't. Contrary to her roommates' opinions of her, Nat did not have sex with men she'd just met. Especially not fifty-five-year-old multimillionaires. But now, Gabe knew where she lived. Another rule broken. But he was not dangerous. He was sending her Thai food. He was thoughtful, kind, generous.

Something pinged in her consciousness. Her wool coat hung on a hook on the back of the door. She yanked it down, shoved her hand into the nylon pocket, and removed five crisp one-hundred-dollar bills. He had paid her, after all.

With the money clutched in her hand, she marched back to the kitchen. "Here's three hundred dollars." She shoved it at Mara, relishing the shock on her face. "That more than covers what I owe you."

Snatching up the Thai takeout, she went back to her room.

Nick

Nat and Ava were in a steamy ramen bar enjoying bowls of hot noodle soup. Normally, Nat did not go out to eat. She brought a packed lunch to school— a bagel with cream cheese or a ham sandwich. At home, she made pasta or scrambled eggs. But her recent windfall allowed her the luxury of a hot meal in a real restaurant. And, of course, she had to update Ava on her disastrous date.

"I was too nervous to eat before I met him," Nat said, pinching up noodles with her chopsticks. "So I had a couple of vodkas to calm my nerves. And then I had a few Scotches with Gabe. And then"— she stuffed the noodles into her mouth—"I was a drunk and disgusting mess."

"Oh shit," Ava said, but she was amused.

"He still paid me, though."

"Classy guy."

"And he gave me a ride home in his town car."

"That's not good, Nat." Ava slurped her soup. "Now he knows where you live."

"I know. The next day he sent me Thai food for my hangover."

Ava set her chopsticks down. "Did you have sex with him in the car?"

"God, no. I was drunk but not *that* drunk."

"Blow job? Hand job?"

Nat felt her cheeks pinken as her mind flashed to the night Gabe had delivered her home. She'd spent the entire ride with her eyes closed, her head against the back seat, all her focus on not puking. But then he'd helped her to the door, his strong hands on her back. She recalled their proximity as he'd guided the key into the lock for her and then ushered her inside. There had been a hug, a bit of chemistry between them, but nothing more. She was sure of it.

"No. I would remember if I had." She slurped some soup. "He was pretty attractive—for his age— but nothing happened."

Ava picked up her porcelain spoon. "Are you going to see him again?"

"I can't." Nat stirred some hot sauce into her soup. "I'm too humiliated."

"Does he want to see you again?"

"He gave me his cell number when I messaged to thank him for the Thai food. He said to text him if I want to get together."

"You should. He sounds like the whole package."

Nat sipped her soup. Gabe *was* the whole package: rich, attractive, a gentleman . . . And that's why she couldn't see him again. This was not about finding a boyfriend, a man who made her feel special and adored. This was a business arrangement. This was about money.

"I'm seeing a different daddy tonight," she said. "In Midtown."

"Look at you go."

"Could I get ready at your place? So I don't have to go back to Brooklyn and then come back uptown?"

"Of course." Ava stirred her soup. "Don't get too drunk tonight."

Nat smirked. "I'm not having anything to drink before the date. And I'll just have one glass of wine when I meet him."

"Good girl." Ava pushed her bowl away. "If you play your cards right, you'll be able to move into Manhattan one day."

Nat gave an ambiguous smile, tossed her napkin into her empty bowl. She knew what it would take to get an apartment in the city. She knew she would never have one.

The man she was meeting that night was a rich tech guy from Silicon Valley, in New York for business. His name was Nick, and he was thirty-nine, according to his profile. He was single, fun loving, a risk-taker who worked and played hard. He was looking for an adventurous girl who could keep up with his wild side. Nat knew she was not that girl, but she could play along for an hour. And she could play along for the four hundred bucks he'd promised her. Nick had suggested they meet at the bar of his hotel, but Nat feared that would send the wrong message. She'd suggested a piano bar on West Fifty-Sixth, only a block from his accommodations. He had agreed.

She was only mildly anxious as she rode the subway uptown from Ava's place. While she'd botched the date with Gabe, it had been a valuable learning experience. She knew how to do this now. She was sober this time and planned to stay that way. And her previous date had given her a certain comfort level. Sugar daddies could be kind, respectful, *normal*. Sure, some may be creepy, some might be perverts, but there was virtually no danger in meeting a man in a public place, having one drink, collecting the cash, and leaving.

She emerged from the subway at Columbus Circle and headed to the bar. It was only a couple of blocks, but her faux patent leather pumps (courtesy of Payless) pinched her toes as she walked. Ava had lent her a black pencil skirt, a low-cut silk top, a sleek, black coat. Her friend's feet were a size and a half bigger, precluding Nat from borrowing a pair of designer heels. Cheap shoes aside, Nat knew she looked the part: sexy, sophisticated, worth the money.

Nick had described himself as "mixed race." The two photos he'd shared showed a slim man with a thick head of dark hair, a groomed beard, and intense brown eyes. He was attractive, and significantly younger than her last date (though still way too old for a real relationship). Nat had been pleas-

antly surprised that most of the men on the dating
site were not the ancient, hideous monsters she'd
envisioned. But why did a young, wealthy, attractive man need to pay for a date? Perhaps it was just
simpler. Perhaps men like Nick didn't want to put
in the effort that a *real* relationship required.

Her phone pinged in her pocket, the sound of
the text reminding her to silence it. She'd been
mortified when her mother had called during her
date with Gabe. It was just one of the many faux
pas she'd committed that disastrous evening. While
Gabe had been understanding, amused even, Nick
might not be so convivial. Digging out the device,
she checked the text. It was her mom. Again.

For Christ's sake Natalie, call me!!!

Allana Heppner had phoned her daughter twice
and texted four times without receiving a response.
Now, she was understandably pissed. Nat had intended to reply, but she'd been busy, stressed, and
a little ashamed. Her mom was not old-fashioned
or judgmental, but there was no way she would ap-
prove of what her daughter was doing. Nat muted
her phone and dropped it into her purse.

Her feet were beginning to throb as she reached
the elegant bar. Pulling open the heavy door, she
entered the sophisticated space: dark wood, deep
red upholstery, live piano music tinkling from a
baby grand in the center of the room. Before the
hostess could greet her, a man at a back table stood
and waved: Nick. Nat waved back and moved toward him. As she approached, she saw that he was

slightly less handsome than in his online photos. But that was to be expected. Nat, herself, was not as polished, pouty, or perfect as her profile suggested. But Nick did not look disappointed. His eyes roamed over her face and body approvingly.

He greeted her with the same familiar kiss on the cheek that Gabe had, his hand on her waist. These rich, powerful men took it as their right, covered under the fee. She could not be offended. Nick pulled out her chair, and she sat. Her date took his seat across from her and picked up a bottle of red wine from the table.

"They had a '96 Penfolds Grange," he said, filling her glass.

"Wow." While Nat was unfamiliar with the brand, she had never tasted wine that was older than she was. She held up her glass and met his dark gaze. "To new friends," she said, flirtatiously.

"And new adventures."

A chill ran through her, some sort of primitive, biological warning system. Nick's tone, his eyes on her, his intense, sexual energy made her feel vulnerable. But she brushed her trepidation aside and took a drink. This was a glass of wine in a public place. Nothing bad would happen.

"How long are you in New York?" she asked.

"A week. I've got meetings each day, but my nights are for fun."

"What do you do?"

"Cryptocurrency."

"Ah . . ." It was obvious she was clueless.

He elaborated. "Bitcoin. Ethereum. Blockchain technology . . ."

"Thanks for clearing that up," she joked, and her date laughed. She felt herself relax a little. "Do you come to New York often?"

"At least once a month." He leaned in, smiled. "If we have a good time this week, I'll make it worth your while to be available when I'm in town."

Her last date had made small talk, had asked about her hometown, about her half siblings. Nick was getting down to business; he was moving too fast.

"Let's get to know each other first."

"Of course." He leaned back with his wine. "I like to be open and up front about everything."

"Me, too."

"I'm into littles, but I can do middles, if you're more comfortable with that."

She giggled awkwardly. What was he talking about?

"I've brought some outfits. Onesies. Baby-doll pajamas. I'll buy some stuffed toys while I'm here."

A picture was forming in her mind: a confounding, disturbing image.

"You don't have to stay in my room while I'm at meetings, but I'd expect you to be there, dressed and ready, when I get back." Nick gave her a lecherous smile. "If you're late, you'll get a nasty spanking."

The vintage wine turned to vinegar in her mouth. A strangled noise escaped her throat.

"I'm fine to just play for a while," he said, trying to appease her. "We don't have to have sex until you're comfortable."

She grabbed her glass of water and drank. She

was in way over her head here. Her voice, when she spoke, was hoarse.

"I don't think we're on the same page."

Nick's brow furrowed. "I told you to read my profile carefully. I was very clear about what I'm into."

She *had* read his profile. She knew he was a tech guy with a net worth of eight million dollars. She knew he liked to travel, to rock climb, to dine at Michelin-starred restaurants. He appreciated fine wine, adventurous people, and a good sense of humor. What had she missed?

Nick spelled it out for her. "I'm into DDLG."

"I . . . don't know what that is."

"Dominant daddy–little girl."

"Oh *God*." She couldn't hide her revulsion.

Nick's expression darkened. "Why did you respond to my message if you weren't into it?"

"I—I wasn't familiar with the acronym. I didn't know."

"Are you some kind of amateur?" He leaned in, lowered his voice. "Or are you just here for some easy money?"

"No," she said, and she could feel her face heating. "I must have read your profile too quickly because I was excited to meet you."

"Yeah, right." He drained his glass of wine. "You're one of those, aren't you?"

One of *what*?

"You think you can waltz in here in your tight skirt and your cleavage, and I'll just hand over four hundred dollars." His voice dripped contempt. "You never had any intention of getting to know me or building something with me. You're a user. . . . You're worse than a whore."

This man, who wanted her to dress up like a little girl and play with stuffed toys for his sexual gratification, dared to insult her this way? She could point out the irony, the hypocrisy, but her words had abandoned her. Humiliation burned her face, clogged her throat, made her eyes liquid. Because she knew, at her core, that Nick was right. She'd never planned to get to know him, sexually or otherwise. There was an honor code in the sugar bowl for which she'd been unprepared.

She stood. "I won't be insulted like this."

"I won't pay you four hundred bucks for nothing."

"Fine," she snapped. Though it wasn't fine. Her next tuition installment was due. Rent was looming. And she knew she could not do this again. Both of her dates had been disasters, leaving her embarrassed, ashamed, hating herself. She didn't judge Ava or other sugar babies for choosing this lifestyle, but Nat was not cut out for it. She was not a user. And she was not a whore.

With her cheap shoes crushing her toes, she stalked out of the bar.

12

......

The Play

Gabe sat next to his wife in the darkened auditorium. Onstage, his eighteen-year-old daughter, Violet, was performing a play she had written. It was undeniably terrible. The theme, Violet had told him, was *intersectionality*, but the six teens onstage appeared to be embroiled in a dance-off. Silently, he cursed the day he'd allowed his only child to transfer to this alternative school from Chapin, the tony private school on the Upper East Side. Violet had been running wild in Manhattan, hanging with a crowd of hedonistic, entitled teens with money for drugs, booze, and clubs. When a boy was accidentally shot at a party Violet was attending, Celeste had panicked. Already fragile from her illness, his spouse had scooped up their daughter and retreated to the Hamptons full-time.

It was an overreaction (the kid had been shot in the *foot*), but Gabe had gone along with it. The move would get Violet "back on track," Celeste had insisted. The Fairhaven School was just a short drive from their Sagaponack home and would be a great fit for their freethinking, creative child.

"They foster multidisciplinary global thinking and engagement," Celeste had said, like it wasn't just a mission statement concocted by some communications firm. Gabe had given in, and now his daughter had become a far-left, political thespian with minimal talent. Perfect.

He glanced over at Celeste. She was smiling, holding her phone, filming the performance for posterity. Perhaps his wife understood the play better as a woman, as a person of color, as someone who'd suffered a serious illness. Celeste had always been more liberal, more open-minded than Gabe was. Though it was an unpopular opinion to voice in his circles, he felt the world was tilting too far to the left, pushing the boundaries of common sense. This opinion was never more solidified than when he spent time with his daughter. Violet had become a social-justice warrior (though he'd never use that pejorative term around her). Since her move from the city at fourteen, the girl had been championing the rights of the marginalized: women, animals, the disabled, indigenous peoples, the LGBTQ community, immigrants, people of color, vertically challenged flight attendants, mimes with Tourette's . . .

Celeste had always been supportive. "She's passionate and curious, with a strong moral compass. We should be proud of that."

Gabe would have been a hell of a lot prouder if Violet had taken an interest in finance or engineering or the law—something that would lead to a career, a salary, a way to pay her own way in life. His only child seemed destined to become a playwright, a poet, or a professional activist, leaching off her parents while she indulged her passions. Celeste might find that path worthy of pride, but Gabe did not. He still hoped Violet would attend his alma mater, but a degree in gender and sexuality studies, even from Princeton, wouldn't take her far.

When Violet was small, she'd been the apple of her father's eye: smart, athletic, precocious. She had worshipped him, too, had hung on his every word, laughed at every joke, no matter how corny. He'd indulged all her whims, unable to say no to her cherubic little face, had been putty in her chubby little hands. "You spoil her," Celeste had gently chided, but she'd admired their father-daughter bond, understood it. Celeste had been a daddy's girl, too. She knew how seminal that relationship was.

And then, something changed. Violet changed. She got "woke." Instead of gazing on him with adoration, his daughter now sneered at him with disdain. She considered him conservative and backward. Capitalist scum. A symbol of the patriarchy.

"She'll come around," Celeste assured him. "Her principles will evolve and change as she gets older."

But it cut him, his daughter's scorn. Gabe had pulled away from his only child in the last few years, repelled by her brittle affect and her constant judgment. He would keep his emotional distance and he would wait. One day, his adoring girl would return.

Violet was alone on the darkened stage now, a spotlight shining down on her lustrous brown hair. In this lighting, you could barely see her pierced septum, the gold ring that branded her "alternative." His daughter had inherited her mother's good looks but not her poise, her confidence, or her common sense. Celeste was practical. She'd chosen a career that was altruistic as well as lucrative. Violet would barely discuss college with him, said she'd *never* consider going into the law. Celeste stayed in a marriage that offered financial stability, physical trappings, the appearance of perfection. Violet (who had recently announced herself pansexual) would insist on a soul connection, emotional intimacy, rainbows, and fireworks. Completely unrealistic.

"Our job as her parents is to love her and accept her," Celeste had said. But, his wife's unconditional devotion had given their daughter carte blanche to turn herself into a morally superior jerk. Had Violet remained with her hard-drinking, coke-snorting peers, at least she'd have been *normal*, at least she'd have made some useful connections. But Celeste was in charge of their daughter's well-being. And Gabe had plenty to distract him: a challenging career; a membership at an exclusive gym; sexy, younger, women eager to please. As Violet performed her soliloquy (something about white privilege though she was, technically, three-quarters white), Gabe realized that the girl onstage was a stranger to him.

His phone, in the breast pocket of his jacket, vibrated silently. It would be work. He was currently embroiled in a massive acquisition, should not be away from the office, but Celeste had guilt-tripped him into staying for this performance. He would head back to the city first thing in the morning, be in the office before anyone else. Surreptitiously, his hand slipped inside his sport coat. Celeste would admonish him if she saw him checking texts during Violet's monologue, but his wife was still filming, seemingly enraptured by their daughter's words. Celeste and Violet had had their issues—the girl could be strong-willed and rebellious; her mother's illness had taken a toll on all of them—but they now shared a connection, a bond that excluded him.

He pulled the phone from his pocket and held it low, next to his right knee. His wife kept filming, didn't even notice. The number on the tiny screen was not familiar but he read the message.

Do-over? I promise not to drink too much this time.

And then, below it.

It's Natalie btw.
The drunken mess from the other night.

He couldn't suppress his smile as he remembered the girl: cute, funny, inebriated, sloppy. . . . But Gabe had liked her. There was something real and raw and refreshing about her. He'd even enjoyed taking care of her: helping her out of the bar and into his waiting car, escorting her to her door where she'd given him a clumsy hug of thanks. It was the way she'd looked at him, with such gratitude, respect . . . almost awe. His wife and daughter did not look at him that way. The other sugar babies he'd dated did, but it was practiced, fake, professional. Natalie's admiration was authentic. He suddenly realized how much he needed it.

Stealthily, he slipped the phone back into his pocket before his wife noticed. When the play was over, he would head to the restroom and text Natalie back. He'd take her for dinner this time, somewhere in Manhattan, close to his apartment on the Upper East Side. If things progressed like he hoped they would, they would have easy access to his place. A thrill ran through him at the thought of her naked, in his bed, her eyes on him, hungry and adoring.

Celeste lowered her phone then and smiled over at him. Her eyes were full of proud, happy tears. He smiled back at his wife, gave her knee an affectionate squeeze. Dutifully, he turned his eyes back to the stage, saw that Violet's monologue was over. She was now being arrested by a teen in a cop uniform and a fake mustache. He watched his kid being dragged off to a cardboard jail, his thoughts firmly entrenched on Natalie.

The Call

Natalie's resolve to leave the sugar bowl lasted roughly two hours after her disastrous date with Nick. When she'd gotten home and showered away the filth of the encounter, the reality of her situation had dawned on her. She had tuition and rent to pay. She could not afford to take a moral stand. All she could do was brush up on acronyms for kinky sex (BDSM equals bondage, domination, sadomasochism; RP equals role-play; DMLB equals dominant mommy–little boy) and read the men's profiles carefully. She would ensure that the next daddy she met would not expect her to dress up like a dominatrix, a toddler, or the slutty pizza delivery girl.

She had scrolled through her messages (they continued to pour in), her cursor landing on the conversation with Gabe. He'd been so kind to her, so patient and understanding. That was not something she was used to with her temperamental father, nor her aloof stepfather. Her boyfriend, Cole, had seemed doting at first, but he had quickly turned cloying, smothering, controlling. Nat had stared at the phone number Gabe had sent after he'd had the Thai food delivered. It couldn't hurt to see him one more time, could it? But when she had gone to text him, her stomach had filled with nervous butterflies and she'd returned to the new messages.

Her search had identified two other potential dates: one, a pudgy business owner who seemed bland and lonely; the other, a neuroscientist, awkward and harmless. The thought of reaching out to these strangers caused her no anxiety, but texting Gabe made her sweat. It was different with him. She knew him, she liked him, and she was slightly attracted to him, despite his age. So why was she hesitating? The other men might be completely benign, but Gabe was a known commodity. He was guaranteed safe, guaranteed to pay. With her heart thudding in her ears, she had sent him a message.

He'd responded to her within the hour, inviting her to meet him for dinner on the Upper East Side on Wednesday night. It was a trek from Brooklyn, but a treat to go out in such a posh neighborhood. And when Gabe offered to send a car for her, Nat was grateful and flattered. As she hurried home from school that evening to get ready, she felt a thrill of anticipation. It was wrong to feel excited; this was not a date, it was an arrangement, a way to pay her bills. But she couldn't help but feel a bit like Cinderella . . . if Prince Charming had handed her a wad of cash as the clock struck midnight.

She was slipping into Ava's black pencil skirt when her cell phone rang. It would be Gabe, canceling their rendezvous. He had commitments: a high-powered job, needy clients. As she rummaged through the clutter in her room for her phone, she was surprised at the depth of her disappointment. She had been looking forward to seeing him again. But when she found her device, buried under her robe on her unmade bed, it was her mom's name on the call display.

It was not a good time to talk to her mother. Nat was about to embark on a date with a man several years her mom's senior. The thought twisted Nat's insides, made her feel guilty and gross. But she knew she could ignore her mom no longer. She picked up the phone and answered.

"Hey, Mom."

"Finally." Allana's tone was not annoyed, as expected. It was relieved. "Why haven't you called me back?"

"Sorry," Nat mumbled. "I've been busy. With school and work."

"Look, honey . . . there's something you need to know."

Her mom's ominous tone made Nat's stomach plunge. "Are you okay? Is it the kids?"

"The kids are fine. I'm fine. Derek's fine." There was a pause. She heard her mom take a fortifying breath. "It's about Cole Doberinsky."

A weight, dark and heavy, fell on Nat at the sound of his name. Nat was angry at Cole, afraid of him, even hated him. But she couldn't deny that he had played a significant role in her life. Her first love, her first sexual experience, her first devastating breakup. And now, something had happened to him.

"He'd been going to school," her mom continued. "Working for his dad part-time. Even dating."

He was dead. Her mother didn't need to say it. Nat knew it in her bones.

"He seemed to have moved on and put the past behind him. But recently, he'd been drinking a lot, hanging with a bad crowd."

Suicide? A car crash? A drunken brawl? It would be something like that. To Nat's surprise, tears welled in her eyes and emotion clogged her throat. A small part of her blamed herself.

"And then . . . he just left."

"*Left?*" Nat's tears and emotion evaporated. "What do you mean, he *left*?"

"He'd been living with his parents. They came home from work to find he'd packed a bag and gone."

"So . . . you're calling to tell me Cole took a *vacation*?" Her grief instantly morphed into irritation.

"He didn't take a vacation, Natalie." It was Allana's turn to sound annoyed. "He left a note. His mom wouldn't tell me exactly what it said, but his parents think he's gone to New York. They think . . ." Her mom trailed off, took a ragged breath.

"They think Cole's trying to find you."

14

......

The Bistro

Nat sat in the back of the town car, her eyes transfixed by the twinkling lights of Manhattan. Usually, she commuted into the city in a cramped, smelly subway car. Now, she was being chauffeured in the back of a sumptuous Lincoln that smelled of leather and wool and expensive cologne. The uniformed driver (she vaguely recalled meeting him the other night) had greeted her officiously in accented English, had held the door open for her to enter the sleek vehicle. Now, he was whisking her into the city to meet a handsome, older man at a chic, uptown restaurant. It all felt surreal . . . because it wasn't real. It was a transaction.

She had vowed to put Cole out of her mind, for tonight, at least. There was no proof that he was in New York, that he was looking for her, that he was still angry with her. And even if he were in the city, how would he find her? The apartment was in Mara's name. Nat had paid fifteen bucks for a new cell number upon relocation. She had blocked Cole from her social media accounts after he'd posted angry rants calling out her abandonment, her duplicitousness, her lack of loyalty in the most colorful terms (*selfish cunt, cheating bitch, lying whore*). Even if he created a fake account to access her Instagram or Snapchat, she never posted anything personal. When she'd first arrived in New York, she'd shared a bunch of touristy photos: the Brooklyn Bridge, the 9/11 Memorial, the Statue of Liberty taken from the Staten Island Ferry. Her limited presence on social media would provide no clues to her whereabouts. She could almost relax, could almost feel safe . . . Except Cole knew where she went to school.

The thought made her feel hot, sweaty, mildly nauseated. She grabbed the plastic water bottle from the console beside her, cracked it open, and drank. It was tepid and tasted like chemicals, did nothing to cool her down or soothe her anxiety. She tried to breathe her way through the panic fluttering in her chest—closing her eyes, inhaling slowly through her nose, out through her mouth. Even if Cole came to the School of Visual Arts, he wouldn't attack her in front of the entire student population. He wasn't that violent, nor that impulsive. But Cole might observe her, follow her, discover her recent lifestyle choice. And with that knowledge, he could destroy her.

She wouldn't allow it. Nat was no longer the

naive, vulnerable girl Cole had known back in Blaine. She'd discovered new depths to her resolve, new lengths to which she was willing to go to sustain her life in New York. Two years ago, she could never have imagined she'd be getting paid to date older men. But now she was. And if Cole Doberinsky came for her, she would be ready for him. If he threatened the life she had built here, she would fight back. She would do whatever it took to protect herself.

They were uptown now, the streets widening, lightening, glowing like they'd been scrubbed clean of the city's grit and grime. Nat did not come here often, but it still felt familiar: the park, the museums, the buildings, all so iconic.

"It feels like a movie," she mumbled, gazing at the passing scenery.

"It does." The deep voice came from her chauffeur.

Nat leaned forward. "I always feel that way when I come up here. I'm from a small town, far away."

"Me, too."

"How long have you lived here?" she asked.

"Many years now," he said, in his undetermined accent. Russian maybe? "But sometimes, I still feel like I've landed on another planet."

"I feel that way about twice a day."

The driver chuckled. "A strange but familiar planet."

Nat liked this avuncular man, felt an instant rapport with him. But then she remembered why she was in the back seat of his car. He was driving her to meet her sugar daddy. He knew what was about to happen. He knew what she was. What did he think of her?

The car pulled up in front of a quaint French bistro set below street level. "We're here," he announced.

"Thanks."

The muscular man, in his mid-to-late forties, was already getting out of the driver's seat, moving around to open the door for her. He took her hand and helped her out without a whiff of judgment.

"Mr. Turnmill is already inside."

Gabe Turnmill. Ava had told her to get his full name, had told her to google him. Oops. Again.

"Thanks for the ride, uh . . . ?"

"Oleg," the driver said with a slight nod. "Nice to meet you, Natalie."

She smiled, appreciating his warmth, his acceptance. "Nice to meet you, too."

With some difficulty, Nat descended the steps to the establishment's front door (a pencil skirt and heels did not pair well with stairs). Inside, she found a classic French bistro: a black-and-white-tiled floor, linen table cloths, orangey-red roses in bud vases. The walls were papered in vertical stripes of gold and cream, the lamplight giving the room, and its well-heeled patrons, a flattering glow.

She spotted him instantly, seated at a secluded back table. Gabe was dressed more casually than the last time she'd seen him. He wore a tweedy sports coat over a crisp white shirt and a pair of jeans. On the table sat that same amber drink, and her stomach churned with remembrance. Gabe was fixated on his phone, but he must have sensed her presence hovering at the door. He looked up and smiled, his blue eyes twinkling, even from this distance. He was handsome, she realized. And not just *for his age*.

The maître d' snapped to attention. "Bonsoir," he said in a smooth Parisian accent. "May I help you?"

"I'm meeting a friend," she said, gesturing toward Gabe.

The man glanced behind him. "Of course. Monsieur Turnmill is expecting you. Right this way, mademoiselle."

Obediently, she followed him down the narrow walkway. Gabe's location afforded them as much privacy as was possible in the packed bistro, its tables close together in the European style. He could have chosen a more discreet restaurant, somewhere bigger, darker, with huge booths where they could disappear. But Gabe did not seem to feel guilty or ashamed to be seen with her. (Of course, it was not *he* who received the disparaging looks; those were directed at Nat.) He stood to greet her, his hand on her waist, his lips on her cheek. She liked his scent: a pricey cologne concocted to smell like he'd spent the day chopping down cedar trees.

As they sat, Gabe ordered them a bottle of Côtes du Rhône, and their host hurried away. Gabe reached out and held her fingers in both his hands. They were warm, smooth, felt strangely comforting. His eyes roved over her appreciatively.

"You look great."

"So do you." She smiled, cast her eyes down. "Thanks for seeing me again."

"I wanted to see you," he said. "I was happy to get your text."

"I wouldn't have blamed you if you'd told me to get lost."

"Why? Because you got a little tipsy last time?"

"A little *tipsy*? I was a drunken disaster."

"An adorable drunken disaster."

He was charming her, his attention making her feel warm and fluttery. She had to stay professional, in control. She could not forget, even for a moment, what this was. She could not fall for this guy.

The maître d' returned then, making a performance of opening the wine, offering Gabe a taste, but Gabe dismissed him with a curt "It's fine." Her date filled their glasses; they toasted their reunion and drank. As usual, good wine was wasted on Nat, but it tasted acceptable, and the first few sips were already relaxing her.

Gabe was perusing the menu. "Do you eat foie gras?"

"Constantly," Nat quipped. Nerves or infatuation were making her silly, sassy. She hoped she wasn't being rude.

But Gabe laughed. "I meant it from an ethical standpoint. My daughter says foie gras is cruel." He took a sip of wine. "But she also thinks chickpeas have *feelings*."

Nat chuckled through an uncomfortable twinge. His daughter. It felt awkward to think of Gabe as a family man, a father. "How old is she?" Nat asked, straining for a casual tone.

"She just turned eighteen."

"It's normal to have a lot of principles at that age."

"Too many, if you ask me."

Nat wondered if Gabe knew how recently she

had been a principled eighteen-year-old. He knew
she was young, obviously, but did he know she was
only a few years older than his daughter? Would he
care? Or would it excite him? A frisson of wrong
shivered through her, but she pushed it away.

They ordered then, a foie gras appetizer (she
couldn't object *now*), coq au vin for her and boeuf
bourguignon for him. Conversation flowed easily.
Waiting for their food, Gabe asked her about school,
queried about her favorite classes, what she'd like to
do upon graduation. When the foie gras on toasted
baguette rounds arrived, she told him she hoped to
become a children's book illustrator. Gabe didn't
smirk or sneer, didn't tell her it was unrealistic or
impractical. He seemed supportive, confident that
she had the talent and drive to bring such a career
to fruition.

As they tucked into their main courses, conversation shifted to travel and their dream destinations.
The topic morphed into a lively debate about
human settlement on Mars. Gabe thought being a
part of the Mars One mission would be a thrill, a
chance to explore a new frontier, establish a new
world, be a pioneer. Nat had felt claustrophobic in
Blaine; she could only imagine how she would freak
out if she had to live in a bubble.

They were laughing, flirting, having fun. Nat
knew this wasn't real, that it was all a game, but she
allowed herself to enjoy the fact that there was no
physical or emotional agenda. She and Gabe could
simply have a good time together. That was the
point of a no-strings relationship. Well, *that* and the
money were the points for Nat. But she was swept

up in the conversation, the wine, the French ambiance. And then . . .

She saw him.

Cole Doberinsky was wearing a smart gray suit. She'd never seen him so dressed up, but she recognized his broad shoulders, his long legs, his rangy walk. His eyes, dark and intense, were unforgettable. And the way they were looking at her, with such loathing, such contempt, was familiar, too. He was coming toward her, his posture tense and aggressive. What was he going to do to her? Slap her? Spit in her face? Call her a whore? Anxiety drew the blood from her face, turned her fingers and toes to ice. She half stood, hands gripping the edge of the table.

"Natalie?" Gabe's voice was concerned, confused. "What's wrong?"

Cole was almost upon them now. She opened her mouth to cry out, but no sound came. Her throat was dry, parched, raw with dread. And then, Cole walked right past them. She watched him move to the back of the restaurant, headed for the restrooms. Before her eyes, he changed. The man in the suit was not an angry twenty-one-year-old determined to exact vengeance on his ex-girlfriend. This guy was in his thirties, with the same build as Cole, the same sandy-colored hair, but a softer jawline, a less handsome face. Her legs turned to jelly with relief, and she sat heavily into her seat.

"Are you okay? You're shaking."

"I'm sorry. I thought . . ." Oh shit. Now she was going to cry. Gabe would think she was a lunatic: raging drunk on their first date, blubbering like a baby on their second.

But her companion's expression was concerned, not disgusted. He brushed her cheek with two fingers and said softly, "Want to get out of here?"

She nodded. If she tried to speak, she would fall apart.

"I live a couple of blocks away. We could go to my apartment. To talk."

Her eyes met his then, and she felt that magnetic pull, the chemistry that had so surprised her. She had not planned for this connection, had not expected to feel what she was feeling. Ava's advice flitted through her mind . . . *Keep your distance. Protect your privacy. Set boundaries.* She had to refuse Gabe's invitation. It was wrong, no matter how right it felt. Her voice, when she spoke, was hoarse.

"Okay," she said.

The Sleepover

Nat was nestled in the back seat of the town car again, but this time, it was morning. Her smart phone told her it was 7:08, the sun hovering over the East River. Gabe's strapping driver—she'd learned he was from Moldova, an Eastern European country bordered by Romania and Ukraine—was shuttling her back to Brooklyn. Their route would take them through Queens, Oleg informing her that this was the quickest route to Bushwick at this time of day. As she watched the drab scenery whisk by the window, everything painted with a patina of winter mud, she let her mind drift back to last night. To Gabe.

She had not intended to spend the night at his apartment (it was larger and even more luxurious than Ava's, but distinctly masculine, a bachelor's pad). She had gone there to *talk*, and they had. This man, this virtual stranger, now knew everything about her: her father's abandonment, her stepdad's resentment, her ex-boyfriend's creepy obsession. Gabe knew that the police—all the adults in Nat's life—had dismissed Cole as an innocuous teenager in love. But Gabe knew that Nat was afraid of Cole. And he knew that the boy was in New York.

"I won't let anything happen to you," he'd assured her. "I have ways of dealing with these nuisances." When he'd leaned in and kissed her, she had let him. At first, out of gratitude, and then, from true passion. Nat had never thought she could be physically attracted to a much older man, but she had never met a man like Gabe Turnmill. He was sophisticated, suave, and, as she had just found out, a little bit dangerous.

A small smile curled her lips as she remembered the taste of his lips, the scent of his neck, his hands in her hair. She'd enjoyed kissing him so much that she'd allowed him to lead her to his bedroom. But she'd stopped in the doorway, suddenly afraid, overwhelmed. Kissing was one thing; sex with a much older man, a man who was paying her, was quite another.

"It's okay," he'd said, "I just want to hold you." It may have been naive, but she'd believed him. And when he'd offered her a large gray T-shirt to sleep in, had worn a T-shirt and boxers himself, she began to relax. They'd crawled into the queen-size bed together, he'd wrapped her in his arms and then, with her head on his chest, she'd slept. Warm. Safe. Protected.

Nat had never been able to sleep in such close quarters. With Miguel, she'd felt crowded and claustrophobic, even in her double bed. On the handful of occasions when she'd spent the night with Cole (his parents did not allow sleepovers, but Mr. and Mrs. Doberinsky spent two weeks in Arizona each winter, allowing the young lovers some intimacy), she'd felt restless and antsy. There was something comforting about Gabe, something reassuring in his posh, masculine apartment, the doorman on sentry duty. Oddly, Nat felt at home there.

Her belly rumbled then, a sick, churning sensation. *It's just hunger*, she told herself. She should have accepted Gabe's offer of whole wheat toast instead of insisting the latte he'd made her was adequate. But it was more than just the caffeine churning in her empty stomach. It was her conscience. Their night had felt so romantic, so special, so meaningful. Until he had handed her the money.

She'd tried to refuse the cash. It felt wrong after the comfort and reassurance he'd provided, not to mention the car service, the dinner, the wine. . . . When he had handed her the wad of bills, it cheapened what they had shared, made her feel like a prostitute though they hadn't had sex. She had shaken her head. "It's fine."

"Take it." He'd smiled and pressed the money into her hands. "I like spoiling you."

So she'd accepted it, trying to push away the sick

feeling in her gut, reminding herself that she had tuition, rent, and bills to pay, that money was the reason she had contacted Gabe in the first place. If she thought of it as a gift, as a token of Gabe's affection and appreciation, she felt better about it. Because she and Gabe had something, something that went beyond a business arrangement. He'd asked to see her again on Saturday, and she had readily agreed.

They were nearing her building now, and Nat suddenly realized how this would look to her roommates. "Could you pull over here?" she asked her driver.

"We're still three blocks away."

"I know. It's just . . . my roommates are really judgmental. I know how this looks . . . even though nothing actually happened."

The big car slowed to a stop. Nat's clarification didn't.

"I was upset. My ex-boyfriend is in New York. He's obsessive and angry, and I'm afraid of him. I thought I saw him at the restaurant. I was rattled, and Gabe—Mr. Turnmill—said I could spend the night. He said that I'd be safe there, since my ex, Cole, doesn't know where Gabe lives, of course. That's all that happened. We just . . . *cuddled*."

Oleg turned in his seat and looked at her. "What you and my boss do in private is none of my business."

"I know. I just didn't want you to think . . . I'm not a . . . I'm not a *whore*."

"I didn't think you were." His expression was impassive. "I know what it takes to survive in this city."

His words of understanding moved her. "Thank you," she croaked.

Oleg watched her struggle with her emotions for a moment. "Are you really afraid of this boy?"

"Yes. It's been three years, and he's still obsessed with me. He's said horrible, abusive things to me online. He broke into my house. And now he's here. He's looking for me."

The man's hazel eyes stayed on her for a beat, and then he leaned over, reached into his glove box.

"Take this," he said, holding out his huge palm. In it was a small pistol.

"Oh my god." Nat had not grown up around guns. Derek had a rifle for hunting, but it was locked away in a cabinet in the garage. Nat associated guns with crime, with mass shootings, with gangsters. Not with people like Gabe Turnmill and his kindly driver.

"N-no thanks," she stammered.

"It's just a little nine-millimeter," he said, like it was a toy, a harmless water gun. He racked the slide. "It's easy to handle."

"I've never fired a gun before."

"And you won't need to," Oleg said, putting on the safety. "Point this at the kid who's harassing you, and you'll never see him again."

Tentatively, she reached out and accepted the revolver. It fit her hand comfortably, felt heavy and cool. Could she point it at Cole Doberinsky and threaten to kill him? To protect herself, her reputation, and her life in New York City, she could try.

Swallowing her anxiety, she said, "Thank you, Oleg."

"Let's keep this between us, yes?"

He didn't want Gabe to know. "Of course," she said.

She placed the gun in her purse and got out of the car.

Facebook

As Nat let herself into the apartment, she practically bumped into Mara in the hallway. Her roommate had a wool hat over her red hair, her winter coat on, and a backpack full of books slung over one shoulder. She was off to class.

"Morning," Nat muttered, sliding past her.

"Morning."

Nat felt Mara's critical eyes on her as she continued down the hall, clocking Nat's high heels, tight skirt, and bed head. Nat knew exactly what the angular girl was thinking: this was the walk of shame after a one-night stand. Her roommate's judgment brought to mind the sneers, the whispers, the disapproving glances Nat's dates with Gabe elicited. Since their first meeting in DUMBO, Nat had decided to ignore them. Because Nat didn't feel ashamed. She'd had a delicious dinner at a delightful restaurant with a charming, handsome man. A man who had listened to her hopes, her dreams, and her fears. A man who had held her, kept her safe in his arms, allowed her to sleep.

A man who had given her five hundred dollars the next morning.

If Mara knew that Nat had accepted money for a date, she'd have been horrified, disgusted, repulsed. And if the ginger-haired girl learned about the firearm in Nat's possession, she'd have gone ballistic. But there was no way Mara would ever know what was nestled in Nat's purse. Nat would wrap the weapon in a T-shirt and hide it in the back of a drawer. And that's where it would stay—unless Cole Doberinsky came for her.

In her room, Nat stripped off her clothes and jumped into her sweats. She would not go to school today. It would be pointless. Her mind was swimming with warm thoughts of Gabe, anxious thoughts of Cole, and of the weapon now hidden in her sock drawer. Ava, Keltie, or Ivan could provide the notes she missed. She had an illustration to work on at home. And she had research to do. She needed to find out, for sure, if her ex-boyfriend was in New York City. If he was there to find her. If he was there to hurt her.

Logging on to her laptop, she opened Facebook. Her peer group was not active on the platform; posting vacation photos and memes and political articles was for *old people*. But Facebook was a utility, a database of everyone she knew (or had met once or twice). And while Natalie had blocked Cole from seeing her social media activity, he allowed her full access. Of course he did. He wanted to stay connected to her anyway he could.

Cole's profile picture featured the two of them at prom, evidence of his continued obsession, his inability to move on. That was over three years ago! Nat felt like a completely different person than the girl in the royal-blue satin dress, her hair up in what she'd considered a sophisticated chignon. Was Cole still the same boy who stood, handsome but awkward, in a rented black suit and a blue bow tie? How could he not have changed? Have grown or matured?

As predicted, Cole hadn't posted anything on his Facebook wall in over a year. There were a few outdated birthday wishes (from his aunt, a couple of their high school classmates), but nothing that provided a clue to his whereabouts. She tried Instagram. Cole hadn't posted, but he'd been tagged in a few photos. In one, he was with a bunch of men—older, rough guys, not their high school crowd—standing in front of a bonfire. Their eyes shone in the firelight. They looked drunk. They looked mean. Is this who Cole spent time with now? Was this who he had become?

Nat's mind drifted back to the day she'd told Cole she'd been accepted to the School of Visual Arts, the day she'd ended their relationship. She'd tried to minimize the hurt, had chosen her words carefully. "It's not about leaving you," she'd said, "it's about seizing this opportunity." But the truth was, she'd been so excited, so full of anticipation, that she'd struggled to contain it. Like a butterfly emerging from its cocoon, Natalie was about to be reborn. She was going to live a stimulating life of creativity and adventure in New York City; it was her destiny. Cole Doberinsky was just collateral damage.

The slightest twinge of guilt, of pity pinched her chest, but she brushed it away. Cole did not deserve her sympathy. He'd tried to hold her back, to take the joy out of her success, to guilt-trip her into giving up her dreams. And then, he had broken into her house while she slept. Even before that fateful night, he'd been possessive and controlling. He'd assumed that Nat, the girl from a broken home, the girl with the absent father, would amount to nothing. That Cole was her last best hope at a decent life. But Nat had a new life now. She was attending the best art school in the country. She was riding in town cars, eating at French bistros, sleeping in an Upper East Side apartment. She would not let Cole Doberinsky take all that away from her.

Her breath was rapid and shallow as she returned to his Facebook page, to the photo of those two naive kids in their almost comical prom outfits. With a shaky hand, she clicked the messenger icon. A small screen popped open, inviting her to type a message to Cole. She took a breath, and then she began.

I know you're in New York. I have a gun. If you try to hurt me, I'll kill you.

Before she could think better of it, she clicked the send button. The threat went flying through the ether to Cole.

Emily

Gabe would stay in the city that weekend. He'd
spent an extra day in Sagaponack earlier in the week
to watch his daughter's ridiculous play, so catching up on work was a suitable excuse. Not that he
needed one: his wife and daughter seemed largely
indifferent to his absence or presence. Once, they'd
waited for his car to pull into the drive, bursting out
of the house to greet him. Now, Violet was busy
with her weird friends and her plethora of causes;
Celeste with a myriad of appointments devoted
to her physical, mental, and spiritual health. Their
ambivalence had wounded him, at first, especially
Violet's. How could she adore him one day, ignore
him the next? At least their apathy afforded him a
certain amount of freedom.

He was looking forward to seeing Natalie on Saturday. The girl was stuck in his head like an ant in honey. He liked her dark hair, her fair skin, her full lips. He appreciated the natural grace that compensated for her lack of sophistication. Even her problems and drama were compelling: the terrified look in her eyes when she'd told him about the jilted high school boyfriend out to get her. When she'd melted into his arms, Gabe had felt like her hero, her savior, her white knight. No one had made him feel that way in a very long time.

On their next date, he would ask her to make things *official*. This was the trajectory of these relationships. A couple of dates to gauge chemistry, and, if all went well, an allowance would be offered, a schedule set. He would see Natalie twice a week subject to his availability. Natalie wasn't greedy; she'd be satisfied with a $3,500 monthly stipend. Add in a few nice dinners out, a Broadway show or two, maybe a weekend in Vermont, and she'd be over the moon. But first, there was something he had to take care of. Or someone.

Emily.

They'd had an arrangement for about four months. Gabe had found her on the sugar website. Emily was sweet, sexy, and exotic. Her mother was from the Philippines, her father, Brazilian. Or maybe he was Argentine? Gabe couldn't recall, hadn't really been listening. He was attracted to Emily, and the sex was good, but their relationship had never felt genuine. The petite woman said and did all the right things, almost like she was playing a part. Emily had been around the block; she knew the drill. Natalie wasn't like that. She was innocent, fresh, real.

The sugar website offered tips on ending relations with one's sugar baby. *Do it in person, over a nice lunch.* This rustic, Italian restaurant in the financial district was one of the best in the city. *Give her a goodbye gift.* A white-gold-and-diamond necklace rested in his pocket. It had set him back almost five grand, paid on his personal credit card attached to a secret account. He never left any evidence for Celeste to find; not that she was suspicious. *Be gentle with your sugar baby's feelings but firm in your resolve.* Gabe was an attorney, a master negotiator. He could handle this.

Emily would not cause him any problems. Gabe was her fourth or fifth sugar daddy; she'd been open about that. It hadn't bothered him. In fact, it had provided him some comfort. This girl wouldn't expect too much or make too many demands. And when he cut her off, she would take it like the pro she was.

He watched her enter the bustling restaurant on sky-high heels, looking hot in a tight dress the color of desert sand. His groin tingled pleasantly as he thought about the body beneath the clinging fabric: tight, compact, strong. She taught some kind of exercise class—kickboxing or boxercise—and it showed. For a beat, he considered keeping things going with Emily on a more casual basis. Financially, he could probably swing it, but the time commitment would be too much. He stood to greet her.

"Hi, Gabe." She kissed his cheek, then took a seat across from him. "Happy Valentine's Day."

Shit. He'd completely forgotten. His assistant

would have sent Celeste flowers. He made a mental note to call her later.

Emily crossed her legs. "You look handsome."

So slick, so professional. He thought of Natalie's shy, slightly awkward presence and felt his heart swell. He was doing the right thing.

"You look gorgeous," he said. "Shall we get some wine?" It was for her, to soften the blow. He had a divestiture to deal with this afternoon, so he had to keep his wits about him. "Red or white?"

Emily smiled. "Whatever you're in the mood for."

He ordered a bottle of white and their lunch—a plate of pasta and clams for him, a caprese salad for her. This place was fast, catering to the bankers, traders, and attorneys who had to get back to the office. He'd picked this restaurant, and this meal, for that exact reason. He didn't want to eat a long, lingering lunch with a breakup hovering over him. Emily asked about his work, but he shifted the conversation back to her and her workout class. As she droned on about boxercise (he knew it was something like that), he wondered what she was wearing under that beige dress. Emily always wore expensive lingerie. Was she expecting their meeting to end in sex, as usual? *Could* it end in sex, as usual? Would it be crass and cruel to break it off with her after she'd serviced him? He nibbled a breadstick and decided it probably would be.

When their meals arrived, Emily picked at her salad, eating the tomatoes and basil but scraping the fresh mozzarella off to the side. Natalie ate real food, ate it with gusto. The way Emily was toying with her entrée made him think of a bratty child.

He chewed a mouthful of pasta and decided it was time. Reaching into his pocket, he brought out the black velvet box with the pendant inside.

"I got you something."

"Oh my god!" Emily dropped her fork, pressed her hands to her surgically enhanced bosom. She flashed him a grateful smile, then dived for the box. Her eyes were alight, glowing with avarice, as she opened it. She took the delicate jewelry from its satin nest and held it before her.

"It's beautiful." She beamed at him. "I love it."

"I wanted you to have a token of my affection." He cleared his throat. "And my appreciation."

The light in Emily's eyes faded as realization struck her: This was not a Valentine's gift. She set the necklace back in the box and closed it. "Thank you."

"You're an amazing woman—beautiful and accomplished. I'm sure there are plenty of men who would love to have a relationship with you."

"Are you ending things?"

"I would love to keep seeing you but . . . it's my daughter. She's going through some difficult stuff. She needs my support and attention right now."

He'd practiced the lie, but even to his own ears, it sounded disingenuous. If Violet were going through *stuff*, Gabe would be the last person to whom she would turn.

Emily read his deception. "I thought she lived with your ex-wife?"

"She does. But she wants to move in with me. Part-time at least."

"We could dial things back. See each other less

often." She was grasping, trying not to lose her allowance. "I respect your relationship with your daughter."

"I think a clean break is for the best."

He expected her to object, to try another tack, but she pressed her lips together and forced a small smile. "Okay." Disappointment made her eyes shiny. "I understand."

This was why he paid for his relationships.

Emily tossed her napkin onto her half-eaten salad, dropped the velvet box into her bag. "I've really enjoyed our time together."

"As have I."

"If you change your mind, you know where to find me."

"Of course." He reached in his pocket for one last gift. "I'd like you to have this." He slid the envelope across the table toward her. "It's two months' allowance."

In one swift movement, she snatched it up, slipped it into her purse. "I appreciate that."

She pushed back her chair and stood. Gabe got up, too.

"My driver will take you back to Hell's Kitchen."

"Thanks." She kissed his cheek, lingering just long enough for the pheromones to kick in and make him second-guess his decision. "Goodbye, Gabe." And then she walked out of the restaurant.

Gabe sat down and signaled the waiter for the bill. He had to get back to the office, had clients coming within the hour. He downed the glass of wine he hadn't planned to drink, feeling a little forlorn. Emily had been sweet, beautiful, compliant.

The ease with which she'd allowed him to end their relationship made him appreciate her more. But he had done this for a reason, and that reason was Natalie. He would see her on Saturday, but he didn't want to wait. He wanted to see her right then, as soon as possible. She would distract him from the niggling sense of loss he was feeling. Pulling out his phone, he texted her.

Drinks tonight?

He waited for a response, but none came. The bill arrived, and he paid it with cash. As he left the restaurant, he checked his phone again. Still nothing. Walking back to his office, he felt agitated, on edge. What if Natalie wasn't infatuated with him after all? Perhaps the wide-eyed ingenue act was exactly that—an act. Maybe the little bitch had been playing him?

"Watch it, asshole," he snarled at a tourist whose eyes were clamped on the digital map on his phone. But it wasn't the distracted Midwesterner he was angry with; it was Natalie. He'd dumped Emily to be with her, and now, she was ghosting him. He was pissed at her, and at himself. He had given this unsophisticated girl the power to hurt him, and he didn't like it.

In the cavernous lobby of his office building, his phone finally buzzed. Pulling it from his coat pocket, he saw the name: Nathan. He'd added the fake name to his contacts on the slim chance that Celeste or Violet glanced at his phone. But it was Natalie. Relief flooded through him. She was into him, after all. Of course she was.

I'd love to. Where?

He would respond to her after his meeting, make her sweat a little, give her a taste of her own medicine.

"Hold the elevator!" Gabe called. With a spring in his step, he jogged toward it.

The Arrangement

The L train rattled and shook its way into the Third Avenue station. Nat stood, along with the other morning commuters, pressing themselves toward the door, straining for their final destinations. She was running late for class, but at least she'd be there. She'd been tempted to skip again—she was exhausted, mildly hungover—but she didn't want to fall behind. Ava had notes from their perspective class for her, and she had an acrylics project due and a lettering assignment to work on. But as she climbed the stairs to street level, she realized she would be present in body only. Her mind, her heart, her moral compass were firmly stuck in the events of last night.

Gabe's text had surprised her. They'd already made plans for Saturday; she hadn't expected a

man so busy and powerful to also be so spontaneous. She had hesitated before replying. Was seeing
him again so soon a mistake? And on Valentine's
Day? She had made a pact with herself. She would
go on two or three dates, make a little money, and
then she would stop. Nat was not sugar baby material. But what she had with Gabe felt different. He
was so attractive, so charming, so attentive. She had
already kissed him, had slept in his arms. She was
already falling for him.

The blossoming relationship was debauched, im-
moral, wrong. But she'd wanted to see Gabe again,
wanted to kiss him again, even. It wasn't about the
money—though she couldn't deny that it was extremely helpful. She had pushed aside her niggling
conscience and agreed to meet him for late drinks.
They'd arranged to meet in the East Village. There
was a poky little bar he liked that played live jazz
at a volume that still allowed conversation. As she'd
gotten herself ready, she'd experienced a confounding twist of emotions: anticipation, excitement, and
something that felt a lot like shame.

She'd splurged on another Uber. She knew that,
at the end of the night, her wallet would be lined
with hundred-dollar bills. It was a luxury she could
grow accustomed to, the kind of perk that made life
in Brooklyn easier. But when her car had stopped in
front of the cool establishment, she paused before
exiting. Her pulse was skittering, her heart ham-
mering in her chest. It was like her intuition had
known that this rendezvous was a turning point.
That it would change everything.

She was at campus now, the walk through the

chilly streets a blur. Hustling toward her illumination lab, she tried to shake off the reminiscence. But as she slid into her desk, booted up the computer, she knew it was fruitless. A smile flitted across her lips, chased away by a queasy feeling in her stomach. As the instructor, annoyed by her late entry, shot her a look, her mind drifted back to the previous night's date.

The club had been dark, almost hazy, though the fog may have been in her brain. She was on her third rusty nail (she had told herself she'd have no more than two, but Gabe had a way of making her feel adventurous, almost reckless). Onstage, a beautiful woman was singing, silky notes effluviating from her throat. The ambience was undeniably sultry.

"I love this place," Gabe said. "I come here when I've got a difficult case. Nothing as relaxing as Scotch and smooth jazz."

"Totally," Nat agreed, as if this was also a habit of hers.

Gabe smiled at her, then took her hand in his. "I'd like to talk to you about making this more . . . official."

The whiskey (she was developing a taste for it) burned her throat. "Umm . . . I'm not sure."

He removed his hand. "You're not interested?" His blue eyes were cold, his tone accusatory. He was angry at her for leading him on, for wasting his time. But she saw the pain beneath it. Her ambiguity had hurt him.

"Of course I am," she said quickly. It was her nature to smooth things over. Ten years with a volatile father had ingrained it in her. "I'm just new to this. I don't really know what that means."

He smiled, his eyes melting. "I'd like to set up an arrangement so I can see you regularly. I'll give you an allowance of thirty-five hundred a month."

Three thousand five hundred dollars. Every. Month.

"In return, I'd like to see you a couple of times a week. Our schedules permitting, of course."

She gave a slight nod, a small smile. Her throat was too dry to speak. And even if she could, how to verbalize the thoughts swirling in her head? This was never her plan, not what she'd wanted. But suddenly, she couldn't find any downside to it. She enjoyed spending time with this man who had introduced her to Scotch and jazz. She loved the way he looked at her, touched her, spoiled her. All her financial worries would be eliminated with this arrangement. And she had made peace with accepting money in exchange for her time, her attention, and whatever else might happen between them. At least she thought she had. . . .

"There are a few things you need to understand."

"Okay."

"I'm devoted to my daughter. I'll be with her most weekends, so I won't be able to see you."

"Right." Nat respected his dedication to his only child, and the schedule aligned nicely with her desire for freedom.

"This weekend is an exception. She's spending it with her mother at their house on Long Island. I keep a small weekend place there. Sometimes, my daughter joins me in the city."

"Okay."

"She can't ever know about you," Gabe continued, his voice firm, adamant. For the first time, she
could see him as a cutthroat attorney. "I keep my
family life and my dating life separate. My daughter
and my job will always be my top priorities."

"Sure." Before this moment, Gabe had made
her feel special and adored. Now, she knew exactly
where she stood.

"If you can respect that, I think we can have
something great together."

"I can. Of course I can."

"Good." He smiled as he reached into his pocket,
extracting a plain white envelope. He held it under
the table, away from prying eyes. "This is for you."

Her hand reached out and took it, depositing it
swiftly into her purse.

"Thank you."

And with that, Natalie had a sugar daddy.

It was surreal and fucked-up and amazing, all at the
same time. Nat needed to talk to Ava. Her friend
had knowledge and experience, would talk Nat
through her jitters and qualms. Ava was not in this
class, but Nat would see her later, in Western civilization. Nat shifted her focus to the task in front of
her, using 3-D lighting techniques to give an ani-
mation depth and dimension, but she was too late.
The professor announced that class was over. She'd
squandered the hour, her thoughts trapped in the
past.

Nat logged off the computer, gathered her bag,
and left the studio. Traversing the hallways on auto-

pilot, her fellow students were faceless blurs, her mind, again, on the night before. On Gabe. He had summoned his driver, had kissed her goodbye, his mouth warm and hungry and tasting like whiskey. His hand found its way into her hair, the other to her waist, pulling her closer into him.

"I'm so happy you're in my life," he'd whispered.

"Me, too." And she'd felt that way then. But not now.

Now, she felt anxious, worried, afraid she was in over her head. Initially, she'd thought she would be repulsed by an older man, disgusted at the thought of his body, of his hands touching her. But that was not the case with Gabe Turnmill. When she was with him, she felt giddy, happy, sparkly. When he kissed her, she melted, when he touched her, she wanted more. She had never felt this way before, not with Cole, not with Miguel. But this was not a real relationship. Gabe was paying her.

Now, Nat was afraid of falling for a man she could never really have.

19
· · · · · ·

The Incident

Ava was not in class, which afforded Nat the opportunity to repay the note-taking favor. Her focus was improved this session, and she religiously jotted down pertinent facts in the professor's monologue on the Enlightenment. Surreptitiously, she texted Ava.

Are you sick? I'll take notes for you.

But her friend didn't reply. When class was over, Nat checked her phone again. Still no response. She had a three-hour window before her next studio session. It would be well spent catching up on what she'd missed yesterday, but without Ava's notes, she wouldn't make much headway. Nat decided to visit the penthouse apartment. Her sick friend would appreciate the homework, and Nat could take care of her. If Ava had a cold, she could fetch her some soup; if she had a hangover, Gatorade or greasy takeout.

She texted Ava again.

Coming over with class notes

The text flew away with a computerized whoosh. Nat looked at the screen; the phone registered it as delivered but not read. Could Ava be sick in bed without her phone? Asleep? Could she have lost the device? With an uneasy feeling tickling her belly, Nat hurried toward the Chelsea pad.

The doorman greeted her in the lobby. "Hello, miss."

She recalled his Brooklyn accent, his weathered appearance, but not his name. "Hi. I'm a friend of Ava Sedin's. In the penthouse."

"Right." He picked up the phone to announce her arrival. "Your name?"

"Nat."

She waited as the phone rang in Ava's apartment. And rang. Could she be out? Too sick to answer? Finally, the doorman said, "Good morning, Ava. Your friend Nat is here to see you."

Ava's voice on the other end of the phone was inaudible, but the doorman—Pete! That was his name—nodded. "I'll send her up."

In the elevator, Nat checked her phone. Ava had not replied to her texts, though her friend was clearly able to answer her telephone. But there was a message from Gabe.

Can't get you off my mind. Hope you're having
a great day.

Her legs went wobbly, her lips curled into a delighted smile. Feeling like a schoolgirl, she texted
back:

Thinking of you 2

The elevator doors slid open, and Nat hurried
into the sumptuous hallway. She was excited to see
Ava, to tell her about her relationship. Ava had become a friend and confidante, the only person who
knew about Nat's secret life. Nat could count on Ava
to guide her through this unknown territory. The
blond girl was savvy, experienced. She might even
have advice on how to handle the Cole situation,
which, Nat realized, had almost slipped from her
mind, thanks to Gabe Turnmill's attentions.

She knocked on Ava's door and waited. And then,
she waited some more. It was quiet in the apartment, no music, no TV, no sounds of life inside. But
Ava knew Nat was there, she had invited Nat up.
Eventually, she heard the shuffle of sock feet moving toward the door, and it opened.

"Hey," Nat began, and then stopped, shocked by
her friend's appearance. Ava's right cheek was red
and raw, her lips cracked and swollen. Both her eyes
were bloodshot, puffy from crying. "Oh my god."
Nat pushed her way inside. "What happened?"

Ava closed the door and locked it, throwing the
deadbolt. "Come in," she said, leading the way toward the low slate sofa. A pillow and fluffy blanket

covered it; a makeshift bed. Ava tossed the blanket aside so they could sit.

"What happened to you?"

Ava gave a rueful smile. "Bad date."

"A *date* did that to you? Did he hit you? Who was it?"

"It was my own fault." The battered girl reached for an ice pack resting on the black marble coffee table, held it to her cheek. "There were red flags, but I ignored them. I got greedy."

Nat reached out, held Ava's free hand. "Tell me. . . ."

"I went back on the site. I don't know why. I've got some good daddies in my life, kind and generous. But I was looking for something different. Something exciting." She moved the ice pack to her swollen lips. "I messaged with a guy—really handsome, into boats and travel. Spring break's coming up. I thought he might take me somewhere if we hit it off."

"What happened?"

"We went for a drink, and he was charming. He said he was into white parties. I was feeling kind of wild, so I said I was, too."

"White parties? Like all white clothes?"

"Like all white drugs. Coke and pills." The ice pack returned to her cheek. "I went to his hotel room. I thought it wouldn't hurt to be spontaneous, just this once, but . . ." Emotion stole her voice, filled her eyes with tears.

Nat squeezed her hand. "It's okay."

"It started off fine. We were fucked-up, but we were having fun. And then, he went crazy."

"What did he do?"

"He punched me in the face. Hard. And then he threw me to the floor and he . . . he raped me. He didn't wear a condom."

"Oh, Ava."

"He held me by the neck, crushed my face into the carpet while he did it. And when he was done"—her face paled beneath the carpet burn—"he spat on me, called me a whore, and then he left."

Nat gathered the bruised girl into her arms and let her cry on her shoulder. After a few moments, Nat asked, "Have you seen a doctor?"

Ava pulled away, dabbed at her eyes with the collar of her sweatshirt. "I've got an appointment at three."

"Do you want me to come with you?"

"I'll be fine."

"Did you call the police?"

"What would I say? *I met a guy on a sugar daddy site. He paid me to go to his room and do drugs with him.* They'd think it was all my fault."

"No, they wouldn't. You're battered and bruised. They'd see what that monster did to you, and they'd make him pay."

"There's no point. I have no idea who he really is."

"Can you report him through the website?"

"I did. But he can always create a new e-mail, up-load some new photos, change his username." She pulled a crumpled tissue from her sleeve and blew her nose. "You have to be really careful, Nat."

But she didn't, because now she had Gabe. He was officially her *sponsor*, her *blesser*. She never had to go on the site again. While she'd been eager to tell

Ava about her new arrangement, it would have been unkind under these circumstances. Instead, she said, "I will be."

Ava insisted she was fine, that she needed nothing, but eventually agreed to let Natalie run out to the deli to get her some soup and fruit. Nat hustled to the corner shop, her mind entrenched in her friend's nightmare. It wasn't Ava's *fault*, of course, but she had been careless, reckless. It was so out of character. Ava had scolded Nat for letting Gabe know where she lived when he delivered her home in his town car. And yet, Ava had agreed to do drugs in some random daddy's hotel room. What had possessed her friend to take such a risk?

Entering the warmth of the deli, Nat's confusion turned to intense gratitude. She'd found Gabe. And she knew, in her heart, that he would never hurt her.

The Sighting

Ava returned to school on Monday, her scraped face camouflaged by makeup, her scabbed mouth covered in lipstick. While her appearance was beginning to heal, her psyche would take longer. Ava was quiet, morose, easily startled. This was not the confident, vivacious girl Natalie had grown to know. Their classmates were noticing it, too. After a sketching session, Nat's friend Ivan approached her.

"Is Ava okay? She seems kind of . . . off."

Nat had to cover for her friend. "It's a family issue, back home in Ohio."

"Anything serious?"

"A sick relative," Nat fibbed. "She's going home for spring break. She'll feel better when she's spent some time with her family."

"I hope so."

"I'm going to get a coffee before next class. Do you want something? My treat?"

"Aren't you the big spender," Ivan said, and Nat felt her face redden. He was teasing, she reminded herself. He didn't know. "I'd love a latte."

"Sure."

Nat strolled toward the coffee shop at Twenty-Third and Lex (take-out coffee, a luxury her new allowance afforded), her mind drifting back to Ava. Her friend had always been dismissive of her home-town, her working-class family, their staid, boring life. So when she'd announced her travel plans, Nat had been surprised. "I need to go home," Ava had explained that morning, tears filling her eyes. "I just want to be with my family right now."

"I understand," Nat had said, and she did. Sort of. It was hard to relate to what Ava had gone through in that hotel room, the damage it had done to her physically, mentally, and emotionally. Perhaps Nat would have wanted to go home, too, if she'd been abused that way. But every negative thing that had happened to Nat had happened in Blaine. It didn't feel like a safe place to run.

She still hadn't told Ava about Gabe, though she was practically bursting to share. It wouldn't be fair, not with her friend so damaged and broken. So Nat kept it to herself, tried to suppress her delighted smiles, hide her dreamy stares when her mind drifted back to their time together. The *relationship* had been going for nearly two weeks, if she counted from their first date, which she did. As clichéd as it sounded, she had never felt this way. Not even in the early days with Cole. Not with Miguel. Those boys couldn't make her feel secure, cherished, adored. That took a man.

But this was not a storybook romance; she knew that. It was a financial arrangement between two consenting adults who had laid out the parameters of their relationship up front. No strings. No commitment, obligation, or drama. And above all, no emotional attachment. This was about enjoying their time together, as limited as it may be, with no thought for the future. Because there wouldn't be one. Her brain knew it, but her heart begged to differ.

On their fourth date, that rare Saturday rendezvous, Nat thought they might consummate their relationship. But she'd been terrified. What if Gabe's fifty-five-year-old body didn't look as good beneath the ten-thousand-dollar suit? Would she be turned off? Men his age were prone to erectile dysfunction, judging by the embarrassment of Cialis ads featuring fit, handsome fiftysomethings that ran during her mom's Shonda Rhimes programs. How would Nat deal with that? Or, what if Gabe took the Cialis or some other sexual-performance-enhancing drug and she had to deal with an eight-hour erection?

Even more terrifying was the possibility that it would go well. That she would be attracted to him and the sex would be amazing. Then what? Gabe would hand her an envelope full of cash in a month's time, thereby turning her into a full-fledged prostitute. It was all too overwhelming.

When Gabe had taken her back to his place after an incredible dinner in the Meatpacking District, she'd expressed her fear. "I'm sorry. I don't think I'm ready."

"I'll wait," he'd said. "I want you to want this as much as I do."

Gabe had slept on the sofa that night, afraid he couldn't control himself in bed next to her. She knew he wouldn't wait much longer. He was a man with needs. For thirty-five hundred a month, he'd want more than a dinner companion, more than a teddy bear. She wanted to be close to him, to share that intimacy, too. But she was afraid of how it would impact her emotionally.

She ordered two lattes and waited in the crowded shop, scanning her phone. Her mom had texted to check in. Since Cole had been in New York roughly two weeks without contacting Nat, they were all beginning to relax. Gabe had texted her, too. They had made plans to go to a show on Thursday night. What did she want to see? This would be Natalie's first Broadway experience. She had no idea what was playing, what was good.

Surprise me, she texted back. *I trust your opinion.* And she did. Gabe was cultured, classy, informed. The more she got to know him, the more impressed she was by him. She couldn't quite believe that a man of his caliber was interested in her, and yet, he seemed to adore her. He looked at her like he'd never seen anyone more beautiful, touched her like she was a goddess. Her stomach fluttered, and her cheeks flushed at the thought of him. It was an infatuation, she told herself. It was not more than that.

"Two lattes for Natalie!"

She stepped up, slipping the hot drinks into cardboard sleeves before grabbing them and pushing her way out into the street. The March sun was high in the sky, doing little to jettison the seasonal chill. But the sun's rays, the coffee in her hands, the Broadway show to look forward to, warmed her, made her feel light and happy. It had been a while since she'd felt that rush of gratitude for her life in New York, that feeling that she was on the right path. Crossing at Third Avenue, she hurried back to campus and her next class.

At the main building, she paused, her hands full of coffees. As she waited for an exiting student to hold the door open for her, she felt it, subtle, but there; a chill, a prickle, a frisson of dread. Some sixth sense, some instinct for self-preservation made her whirl around and scan the streets. No one was looking at her—students, construction workers, tourists, all going about their day. But her eyes moved to the opposite side of Twenty-Third Street, and she spotted him. This time, she was not hallucinating. This time he was not a mirage. There, loitering outside a thrift shop, was Cole Doberinsky.

The lattes slipped from her grip, the paper cups hitting the sidewalk, dislodging their plastic lids, sending coffee splashing over her shoes and jeans. Cole wore a black hoodie over his sandy hair, but she knew it was him. His physique was familiar, strong and wiry. His posture was tense, tightly coiled. For a brief moment, their eyes connected, and she saw her shock and fear reflected back at her. Cole had not wanted her to spot him. But she saw something else in his dark eyes. Anger and resentment. Cole Doberinsky still hated her.

She thought of the gun hidden in her sock drawer. Should she have been packing it to school? What would her liberal, art-school friends have thought of that? And would she have the guts to walk over to Cole, pull the gun from her pocket, and point it at his face?

"Are you okay?" It was her classmate Keltie. She bent down and picked up the dropped cups. "What happened?"

"I don't know," Nat mumbled. "They . . . slipped."

She turned back toward Cole, but he had disappeared.

Broadway

Nat was shaken by the encounter with Cole. She'd been lulled into a false sense of security when her ex had failed to materialize, but now she knew. He was in New York because of her. The only mystery left was what he planned to do to her. And what she was willing to do to protect herself. Nat had no one to talk to about the boy's sinister appearance. She couldn't burden Ava with it, given all she'd been through. Her roommates already disliked her and would see "stalker ex-boyfriend" as definitive third-strike material. And Gabe Turnmill had not signed up for all her drama. He'd been tender and supportive when Nat had conjured Cole in the French bistro, but she didn't want to belabor the issue.

She had other friends at school, like Ivan and Keltie, but they wouldn't understand the mess she was in, would be repelled by it. Her only confidant was Oleg, the driver. Despite his muscular, menacing aspect, despite the weapon kept casually in his glove box, Nat had developed a rapport with him as he'd shuttled her to and from her liaisons with his employer. Tuesday night, after a quick drink downtown with Gabe, she vented to her chauffeur.

"I told Cole I have a gun. I told him to stay away from me. But still . . . he came to my school. He's obsessed with me."

Oleg's voice was level, his eyes on the road. "If you really think he's dangerous, you should learn to use the pistol."

The alcohol in her stomach churned at the suggestion. Nat could never shoot someone, not even Cole. While her ex-boyfriend's presence filled her with anxiety, her rational mind knew he wouldn't really hurt her. Not physically anyway. He would probably scream at her, humiliate her, publicly disparage her. Or he might be more devious. He might watch and wait and gather evidence—of her relationship with Gabe, of their financial arrangement. And with that, he could ruin her.

"I'll think about it," she muttered.

She had reported the Cole sighting to her mother.

"Maybe you should come home," Allana said, sounding shaken.

"How would that solve anything?" Nat responded. "He'll just come back to Blaine and harass me there."

"You're right. . . . Have you called the police?"

"And say what? My ex-boyfriend *stared* at me from across the street?" She was being snarky, and she knew it. But she couldn't seem to stop it.

The line was quiet for a moment. "Do you have any male friends who could protect you? Do you . . . have a *boyfriend?*"

Her mom's reticence to delve into her daughter's private life articulated the distance between them. If things had been different, her mom would have known everything that was going on in Nat's life. They had been so close. But now, Allana's new family came first.

"I can protect myself," Nat said, her voice hoarse with repressed emotion.

She heard her mother's deep intake of breath. "I'll call Trish again." Trish was Cole's rather domineering mother. "I'll see what I can find out."

"Thanks, Mom."

"I love you, Natalie. You'll get through this."

The week progressed without another Cole sighting. That didn't mean he wasn't lurking, watching, planning a way to get to her. Her mom informed her, via e-mail, that Trish Doberinsky was worried about her son, felt he was more destructive to himself than anyone else. But Nat wasn't so sure. She went to school, tried to focus, but she was distracted, on edge. Much like her friend, Ava. The girl's pretty face was back to normal, but her spirit was not. Ava had taken to scurrying home between classes, skipping more of them than was acceptable for a decent GPA. Nat understood the temptation to hide away. At times, she wanted to hole up in her chaotic Brooklyn bedroom, where she knew Cole could not find her. But she couldn't risk her scholarship money. Even with her new allowance, tuition would be out of reach on her own.

On Thursday, Gabe sent Oleg to collect her for their date on Broadway. She'd spent an hour getting ready, making sure she looked appropriate for a night at the theater with a distinguished man. She'd gone shopping, purchasing three little black dresses and a pair of quality stilettos that would work for dates with Gabe. She did her hair and applied her makeup, using Ava's expert techniques. Looking good for him, making him proud of the woman on his arm, was all part of their arrangement.

Gabe would meet her at the theater. The show started at seven thirty, so he would come straight from the office. He worked late most nights, he'd told her, getting home at ten, even eleven o'clock. His long days worked for Nat, allowing her time to study and do homework before joining him for a late dinner. But that night, he was knocking off early to take her to the show.

When the car pulled up near the theater, Gabe was there, waiting. He was still in the suit he'd worn to the office, looking professional, sophisticated. He opened the door for Nat, helping her exit the car in her tight dress and heels. "You look beautiful," he said, kissing her cheek. He waved Oleg away, and then, taking her arm, he escorted her past the line and into the opulent theater.

As they crossed the carpeted lobby, Nat was chagrined to see that many of the patrons were dressed casually: tourists, given their comfortable running shoes, Big Apple sweatshirts, and plastic bags full of souvenirs. She felt conspicuous and overdressed in her LBD and heels, until she looked at the man beside her. Her ensemble was a match for her date's.

And Gabe had told her she looked beautiful. His opinion was all that mattered.

Inside, the theater was even more spectacular: glittering chandeliers, ornate cornices, pillars, and porticoes. Gabe led them to excellent seats, fourth row in the orchestra section. "This place was built in the twenties," Gabe said, leaning in close, his breath warm in her ear. "It was built for the composer Irving Berlin." Nat raised her eyebrows, impressed, though the name meant nothing to her. She made a mental note to google this Irving guy when she got home.

The show was a musical comedy, smart, witty, expertly performed. As a spectator, Nat was awed. As a creative person, she was filled up, energized by the talent it took to craft such a production. Gabe held her hand in the darkened theater, their shoulders pressing against each other. She felt grateful, shy, and infatuated, all at the same time.

Halfway through the show, the lights went up for intermission. "Champagne?" Gabe asked.

"Yes, please."

They moved with the crowd to the lobby. "I need to use the restroom," she called over the buzz of the other patrons.

"I'll get us a drink and meet you back here."

In the bathroom, she waited in a queue of women—tourists and locals—all chattering about the show, about New York, about the weather. Nat peed, washed her hands, freshened her lip gloss. She paused, staring at her reflection. Who was this confident girl with the contoured cheekbones, the smoky eyes, the figure-hugging dress? How did she end up there, at a Broadway show, with a rich, handsome, older man? A small, self-satisfied smile crept across the face of the girl in the mirror.

When she emerged, she spotted her date across the bubbling stew of people. Gabe was embroiled in conversation with a sophisticated older couple: a man in a sharp suit and a painfully thin woman in a stylish wrap dress. They had to be friends, or colleagues, perhaps. Nat pushed her way through the thick crowd toward Gabe and his companions. When she was about fifteen feet away, Gabe looked up and met her gaze. What she saw in his eyes stopped her dead in her tracks.

A warning. Even a threat.

Gabe did not want her to approach, did not want to introduce her to this classy pair. If Natalie walked up to him, he would shun her, dismiss her, even disparage her. Because she was a paid escort, nothing more. Gabe was embarrassed to be seen with her, ashamed of her. She stood still, in the middle of the crowd, her face hot with humiliation. Ahead of her, Gabe clapped the man on the upper arm and kissed the woman on the cheek. As the couple moved back toward the theater, Gabe made his way toward Nat.

"Ran into an old client," he said, his upbeat tone forced. "Shall I get us that champagne?" But a musical tone rang out then, and the house lights flickered. "I guess I left it too late," Gabe said lamely.

"That's okay."

Nat led the way down the aisle, Gabe close behind her. His hand was not on the small of her back as it had been when they arrived. He seemed tense and distracted; she could feel him looking around the theater. When they sat, he didn't lean over to whisper in her ear.

For the second half of the show, he didn't hold her hand.

Honduras

Running into Michael and Suze Weintraub while he was at the theater with Natalie had been a close call. Luckily, Gabe's date had gone to the restroom, allowing him to catch up with his former client and the man's wife without raising any suspicions. Gabe's firm had helped Weintraub's company with a hostile takeover that had gotten messy. Spending all that time in the trenches together, crossing the lines that had to be crossed, had developed a rapport between them. They shared a bond that went beyond the professional. Michael had suggested dinner with their wives, and they'd found that the women hit it off, too. Suze Weintraub was in publishing. Celeste was well-read. They'd had four or five dinners before Celeste got sick and retreated to the country full-time.

Gabe glanced over at his wife, standing at the gleaming Italian marble countertop in their spacious kitchen. She was in her element, surrounded by fresh produce and cookbooks. Despite some puffiness around her eyes from lack of sleep, she was lively, almost glowing, planning tonight's dinner party. They were hosting an old cop friend of Celeste's—Manny Dosanjh, from the crime lab, and his newish wife . . . Trudy or Judy or something like that. Gabe found Manny coarse and pedantic, but Celeste thought he was *salt of the earth*.

His wife had become a homebody, but she wasn't antisocial. She loved cooking and entertaining, welcoming friends into their six-bedroom Victorian farmhouse for gourmet feasts. Celeste was a significant asset when he had to schmooze clients or colleagues. She handled every detail with aplomb. Gabe's only duty was to make sure the drinks and conversation kept flowing.

He turned his attention back to his laptop, where he was reading through a brief. Or trying to . . . His mind kept wandering back to Natalie. He'd hurt her, that night at the theater. He'd seen the sting in her eyes, sensed the pain in her rigid posture. She thought he was ashamed to be seen with her, but that wasn't the case. The girl didn't know he was married, didn't know why he had to hide her from the prying eyes of the Weintraubs. After the show, he'd feigned a work emergency, hustled out the door of the theater before his old friends could spot him. Oleg had come when summoned, had delivered Natalie back to Brooklyn. Gabe had kept his distance since then, rattled by the near miss. Natalie would feel abandoned, rejected, insulted. It was unfortunate, but better safe than sorry.

Leaning back into the cream sectional sofa, he closed his eyes and massaged his temples. If Suze Weintraub had spotted him with his young mistress that night, she might have told Celeste. Then again, she might not have. The women hadn't been close in years, and no one wanted to be the bearer of that kind of news. "I saw your husband at the theater with a sexy, younger woman." If Suze cared for Celeste at all, she wouldn't hurt her that way, especially given all his wife's health struggles. If, somehow, Celeste had gotten wind of his date and confronted him, Gabe would have come up with an excuse: an extra ticket, a young associate, a client's niece in from out of town. But he was sure the Weintraubs had not seen him with Natalie. As usual, luck was on his side.

"I'm leaving."

He opened his eyes to see Violet. His tall, pretty daughter strode into the room, her hair pulled back from her face, a pouf of ponytail like a halo behind her. Her face was free of makeup and she was dressed in head-to-toe black. As usual.

Celeste looked up from her Ottolenghi tome. "I thought you were staying for dinner."

"We don't want to get stuck in traffic."

"But I wanted you to see Manny and Judy. He hasn't seen you since you were little."

"I don't even know them, Mom."

"Where are you going?" Gabe ventured.

She didn't look at him when she answered. "A poetry slam in Dix Hills."

A poetry slam? Gabe would almost have preferred she go to one of her drug-fueled parties and get shot in the foot.

Celeste asked, "Is Fern reading?"

"She's performing," Violet corrected.

"What time is she on? You could say hi to Manny and Judy and leave after."

"Let her go," Gabe chimed in. He wasn't ashamed of his daughter, per se, but he didn't like to invite comparison with the children of their peers. Their friends' kids were all bound for business school, med school, or law school. They were all accomplished equestrians, swimmers, or fencers. They engaged in pleasant small talk, didn't rant about *issues*, didn't dress like grieving Italian widows. Of course, Manny Dosanjh was a newlywed at forty-eight, and this Judy might be too old to have children. But still . . . it was easier to spin Violet's creative prowess, her altruistic nature, when she wasn't skulking around the house.

Violet grabbed her car keys off a hook inside one of the cupboards. Gabe had bought her a BMW for her sixteenth. She'd traded it in for a Prius. She dutifully kissed her mother's cheek.

"Say hi to Manny and Judy. Whoever they are."

"Drive safely."

"And don't neglect your studies," Gabe called after her.

"It's spring break," she snapped. "But I wouldn't expect you to know that."

His wife shot him a look as the door slammed behind their girl. "Don't put so much pressure on her."

"What? She needs to keep her grades up if she's going to Princeton."

His wife didn't respond, busying herself with her mise en place.

"What?" He could read her, knew when she was hiding something.

"Violet's considering a gap year."

"A *gap year*?" He set his laptop aside and stood. "To do what?"

"She'd like to do some volunteer work," Celeste said breezily, chopping fennel. "With a young people's theater. In Honduras."

He moved from the seating area to the kitchen island, perching on a barstool. "What about college?"

"It will still be there when she gets back."

"*If* she gets back. These do-gooder organizations can brainwash you into devoting your life to them."

"She's volunteering to work with children, Gabe, not joining ISIS."

"Kids in Honduras need fucking *plays*?" He grabbed a piece of carrot, crunched it. "Don't they need houses? And food? And human rights?"

"It's a well-rounded program. She'll be helping on farms and building houses, too. They just happen to offer a theater program for at-risk youth. She's excited about it."

"I spoke to a friend on Princeton's board. He put a word in for her."

"His word will still be good next year."

They took him for granted, his wife and daughter, expected him to roll with their whims, pick up the pieces when it all went wrong. "If she'd stayed at Chapin like I wanted, this wouldn't be happening."

"If she'd stayed in the city, she might be an alcoholic. Or a drug addict. Or dead. And she's loved her time at Fairhaven. It's a better fit for a girl like her."

"It's turned her into an artsy-fartsy weirdo. It's fostering useless fucking skills like acting and beat poetry and performance art!"

"Gabe . . . ," Celeste began, but he was already leaving the room, heading for the bathroom.

"I'm not paying for her *voluntourism*!" he bellowed from the hallway. "If she wants to save the world, she can pay her own fucking way."

Celeste didn't follow him. His wife didn't like to fight.

In the first-floor powder room, he peed, trying to quell the pressure in his chest. It was rage. And panic. Gabe liked situations he could control, people he could manage. His daughter was doing this to get under his skin; he knew it. But why? How had her admiration of him turned to disgust? And was she really willing to sabotage her own future just to piss him off? Violet was a bright kid. There was no way she thought that deferring college to teach Tennessee Williams to Hondurans was a good idea.

He flushed, washed his hands, then splashed some cold water on his face. He needed to calm down, needed a way to deal with his frustration and anxiety. Perhaps a run. Or a swim in the heated pool. He was too irritated to focus on his waiting brief. What he needed was a distraction. On cue, the girl flitted into his mind: beautiful, sexy, compliant. He pulled out his phone and texted.

Do you have classes next week?

She responded quickly.

No. It's spring break.

He smiled, could feel himself relaxing just by connecting with her.

Want to get away for a couple of days?

The answer came instantly.

Yes!!!!!!

He tucked his phone into his pocket and went back into the kitchen. Celeste was elbows-deep in a raw chicken. "I'll go pick up the wine," he said, grabbing his car keys.

All traces of his previous frustration had evaporated.

Vermont

Nat came from a picturesque part of the world, but nothing could have prepared her for the bucolic splendor of Vermont. It was cold, temperatures hovering near freezing, as Gabe drove them to their B and B outside the small town of South Woodstock. Nat gazed out the passenger window of the Mercedes, taking in the snow-dusted trees, the quaint farmhouses, the spired churches, and covered bridges. She felt like she was in an alternate reality, where life was simple and wholesome. Where she and Gabe were not in a sugar relationship but were a real couple . . . at least for two nights.

That evening at the theater had upset her. It was clear Gabe did not want to be seen with her in front of his society friends, and it hurt. She'd convinced herself that what she and Gabe had was more than financial; it was genuine and beautiful. But that night forced her to face the truth. Gabe was paying her to be there when he wanted her, to go away when he didn't.

The driver, Oleg, had taken her home after the show. "Successful men like Mr. Turnmill can be cold and hard," he said, in his deep, masculine voice. "That doesn't mean he doesn't care for you, in his way."

"I'm just . . . I'm not sure I'm cut out for this."

Oleg was the only person who knew that Gabe was her sugar daddy. There was no one else to whom she could confide. "I thought I could handle it, but . . . it feels so demeaning."

The big man pulled up half a block from her apartment (her drop-off spot had inched closer with each subsequent date) and turned to face her. It looked like he wanted to tell her something but was unsure, afraid even. Finally, he spoke.

"Sometimes, we do things we don't feel good about to survive. It doesn't mean you're a bad person."

His sympathy, his assurance had brought her perilously close to tears. But she couldn't cry about this. She had known what she was getting into. *No strings*.

"Thanks, Oleg. You're really nice."

Climbing the steps to the building entrance, she had caught the movement of the front curtains out of the corner of her eye. If Mara or Toni had been looking out the window, they would have witnessed her emerging from the chauffeured town car, wearing her slinky black dress and high heels. It looked tawdry and gross. Because it was. *She* was.

Her self-loathing was exacerbated by Gabe's distance. Since that date, there had been radio silence for more than a week. She knew he was a busy man, but this felt deliberate. It felt cold. And then, three days ago, the invitation had arrived. He didn't apologize or kowtow, he just asked if she'd like to go away with him for a couple of days. This powerful attorney was going to take time away from his cases and clients to spend some of her spring break with her. It all felt real again.

"The B and B is just up here," Gabe said, smiling over at her. He seemed to know his way around Vermont. Maybe he'd brought his daughter here. Or his wife. Or a girlfriend. She felt something unpleasant in her gut—jealousy. But, of course, a man Gabe's age had had a life before her. It would have been creepy if he hadn't. She shook it off.

Their accommodations were in a quaint cottage on a well-groomed hobby farm. As Gabe checked them in, Nat wandered around the grounds. Horses grazed in a sunlit paddock, nibbling the tender spring shoots just beneath the skiff of snow. Chickens clucked in a henhouse, promising fresh eggs for their breakfast in bed. Fluffy sheep dotted a hillside, bleating from time to time. It was serene. It was sublime. It called for a selfie.

Nat knew she couldn't post any photos with Gabe, but that didn't mean she couldn't share solo holiday pics on social media. Her friends back home would be interested in how she spent her spring break. And curious. And jealous. She experienced that perverse sort of thrill she always got from Instagram, knowing her followers would admire, envy, and resent her.

Gabe emerged from the main house then, jingling a key. "Our palace awaits."

The cottage was a perfect mix of modern amenities and old-school charm. The decor was kitschy, French country meets hippie commune. Nat wandered through the tiny home, set back from the main building, allowing the couple complete privacy. She took in the claw-foot bathtub, the flatscreen TV nestled in an antique armoire, the massive sleigh bed. One bed. Her stomach fluttered.

Suddenly, Gabe was behind her, his hands on her waist, his breath on her neck. "Are you hungry?"

"Yes," she said quickly. It was after five. She'd been too excited, too busy packing to eat much lunch. She suddenly realized she was famished.

Gabe drove them to an adorable inn with a cozy farm-to-table restaurant. Conversation flowed easily, flirty banter mixed with heavier topics—fossil fuel reliance, foreign intervention. Nat had grown up in a home where the TV was a ubiquitous dinner guest. They did not discuss politics over their meals, did not discuss anything of consequence. Her father had liked sitcoms. Derek liked sports. And her mom seemed perfectly fine with the constant electronic babble. Gabe's daughter would have been raised on stimulating, thought-provoking dinner conversation. The girl would be informed and sophisticated; not like Nat.

They lingered over a shared dessert (apple pie with local cheddar) and wine. Nat was drinking most of it—Gabe was driving. And she needed the alcohol to calm her nerves. As the night wound down, her anxiety about what was to come increased. Gabe had planned this getaway with certain expectations. He had picked her up, paid for the room, and bought her dinner. In return, he would want sex. Nat understood this, accepted it. But still . . . she was afraid. Making love would change their relationship, it always did. And it would change *her*. Once she slept with Gabe, the man who paid her monthly allowance, she would be a prostitute . . . no matter how much she cared for him.

On the drive back to the house, she felt an odd mixture of nerves and sedation, simultaneously wound up and wiped out. The country road was dark, with no streetlights or oncoming traffic to illuminate their journey. She glanced over at Gabe, at his profile in the glow of the dashboard lights. He looked strong and handsome, younger in the dim lighting. She felt a flutter in her chest—attraction, infatuation, genuine fondness. If she focused on those feelings, and not that envelope full of cash, maybe . . . just maybe.

When they reached the farm, Gabe parked the car and they scurried through the frigid night to their cozy cottage. Gabe turned on the gas fireplace and opened the bottle of red their hosts had left for them. Reading the label, he shrugged. "It'll have to do."

"I'll be right back," Nat said, grabbing her purse and heading to the bathroom. She ran the faucet and peed (she didn't want to subject Gabe to the sound of her bodily functions). Scrounging in her bag, she found her travel toothbrush and compact floss. She cleaned her teeth, then freshened her lip gloss. She took in her reflection in the mirror—a little wan, glassy-eyed, but fine. Before she returned to her partner, she checked her phone.

Her Instagram photo had received a decent number of likes. She scrolled through a handful of comments. Her classmate Ivan had commented:

Vermont?!?! Why didn't you invite me bish!

She chuckled at his faux snark. Her roommate Toni had liked the photo, too. Nat knew that a *like* was sometimes just an acknowledgment. *I see your photo. I see you're on a holiday. You'd better be able to cover your rent next month.* Closing the app, she checked her texts. There was one from Keltie inviting her to go see a band the next night. And three more from an unknown number.

Got your message psycho bitch
You can't kill me if I get to you first

And finally:

I know what you are whore

Nat's knees went weak and she staggered backward, perching on the edge of the claw-foot tub. Cole. They had to be from him. But how had Cole gotten her cell number? She'd given it to a handful of people: her mom; Derek; her one trusted friend, Abbey, back in Blaine. None of them would have given it to Cole Doberinsky. They all knew he was unstable; they all knew he scared her. Cole was more resourceful than she'd thought.

He must have been observing her at school for days, undetected, must have followed her home on the subway. What had Cole seen as he sat outside her apartment, waiting, watching? Had he seen her getting into that town car? Had he tailed her and spotted her with Gabe? Would he tell her mom, their former classmates, the whole town that Nat was a slut? A sugar baby? A prostitute?

Her fear morphed into white-hot anger. Her whole life, she'd been powerless—when her dad walked out on her, when her mom remarried and started a new family, effectively forgetting about the daughter she already had. And now, Cole Doberinsky was threatening to ruin her. She thought about the nine-millimeter handgun, thought about pointing it at him, thought about pulling the trigger. Could she do it? Could she finally stop being the victim?

There was a soft rap at the door. "Are you okay in there?"

Shit. She had to pull herself together. Her role in this arrangement was to be charming, sexy, sweet; not shaking with rage, dread, and fear.

"I'll be right out." But her voice trembled, belying her angst.

When she emerged, Gabe's face was full of concern. "Are you sick? What's wrong?"

"I'm fine." She forced a smile. "It's nothing we need to worry about right now."

"You're clearly upset." Taking her by the hand,

Gabe led her to the sofa. When they were seated side by side, he said, firmly, "Talk to me."

Instead, she passed him her phone. "It's Cole," she said as Gabe read the texts. "It has to be."

His handsome face darkened as his eyes drifted over the venomous words. "Shit."

Nat could have told him then about the gun Oleg had given her. But she wasn't sure her powerful partner would appreciate his employee's intrusion. Besides, the gun was little more than a prop, if she wasn't willing to use it. And Gabe's obvious concern for her well-being warmed her, made her feel special, even loved.

"If he knows about us . . ." She trailed off.

Gabe got up and went to a side table to retrieve a notepad and pen. Returning to the sofa, he asked, "What's this kid's name?"

"Cole Doberinsky."

He asked her to spell it as he wrote it down. "Middle name?"

"Jonathan."

"His parents' address?"

She provided the street address and the zip code (there were only two in the town). Gabe recorded it all. Then he tore off the piece of paper, folded it, and slid it into his pants pocket.

"I'm going to take care of Cole Doberinsky," he said calmly. "You don't have to worry about him anymore."

"What are you going to do?"

He took her hands in his. "Do you trust me?"

She looked into his blue eyes, so confident, so commanding. She did trust him. Gabe Turnmill was more composed, more capable than anyone she'd ever met. And he cared for her. She knew it. This wasn't just a financial arrangement. It may have started that way, but there was more between them now.

"I trust you," she said softly.

"I'll keep you safe, Natalie. I won't let that kid hurt you. I promise."

She nodded, too overcome with gratitude to speak. She kissed him then and felt something swell inside of her. It was intense, powerful, a feeling she'd never experienced before. Standing, she took him by the hand and led him to the bedroom.

24

. . . . . .

Ohio

Everything was different now that Nat could admit what she felt for Gabe. She was in love with him. His limited availability, the money he gave her, the age difference between them . . . all of that was irrelevant. What mattered was her heart, and it had never felt so safe, so cherished, so protected. And it wasn't the only organ affected: her mind craved his stimulating conversations; her body pined for his touch. Even now, thinking about him as she worked on a painting in the studio, pinkened her cheeks and made her pulse race.

When they'd made love in Vermont, he had been tender and attentive. Unlike her previous partners who'd seemed to consider sex an athletic endeavor, Gabe treated it like an art form. Nat's body was his instrument and he'd played her like a master. With

Gabe, she had felt things she never had before. Were older men better in bed due to their experience? Or because they weren't raised on internet porn? Nat didn't know, didn't care. She just wanted more.

Thoughts of her boyfriend (such a juvenile term but she would not call him her sponsor, her blesser, or her sugar daddy, not anymore) had replaced her fears about Cole. It had been a week since she'd received his menacing texts, and he had not made an appearance at her school or her Brooklyn home. No one in her orbit had confronted her about her sugar arrangement, meaning Cole had not outed her. Gabe had promised to protect her, to keep her safe, and he had.

Her *boyfriend* was a powerful man, a brilliant legal mind. He would have contacted Cole's parents, threatened some sort of legal action if Cole didn't cease and desist his harassment. Cole's dad must have flown to New York, found his son, and dragged him back home. The Doberinskys would have taken Cole's credit cards, his ID, ensured he could not return to New York. If Cole told anyone about Nat's sugar baby status, it would be dismissed as the angry ramblings of an ex-boyfriend. Now, she could relax.

Ava had not been to class since school resumed. It was not unusual for a student to tack a few extra days onto spring break, especially when they were traveling out of state. But with each day that passed, Ava was falling further behind. Nat had texted her several times, inquiring about her return, but she'd received no response. Until Wednesday afternoon.

Can you come over?

Nat could. She just had to clean her brushes after her painting class, and then she was done for the day. Grabbing her coat (a new camel trench, courtesy of Gabe), she hurried to Ava's building. She was eager to see her friend, sincerely hoped the girl had recovered from the traumatic encounter with the violent bastard who had hurt her. Nat wanted the best for Ava. And selfishly, she wanted her friend and confidante back. Ava was the only person who would understand her relationship. And without Ava, Nat would not be with Gabe, would not be so ridiculously happy.

The doorman, Pete, called upstairs, announcing her by name. She had been there often enough that he remembered her, and she him. Nat hurried to the elevator and rode to the penthouse. Maybe she should have brought welcome-home flowers. Or chocolates. At least she was armed with notes from the classes Ava had missed. In the hallway, she practically skipped in anticipation of seeing her friend. But when Nat knocked on the door, it was opened by a heavyset woman with a warm face and softly curled blond hair.

"Umm . . . hi," Nat said. "Is Ava home?"

Her friend materialized behind the older women, illuminating their resemblance. "Mom, can you go get us some coffees?"

Without a word, Ava's mother grabbed her coat and purse and left, giving Nat a sidelong glance.

"Come in," Ava said, ushering Nat inside. The blond girl wore baggy sweatpants and a slouchy cardigan. Her skin was free of makeup, but Nat could see no traces of the damage that creep had done to her face. Ava looked fresh, pretty, natural—but this was not the confident, savvy girl Nat knew. There was something vulnerable, defeated in Ava's eyes and in her posture. And then she noticed the packing boxes.

"I'm going home for a while," Ava explained, crossing her arms over her chest.

"You're dropping out of school?"

"I'm deferring," Ava corrected her. "I'm going to move in with my parents, get a job, and save some money. Hopefully, I can come back in the fall."

Nat perched on the arm of the slate sofa. "Is this because of what that asshole did to you?"

"Partly."

"You can't let him ruin your life, Ava. You can't give him that kind of power."

"It's not just that." Ava moved to the leather wing-back and sat. "I did a lot of thinking while I was home. I . . . can't do this anymore."

"Do what?"

But Ava didn't answer. She didn't need to. Nat already knew. They sat in silence for a moment, letting the words settle. Finally, Ava spoke.

"I couldn't tell my parents what had happened to me." Her voice was soft, her eyes cast down. "There I was, physically and emotionally battered, and I had to make up a story about a random mugging." She looked up then, her eyes shiny with tears. "I was too ashamed of what I'd done—of who I was—to tell them the truth. I can't live like that anymore."

"Okay," Nat said gently, "I understand."

"I feel awful that I got you into this, Nat." The tears spilled over then. "I don't want you to get hurt."

"I won't," Nat quickly assured her. "I've met someone amazing. We've been together for a while now. He's kind and generous and I'm attracted to him. And he really cares about me."

"He doesn't, though," Ava said, fat tears rolling dramatically down her cheeks. "It's not real."

Nat was instantly defensive. Ava didn't even know Gabe, didn't know anything about what they shared. But she couldn't snap at her friend. The girl was damaged and broken, blaming herself for the violence she'd endured.

"You don't need to worry about me," Nat said, only the slightest edge to her voice. "I'm safe and I'm happy."

"When he's tired of you, he'll throw you away like a piece of garbage. That's how it works. That's what he's paying for."

Nat's temper flared. "Every relationship is different," she retorted. "You told me one of your daddies wanted to marry you."

Ava snorted, swiped at her nose. "He was old and lonely, and he knew I'd never say yes. It was just a game to him. It's all just a game. You have to understand that."

Nat stood. "I'm sorry things turned ugly for you, Ava, but that doesn't mean that's going to happen to me."

"Okay," Ava acquiesced, hearing the anger in Nat's voice. "Maybe it will be different for you. Maybe you won't end up hating yourself."

There was a key in the lock then. Conversation

ceased as Ava's mom entered with two deli cups of coffee. The woman's expression made it clear that the tension in the room was palpable.

"Good luck in Ohio," Nat muttered. She hurried out of the penthouse.

The Face-off

As Nat took the subway back to Brooklyn, her irritation toward Ava continued to simmer. She understood that her friend had been hurt and humiliated. She got that Ava's words were meant to protect Nat from a similar fate. But Gabe Turnmill was not some coke-snorting misogynist who had lured Nat to a hotel room to degrade her. He was a hardworking, single dad who wanted companionship. Even love. Her heart knew this. It was her head and her gut that needed to shut up.

Nat was not Gabe's disposable toy, not a trinket to be tossed aside when he grew tired of her. The way he looked at her and made love to her; the way he listened to her and promised to protect her. If Ava was right, if this was just a game to him, why would he bother? No. Gabe had to feel like Nat did.

She was young, but she wasn't gullible, she wasn't a fool. She had enough life experience to know that her relationship was real, and she resented Ava for planting the seed of doubt.

She decided to text Gabe. He communicated with her frequently.

> Can't stop thinking about you.
> Can't wait to see you.
> Can't wait to touch you.

She always responded promptly, but she never initiated contact. He was a high-powered attorney with meetings and clients and cases. But if she reached out, he would make time for her. Because she was important to him. That night when they'd solidified their arrangement, he'd told her that his daughter and his work came first and second. Nat respected that. But she had to be a close third, didn't she? A simple text would confirm it.

Walking down Wyckoff Avenue past hip galleries and happening bars, she pulled out her phone. Her hands felt weak, almost trembling. This was a test, she realized, of the validity of her relationship. If what they had was real, Nat could text Gabe without seeming needy and insecure. And he would answer. She stopped walking and typed.

> I miss you.

Her heart hammered in her chest, as if she were about to press the big red nuclear button, not just send. But she did it. She launched the missile.

Gabe was going to respond, but she wouldn't stand on the street waiting for those three little dots that indicated he was typing. Stuffing the phone into her pocket, she hustled toward home. As she walked, she played a game with herself. If she didn't look at her phone until she was ensconced in her bedroom, his message would be there. Looking now would jinx it.

Letting herself into the apartment, she listened for the presence of her roommates. She was feeling fragile, upset by her meeting with Ava. She didn't need an encounter with Mara or Toni right now. Things were civil but tense these days. The girls still disliked her, but she'd given them no cause for a confrontation. Nat heard a shuffling noise from the back of the apartment—Mara's room. The angular redhead would be in there studying or tidying or plotting creative ways to evict Natalie now that her rent and bills were paid in a timely manner. As quietly as possible, Nat slipped into her room.

She removed her phone from her coat pocket, her brain already making excuses for Gabe. He could be in an important meeting. He might be with his daughter. At the gym. Or dead in an alley after a mugging gone wrong. With a deep breath, she looked at her screen.

No messages.

Her heart sank. It was entirely possible that Gabe would still respond to her, or that he really was in a meeting/with his daughter/at the gym/dead. But she had needed to hear from him *now*. If they really had a connection, wouldn't he somehow know that?

Wouldn't the universe offer her the sign that she needed to take away all this doubt?

There was a knock at the front door. Normally, Nat would have left it for Mara to answer. This was her place after all, and the roommates were more likely to have visitors than was Nat. But something— a desire for distraction, perhaps?—sent her to the front of the apartment to answer the heavy, almost pounding knock.

Opening the door a crack revealed a man's face: battered, bruised, disfigured. Ava's pretty visage had been damaged by violence, but this was on a whole other level. Both eyes were swollen shut, but one was open just enough to reveal a bloodred eyeball. The nose was flattened, the lips swollen and scabbed. Purple and yellow bruising colored the man's skin. His arm was in a cast to the elbow, a beige fabric sling holding it stationary across his chest. He wore a ball cap, a pair of jeans, and running shoes. It was the legs, the athletic, slightly bowlegged stance, that sparked recognition.

Cole Doberinsky.

She was about to slam the door, to turn and run for the gun in her dresser, until Cole spoke.

"I wanted you to see what you did," he said, his voice muffled through his damaged mouth.

Nat opened the door wider. "What *I* did?"

"Your guy found me and beat the shit out of me. He told me to get out of New York. He told me to go home and keep my fucking mouth shut. He said if I ever spoke your name again, he'd kill me."

Oh god. . . .

"I just wanted to talk to you, Nat." Cole's voice

shook with emotion. "I just wanted to understand why you threw away everything we had. And now I know." A tear leaked from his closed eye. Nat wasn't sure if he was crying or if it was a result of the damage. "You're a cruel, heartless bitch," he spat. "You're superficial and materialistic and ruthless."

"Cole, I didn't—"

But he cut her off.

"You'll get what you deserve," he growled, and she wasn't sure if he was talking about retribution or karmic payback.

"What's going on here?" Mara had materialized behind Nat, her pallor almost ghostly from the sight of the mangled face right at their front door.

"Ask *her*," Cole said, indicating Nat with his chin. "Ask her what kind of person she is. Ask her what she's capable of." He turned then and hurried down the stairs. He was terrified; she could see it in his gait, in the way he glanced around himself, as he hustled down the street.

"Who the hell was that?" Mara snapped, closing the door and turning all the locks.

"I have no idea," Nat lied.

"Should I call the police?"

"He's gone now," Nat said, walking back toward her room. "There's no point."

Closing the bedroom door behind her, she sat on the edge of her bed. She felt hot, flushed, jittery. It was the violence that disturbed her, the horrific extent of Cole's injuries. But she was experiencing something else, too. Relief. Cole was terrified, traumatized. He would leave her alone now. Her mind, body, and reputation were safe.

Gabe had done it. Not personally, but he had hired someone to find Cole, to beat him bloody, to make sure he didn't hurt her. She'd had an inkling before, but now she knew for sure: Gabe Turnmill was dangerous. Nat should have been fearful, appalled at his propensity toward bloodshed, and she was. But she was also flattered. The fact that Gabe was willing to go to such lengths to protect her made her feel special. And this display of his power made her feel something else.

It was wrong, she knew that, but it turned her on.

Park Avenue

Nat woke up alone in Gabe's bed. It took a moment to orient herself to her luxe, masculine surroundings. Then she remembered the night before. Cole on her front steps, swollen and battered. And afraid. She had sent Gabe a text after the encounter with her former abuser.

> Thank you.
> I'm safe now.   —

She had known enough not to mention Cole's name, not to implicate Gabe in any way. Her hero had responded twenty minutes later, suggesting a late dinner. Nat had replied:

> Or I could just come to your place? Show my gratitude?

Those three shivering dots had prefaced his response.

Sounds good.

And it had been good. More than good, it had been *great*. They'd made love with unprecedented intensity. Nat had been fervent with gratitude, ardent with affection, ravenous with desire. "I love you," she'd whispered, the words bubbling out of her in a torrent of ecstasy. She had been shocked by her own utterance, embarrassed, mortified. Panic tensed her body as she prayed that her words had been inaudible, indistinguishable from a moan or a sigh. And then, Gabe had responded. His voice was muffled by her hair, her neck, but still, she heard him.

"I love you, too."

Now, alone in the bed, she stretched languidly, reminiscing about the things she had done to Gabe until he had regained control—as a man of his stature should—and taken over. Forcefully. Masterfully. The shower was running, and Nat considered slipping under the rain showerhead with Gabe, but he had to get to work. She had to get to school. And after the intensity of last night, she wasn't sure how much Gabe would have left in the tank. She didn't want to push it with a man his age. Instead, she climbed out of bed, slipping into Gabe's button-down shirt tossed hastily on the floor. Barefoot, she padded to the sleek marble kitchen and the built-in coffeemaker. How did this thing work again? She selected from the digital screen, made herself a double shot.

Coffee in hand, she strolled to the living room, waiting for her lover to emerge. She needed to shower away the night's passion before school. She'd had the foresight to pack some clothes, art supplies, and textbooks so she could go straight to Gramercy Park from the Upper East Side. Perhaps Gabe's driver, Oleg, could drop her off on the way to the financial district? She felt a flutter of anxiety at the thought of her classmates seeing her exit the impressive town car. What would they think? She didn't care. There was no need to be ashamed of this relationship, not anymore.

Walking through the apartment, she moved to the window that looked out over Park Avenue. It was 6:10 A.M., according to the coffee machine. The street was quiet, dim, damp from overnight rain. The occasional car whisked past, cabs mostly, their tires inaudible from this height. The scene was dreamlike, a fantasy: the multimillion-dollar apartment, the tony address, the powerful man in the shower. And, at the window, the small-town girl with the messy past. Nat was incongruous with her surroundings, but she was strangely comfortable here. She let herself try it on, and she liked it. It felt right.

The shower turned off, and she moved back toward the kitchen. Having mastered the high-tech coffee machine, she could bring her boyfriend a cappuccino. But as she was passing the flat-screen TV perched on a lacquered black table, something caught her eye. Behind the device was a stack of picture frames, facedown, their velvet backs and stands just visible. Had Gabe hidden these photographs away from her view? Her pulse quickened.

Before she could think better of it, she reached for the top frame, turned it over. It was a high school photo, a girl in a black top, with dark hair and flawless skin. Her face was free of makeup, but her beauty emanated from the photograph like phosphorescence. Printed at the bottom of the photo was:

VIOLET TURNMILL

SENIOR CLASS

THE FAIRHAVEN SCHOOL

This was the daughter Gabe had mentioned.

Nat stared at the girl, dismissing the uncomfortable feeling tickling her belly. Violet's natural look and septum piercing were in keeping with her anti–foie gras, pro-chickpea stance. The name of the school was not familiar—why would it be? Nat had gone to a public school, knew nothing about the world of elite private education, of Ivy League prep. But Violet's must have been an artsy school, fostering free expression and creativity. Nat had expected a school uniform, had envisioned a preppy blonde with her father's blue eyes.

Hurriedly, Nat reached for the next photo. It featured Violet, Gabe, and a striking black woman with full, natural curls. She was clearly Violet's mother; their resemblance was evident. Why did Gabe keep a framed photo of his ex in his apartment? Nat's heart was pounding, her stomach fluttering as she turned over the next frame. Gabe and the same stunning woman—younger, even more beautiful—with baby Violet.

Nat knew that not all divorces were filled with hate and ugliness like that of her parents. Gabe would have kept good relations with his ex for the sake of his daughter. He would have displayed these photos for the same reason. But the sick feeling in her gut was creeping its way into Nat's throat. Was it jealousy? Envy? Nat wasn't sure of the difference, but she felt insecure, threatened, possessive as she stared at the two females.

The ex-wife had secured her place as the mother of Gabe's only child. They had shared something once, but it was over now. It was the girl who elicited the most powerful response in Nat. Without any effort, this young woman was number one in her father's life, would be always. Nat's status was tenuous, ephemeral. Would she trade the intimacy she shared with Gabe for the effortless security that Violet Turnmill enjoyed? The knowledge that she was a permanent fixture, that her role in her father's life was untouchable? If she could get rid of Violet Turnmill and take her place, would she?

Nat brushed away the rhetorical question. She had not been born into luxury or privilege, but she was here, on Park Avenue, naked beneath Gabe's shirt. Her lover cared enough about her feelings to hide these photos from her view. He cared enough about her well-being to deal with Cole. She heard the creak of the bedroom door. Gabe would emerge soon. Hurriedly, she returned the photos to their spot behind the TV.

Gabe entered the living room dressed in a smart navy suit, his damp hair curling up at the collar. His eyes were slightly red from lack of sleep, but he looked handsome, young, fresh. "Morning." He kissed her lips like it was normal for her to be there, like he enjoyed her presence.

"Cappuccino?" she asked. "I've figured out your state-of-the-art coffeemaker."

"Sure," he said, playfully smacking her butt as she headed to the kitchen. "I could get used to having you around."

Nat could get used to it, too.

The Sex Trade

That Saturday, Nat spent the day on campus with Ivan and Keltie. They were working on a collage project that was due on Monday. Ava, the fourth member of their team, was gone, and they had to make up the shortfall. Afterward, they'd gone for a couple of cheap beers (okay, four cheap beers), at a dive bar on Second. Nat had been happy to pick up the tab. Keltie and Ivan had half-heartedly objected, but in the end, they were too grateful to grill her about her finances. They had to have noticed the shift in Nat's circumstances, her new clothes, her highlighted hair, her pricey leather bag, her new-found generosity . . .

Now, she was on the train, heading back to Brook-lyn. She was tired, a little drunk, but content. While she missed Gabe on weekends, she appreciated the time to focus on school and her friends. And she understood his need to spend time with his daughter. Violet . . . that pretty girl with smooth brown skin and luminous eyes; the strong resemblance to her mother, so sophisticated, almost regal. Nat's mood was shifting to a darker place as she thought about those hidden photographs. She shook her head, trying to dislodge the images of that woman. That girl.

Exiting the train at Jefferson, she hustled through the darkened streets. The neighborhood was safe—fairly safe—but this was not Park Avenue. She allowed herself to imagine going home to Gabe's apartment . . . to Gabe. They could open a bottle of wine, order some food, and then climb into his deep bathtub together. But it was the weekend. Violet would be with her father.

If Natalie's arrangement was going to turn into something more valid, more permanent, she would have to build a relationship with Gabe's daughter. It would not be easy. They were too close in age, too disparate in upbringing. And Nat knew the tribulations that came with *having* a stepparent; *being* one wouldn't be any easier.

Suddenly, an incredulous bubble of laughter erupted from within her. How could she think of herself as a stepparent? She was twenty-one years old! Her potential stepdaughter was eighteen! Were her feelings for Gabe really so strong that she would consider it?

The man. The apartment. The life. What would she be willing to do . . . ?

Turning onto her street, she saw the warm glow of lights from within the building. As always, she experienced the queasy feeling that prefaced an encounter with Mara and Toni. She would head to her room and hide out there until the girls went to bed. Only then would she emerge to pee, to have a snack, to brush the beer scunge from her teeth.

As soon as Nat stepped into the entryway, she felt the aggressive energy. Something was about to go down here, something pivotal. It so rattled her that she considered slipping back into the night, heading to a coffee shop or an all-night diner. But avoidance was pointless. And impossible. Because Mara and Toni had materialized before her.

"Can we talk to you?" Toni's voice was indignant but timorous. Nat could see the anxiety in her dark eyes.

"Okay." To her surprise, Nat sounded calm, even casual, despite her racing pulse.

"You might want to sit down for this," Mara said, pointing to the sofa.

But Nat shook her head. "I'll stand."

The roommates exchanged a quick look before Toni said, "We need you to move out."

"Why?" Nat was not surprised, but she was not going down easy. "I've paid my rent and my bills. You can't kick me out for no reason."

"We know about your *lifestyle*," Mara snapped, a gleeful light dancing in her eyes. "And we're not comfortable with it."

"What *lifestyle*?" But Nat's face was turning red, belying her guilt.

Toni's voice was almost sad. "We know that you're an escort, Nat."

"No, I'm not!" She sounded offended, incredulous, but shame and humiliation burned her face.

"We're not stupid," Mara retorted. "We've seen you dressed up, getting into that big black car. Some nights you don't even come home."

Toni elaborated. "A month ago, you couldn't afford rent. Now, you've got money for new clothes and fancy bags . . . and trips to Vermont."

"We saw your Instagram," Mara said, struggling to hide her enjoyment of this moment. "Cute little inn you stayed at."

Why had Nat posted that photo? She'd been showing off, and now she would pay for her arrogance.

"What you do with your life is up to you," Toni remarked, "but we don't want to be around it."

Mara went in for the kill. "We don't feel safe living with someone who's in the sex trade."

"I'm not in the *sex trade*!" Nat cried. "I'm not doing anything wrong or dangerous."

"Really?" Toni barked. "Then why do you have a *gun*?"

"How did you—?"

But Mara cut Nat off. "We packed up your shit and we found it."

"I can explain. . . ."

But she couldn't. How could she explain that Gabe's driver, his hired muscle, had given her the gun because he cared about her safety? That Oleg had become her friend and confidant, their bond developing as he delivered her, like a precious package, to his employer? And how could she explain what she had with Gabe Turnmill? That she slept peacefully in Gabe's Egyptian cotton sheets; that she knew how to work his high-end coffee machine;

that she felt like she was home when she spent the night in his Upper East Side apartment. They wouldn't believe her if she told them that it wasn't about the money, she only accepted it to make him happy. Gabe liked to spoil her, and he wanted to ensure she was comfortable. So she said nothing.

"Even if you make a lot of money," Toni said softly, "you're still selling yourself." Then she turned on her heel and left the room. Nat felt a sharp, stabbing pain in her chest as she watched her go.

"You can arrange to have someone pick up the boxes in the next few days," Mara said, her tone triumphant. "But you need to leave now."

"It's eleven o'clock at night. Where am I supposed to go?"

"You've got money. Get a hotel," Mara said, "Or I'm sure one of your *clients* will take you in."

Rage filled Nat's chest, made her throat burn and her eyes sting. She wanted to tell Mara that her judgment and condescension were anti-feminist, that women should support each other's choices, even if they were controversial. But like all the people who had sneered and whispered when Nat and Gabe entered a restaurant or a bar, Mara was disgusted. And her roommate held all the power. There was nothing Nat could do but leave. Where would she go? Keltie and Ivan both lived in double rooms on campus and could not accommodate her. Ava was gone.

There was only one option.

The Real Estate Agent

The call came in at 11:20 P.M.: Nathan. Gabe wouldn't have answered it, but Celeste had gone to bed early. She'd been tired lately, napping in the afternoons, abandoning him at ten for the comfort of their king-size bed. Violet was out; not at a party or a club like a normal teen. She was at a meeting to organize a protest outside a Jersey meatpacking plant (he'd seen the MEAT IS MURDER placard in the hallway). Since he was alone in the family room with his glass of Scotch, he decided to answer. Natalie was not the type of girl to call for no reason.

"I'm so sorry to bother you," she began, "but my roommates threw me out."

"Why?"

"They know about us," she said quietly. "They think I'm a hooker."

Which made Gabe a john. "Where are you?"

There was panic in her voice when she said, "I'm at an all-night diner. I have nowhere to go."

"Can you go to a hotel tonight?"

"My credit card is maxed out. I might have enough for a hostel."

He couldn't let his sugar baby slum it in a hostel. It would degrade them both. "Get an Uber and go to my place. I'll call the doorman and tell him to let you in."

"Where are you?"

He thought about Melody, the crazy paralegal. She'd turned up at his Hamptons house with her fake brief and nearly destroyed him. "My daughter and I went away for the weekend," he fibbed. "But you're welcome to stay at my place for a couple of days."

"Thank you so much."

"On Monday, I'll make some calls. We'll find you somewhere to live."

After he hung up, he finished his Scotch, thinking about Natalie alone in his apartment. He liked the image in his mind, the pretty brunette naked under one of his work shirts, or maybe in his robe. In reality, Natalie would likely be wearing her own clothes, but this was *his* fantasy; *he* chose the wardrobe. Tinkling the ice in his glass, he allowed himself to imagine himself there with her, even living there with her.

It wasn't out of the realm of possibility. Violet was growing up, was going to college (or to fucking Honduras). It was not uncommon for couples to split once the kids left home. The gray divorce, they called it. No one would be shocked; no one would be to blame. Everyone would put it down to living separate lives. He could keep Natalie on the down-low until sufficient time had passed and it was socially acceptable to introduce his new girlfriend. There would be whispers about her age, comments about an affair, a midlife crisis, but he wasn't the only guy he knew to turn into a cliché.

It was the Scotch muddling his thoughts. He barely knew Natalie. And while she was sexy, attractive, charming, she would never fit into his world. His friends and colleagues might grudgingly accept her, but Violet would lose her mind. And, as an attorney, he knew all too well what he would lose if he divorced Celeste.

Under New York's equitable distribution system, his wife would make out like a bandit. She'd been a decent earner when they married but had devoted the last six years to her health, their daughter, and their home. Gabe would get brownie points for sticking by her through her illness, but at the end of the day, Celeste would get half. Half of what she knew about, half of what she and her lawyers would be able to find, but still . . . half.

And Celeste had always been a personal and professional asset. At the firm, the partners and their wives adored her. She was accomplished in her own right but happy to play hostess to his friends and clients, always remembering their names, asking after their children, charming them. She kept their home beautiful and immaculate, organized their social calendar, had wrangled their rebellious daughter. And Celeste legitimized him. She'd been a public defender, a crusader for justice. No one would suspect her husband of being less than squeaky clean. And he had stood by her while she battled cancer. He wasn't afraid to use that anecdote when he needed to.

But Celeste had sexually forsaken him in the last few years. She went to bed, alone, at ten o'clock. She'd let herself go, gaining weight, eschewing makeup as if to repel his romantic interest. During the week, there was physical distance between them; on weekends, it was emotional. Gabe had always filled that void with young, attractive women who did not pose a threat to his marriage. But there was something different about Natalie Murphy.

He'd been stupid and reckless, had let her get under his skin. Natalie should never have spent the night with him at his apartment; it was too intimate, too much like a real relationship. The girl knew her way around his place, knew how to make cappuccinos, for Christ's sake. And that night, when she'd told him she loved him, he should never have said it back. They'd been drinking; they were in the throes of passion. He didn't really mean it . . . but then, he didn't *not* mean it, either. Jesus . . . He'd created a problem.

He would set boundaries with Natalie, and he would stay with Celeste. For now, anyway. He'd always been comfortable compartmentalizing his life: the woman in the country, and the girl in the city. He glanced at his watch. The girl in the city would be on the subway now. In about forty-five minutes, she'd arrive at his luxurious building. Setting down his empty glass, he called his doorman.

After that, he called his real estate agent friend, Calvin. The younger man owed him a favor—or ten—after Gabe had helped him salvage the sale of a Midtown building to Chinese billionaires that had turned ugly. After ensuring his strictest confidence, Gabe instructed him to find something small, rent-stabilized, if possible, in the West Village or Chelsea. Natalie would be fairly close to campus, and not too far (and not too close) to his Upper East Side home. He could stop by her place on his way home from work, if he felt like it. She could ride the subway uptown to be with him. And at the end of the night, he could send her home.

He got up and made himself another Scotch.

The Delusion

The alarm on Nat's phone beeped: 7:00 A.M. She stretched dreamily, relishing the soft sheets that smelled subtly of Gabe's cologne. It was Monday; she didn't have time to lie around. She had classes in a couple of hours. She had to find a new place to live. She had to get her boxes out of Brooklyn. But, as she had for the past two days, she allowed herself a moment to enjoy being there, in that sumptuous apartment on Park Avenue. She allowed herself to pretend it was her home.

Climbing out of bed, she padded to the kitchen in her T-shirt and panties and turned on the coffee machine. She opened the fridge and peered inside. There was a jug of organic milk, a dozen eggs, some cheese, and an onion. She could make an omelet or scrambled eggs. Did she have time? She didn't, really, but the thought of cooking in Gabe's kitchen was strangely appealing. She was rummaging through his kitchen cupboards when her phone buzzed.

Reaching for it, she saw Gabe's name on her call display.

"Hey, babe," she said, her voice still throaty with sleep.

"Did I wake you?"

"No, I'm up. I was just going to make coffee." She didn't mention the eggs, suddenly feeling guilty for being so familiar in his kitchen.

"How'd you sleep?" He was driving. She could hear the hum of the freeway, could tell his attention was divided.

"Great. But I was lonely here without you."

"I spoke to a real estate agent," he said, getting down to business. "He's going to find some apartments in Manhattan. Somewhere small but comfortable and close to school. Are you around this week for viewings?"

"Of course."

"I was thinking Chelsea or the West Village. They're safe areas and there are a few rent-stabilized buildings."

"Sounds good." But her voice trembled.

"What's wrong?" He sounded surprised, mildly perturbed.

"Nothing," she said, but found her throat was clogged with emotion. "I'm just . . . grateful."

And she was. But she was also disappointed. Without articulating it to herself, she had hoped Gabe would invite her to stay with him. For good. Some naive, overly romantic part of her had longed for an offer to become a permanent part of his life. His live-in girlfriend. It was a delusional concept. It was way too soon; they barely knew each other. But she'd allowed herself to believe that all the drama— Cole, her roommates' confrontation—had happened for a reason. She had hoped it meant they would be together.

"It'll be great to have you living closer," Gabe said. "It's been a pain in the ass having to schlep you back and forth to Brooklyn."

Like she was a parcel. A document. An annoying child whose divorced parents shared custody.

His words, so businesslike, so matter-of-fact, forced a sudden burst of clarity. Gabe did not consider her live-in girlfriend material. He viewed her as a sex partner, a companion, paid to keep her physical and emotional distance. She was an escort. It was stupid and pathetic to try to turn their debauched relationship into something real. She was desperate and needy, clinging onto her older lover because of her daddy issues.

But, no . . . Gabe had protected her from Cole, had rescued her from homelessness. He had told her he loved her. True, it had been said in the heat of passion, after numerous glasses of Scotch. But he'd said it. And the way he looked at her, the way he touched her . . . What they shared was real. It had to be.

"It'll be a lot more convenient," she said, forcing an upbeat tone. "I'm excited."

30

......

The Studio

Nat's new apartment was in a four-story building situated on a leafy street several blocks from the School of Visual Arts. It was a studio, barely big enough for the double bed and plush sofa Gabe had had delivered. Nat had scoured thrift shops and secondhand stores, cobbling together a fun, kitschy collection of furnishings. The space had a cool Southeast Asian vibe thanks to a hand-carved teak coffee table she'd discovered, some brightly colored jacquard throw pillows, and a decorative Buddha next to the beaded turquoise lamp.

This was the first time Nat had ever lived alone. At first, she was afraid she'd feel isolated, but she'd felt far lonelier living with her mom and Derek in their new house in Blaine. She'd been much more solitary in the Bushwick apartment, hiding herself away from her judgmental roommates. Nat savored having her own space. She could watch TV in her underwear while eating Chinese takeout straight from the carton. She could invite Keltie and Ivan over under the auspices of working on a project and then end up drinking white wine until 2:00 A.M. It was the first place Nat could call her own. *If* she could call it her own.

It was her name on the one-year lease, but, without any discussion, Gabe had handed her a stack of cash for her damage deposit and first month's rent. When May 1 rolled around, Gabe had taken care of her rent again. He was wealthy, she knew that, but could he afford to house his ex-wife and daughter, his mistress, and himself? She hoped so. Without his support, there would be no way she could afford her new home. When classes finished, she would offer to get a job to help with expenses. Hopefully, he'd tell her it wasn't necessary. She'd allowed herself to envision a summer spent sketching, painting, enjoying the city with Ivan, when he wasn't at one of the two jobs he'd taken on to allow himself to stay in New York over the school holidays. (Poor Keltie would be going home to Pittsburgh.) And, of course, Nat would spend time with Gabe.

Skipping down the stairs and through the small tiled lobby, Natalie let herself out onto Twentieth Street. It was only a ten-minute walk to the main school building, heaven after her long subway commute from Bushwick. Afternoon sun was filtering through the leaves of the linden trees, dappling the sidewalk as she strolled to class. As happened often since her relocation to Chelsea, she felt an odd sense of déjà vu. It was different, though . . . more like simultaneously being out of her element and exactly where she was meant to be. The life she was now living felt both surreal and right. Even fated.

Her relationship with Gabe had intensified since she'd been living in the city. It had also normalized. They'd been together for three months now, and they were slipping into a comfortable groove. On Tuesdays or Wednesdays, they went out: to dinner, to the theater, even the opera once (though she'd only pretended to enjoy it). Every Thursday night, around ten, he would come to her apartment on his way home from work. She would set her studying aside, put on something sexy, open a bottle of wine. They would talk—about his day, her day, books, or even politics—and then they would make love. On the weekends, she let him be with his daughter.

Her fascination with the girl had not diminished with time. Perhaps this was due to Gabe's increased openness about his only child. He had mentioned Violet's impending graduation ceremonies, a party his ex-wife was going to host at her home somewhere on Long Island. Gabe had wanted his daughter to go to Princeton like he had, but the girl was planning to do volunteer work in Honduras (*fucking* Honduras, he called it, but Nat admired Violet's social conscience). The way he spoke of his daughter confounded Nat. Sometimes with affection, often with confusion, even with a sense of loss. Nat's curiosity had to be slaked.

Violet Turnmill was easy to find on Facebook. Nat had thought only older people were active on the platform, but apparently teens with a lot of strong opinions used it, too. Violet had lax privacy settings and posted regularly: articles about the environment, memes on women's rights, and feminist Insta-poetry. She shared photos of the intersectionality play she had written, directed, and starred in. She railed about bi erasure, about racism, and battery cages for chickens. From scanning the girl's posts, Nat was able to discern that she was pansexual, a vegan, passionate about theater and the disenfranchised.

When the younger girl finished high school, went off to Honduras or Princeton, Nat's relationship with Gabe would evolve. They'd be able to spend weekends together like a legitimate couple. Maybe they'd fly out to Blaine so Gabe could meet her mom. It would be awkward, given Gabe's age, but her mom would accept him eventually. Given time, Gabe would be comfortable introducing her to his friends and colleagues . . . even to Violet. Nat was happy with the status quo, but craving romantic progress was only natural. She was in love.

Nat had reached campus now. She had just one exam left, and then the semester was done. The school year had flown by. When she thought about her arrival at the School of Visual Arts, so young, so naive, so broke, she couldn't believe she was the same girl. She had a sophisticated, older boyfriend. She had money, new clothes, and an apartment. With them had come a new sense of self-confidence, of self-worth. Contrary to her earlier suppositions, she found her paid relationship with Gabe empowering.

Entering the classroom, she slipped into a vacant

desk. Just ahead of her and across the aisle, she spotted her pal. "Keltie," she called in a loud whisper. The pierced girl glanced over her shoulder, briefly, but didn't reply. There was something tense and purposeful in her ignorance of Nat's overture. Had Nat done something to piss her off? That's when she felt the weight of eyes on her. Several of her classmates were looking at her, whispering among themselves. She shifted in her seat, self-consciously.

As the exam booklets were handed out, Nat brushed away her paranoia. Keltie had no reason to snub her. Her friend was probably just stressed about her final exam, about packing up her dorm room and moving back to Pennsylvania for the summer. Nat, though jobless, could afford to stay in the city year-round. Keltie might be jealous.

The exam was surprisingly easy. Nat had worried she hadn't studied enough (she'd been busy with Gabe all week), but she was sure she'd done well. When it was over, she loitered outside the room, waiting for Keltie. Her friend emerged about five minutes later.

"What did you think?" Nat asked.

Keltie kept walking, so Nat fell into step beside her.

"Easier than I expected," the girl said.

"Let's celebrate. Ice cream? Margaritas? I'm buying."

Keltie stopped then. "Have you looked at your Instagram this morning?"

"No, I was running late. Why?"

Her friend leaned in, lowered her voice. "Have you heard of *Tag a Sugar Baby?*"

Oh, shit. "No."

"It's an Instagram page that outs escorts and sponsored girls." She took a deep breath. "Someone sent a screen shot of you to that page. They posted it."

"How did you see it?" Nat's voice was shrill with panic. "Do you follow that page?"

"No, of course not. I think it's mean and ugly. But someone tagged me in the photo. And your Instagram profile is public. A bunch of your followers were tagged to make sure they'd see it."

With trembling hands, Nat pulled out her phone and tapped the app. In the search bar, she typed in: Tag a Sugar Baby. The page had 8,045 followers. Beneath a tiny profile photo showing a girl in a bikini lounging on the hood of a Ferrari, it read:

Think you can get away with it, bitch? Think again.

And then:

Direct message us a screen shot if you want us to post a sugar baby.

With a sick feeling in her throat, Nat found the tiny photo of herself and tapped it. It was taken at the Metropolitan Opera. She wore a tight black dress, flawless makeup, and a self-satisfied smile. She remembered taking the selfie—Gabe had gone to the lobby to make a phone call, so she'd snapped it, sitting in her deep red seat in the opulent theater. It was the first (and only) time she'd been to the opera, so she'd posted it. She'd thought sharing her glamorous experiences couldn't hurt, now that she didn't have to worry about her roommates. She'd thought wrong.

Beneath her photo was a caption:

> Full-time student with an NYC apartment, nights at the opera, Michelin-starred restaurants, alone in every pic = #sugarbaby #sponsoredgirl #thanksdaddy

Nat went pale. Her mom was on Instagram. (What better way to show off her highly photogenic blond children?) Had she seen this? By tapping the image, Nat was able to see who had been alerted to the salacious post. Her mom's name appeared, along with another classmate from SVA, an old friend from back home in Blaine, a cousin. . . . Someone had covered all the bases. Soon, everyone would know.

"Who would do this?" Nat gasped, but it had to be Cole. Even after the beating Gabe had ordered, her ex had found a way to ruin her. He would pay for this. . . . But there was no way to prove it was Cole. And there were other possibilities, too many. Mara and Toni. Miguel. Even Ava might have betrayed Nat, may have felt she was protecting her.

"There's a website too," Keltie said. "You're on it."

"Oh my god . . ."

"I don't care what you do to make money. It's your body; it's your life. But not everyone feels that way."

"It's true, isn't it?" The voice was male, hostile. Ivan. Keltie must have shared the page with him.

Nat opened her mouth to respond, but she couldn't find the words to defend herself. Ivan, while progressive in many respects, obviously maintained some traditional values. His voice was shrill, loud, cutting.

"I knew something was up when you went to Vermont. And then when you moved into that apartment . . . It didn't make sense. But I never thought you were a *hooker*."

"I'm *not* a hooker," she whispered.

"Just because you don't get paid by the blow job, doesn't mean you're not a prostitute."

"Ivan, stop," Keltie scolded. "You're being an asshole."

"She's having sex with old men for money! It's disgusting!" A crowd of classmates was gathering around them, all of them looking at Nat, some looking at their phones. All of them judging her. She felt Keltie's hand squeeze hers, and it was that small show of support that unraveled her.

Tears blurred her vision as Nat turned and fled. Scurrying blindly down the streets, back to the apartment Gabe paid for, she told herself it would be okay. That it would all blow over. When school resumed in the fall, they'd all have forgotten. She would call her mom and make up a story—a vindictive former friend out to disparage her. A free ticket to the opera.

But alone in the tiny studio, her shame felt overwhelming. She'd made peace with the nature of her relationship, had stopped feeling guilty about the money Gabe gave her. Because he cared for her, loved her even. He'd told her so. Just because he hadn't repeated the sentiment since that night when they'd had amazing sex in his apartment, didn't make it less true. Gabe loved her; she knew he did.

She needed to see him. He was her boyfriend, and it was normal to crave his support at a time like this. It was Friday afternoon—he would likely be heading to Long Island to pick up his daughter at school. But just this once, Violet could spend the weekend with her mother. Just this once, Natalie could come first. She dialed his number.

He answered after one ring. "Hello?"

Did he sound annoyed? Or was it concern that gave his voice that edge? Gabe had made the parameters of their arrangement clear: weekends were for his daughter. But that conversation had happened months ago. Their relationship had evolved since then. Hadn't it? She suddenly felt afraid, was tempted to hang up, but she couldn't. Not now.

"I need you," she said.

31
· · · · · ·

Self-harm

When the call from *Nathan* came in, Gabe was on the Montauk Highway, just past Bridgehampton. Had Natalie called ten minutes later, he would have been at his picture-perfect country house and wouldn't have answered it. Her voice was shaky, tearful. Someone had outed her sugar baby status on social media and she was humiliated. (He'd found a tactful way to ask if he'd been identified; he hadn't.) Natalie had wanted to see him, needed his comfort and support, but he was already in the Hamptons. She'd pleaded for him to come back early, to spend the weekend with her, just this once. He'd made up an excuse, an important fund-raiser at his daughter's school.

"Don't let their judgment bother you," he'd assured her. "You know that what we have is real."

"I know," she'd said, and he had heard relief and gratitude in her voice. "I don't care what anyone thinks. I know how I feel. I know how you feel."

"I'll try to come back Sunday morning if I can."

"It's okay," Natalie had said. "Soon Violet will be off to college or on her trip, and we can be together every weekend."

"Right," he'd replied weakly. "I'll see you in a couple of days."

It was Saturday afternoon, and he'd been trapped at the Sagaponack house until now. Celeste's parents had been visiting from Montreal, were just now heading home. They'd been there all week while Gabe had been in the city; he'd left work early Friday afternoon to have dinner with them. He'd been relieved it was just one dinner. Gilbert and Sylvie were fine but, even though they spoke perfect English, they insisted on speaking French, which drove him nuts. He had no idea what they were saying and often assumed they were mocking or disparaging him without his knowledge. Violet was fluent, but she always responded in English. He doubted it was for his benefit, but he appreciated it nonetheless.

He was in the massive kitchen, making himself a sandwich with the leftover pork loin Celeste had made last night. As he spread Dijon mustard on his multigrain bread, his mind returned to Natalie's words on the phone.

Soon Violet will be on her trip, and we can be together every weekend.

His daughter's graduation was a ticking clock on his affair. Once Violet was at college or in fucking Honduras, he would have two options: end it with Natalie or end his marriage. There was a third option—tell Natalie he'd been married all along, that he'd like to keep her on as his mistress. But the girl was in love with him. She'd feel betrayed. She might freak out, contact Celeste. He could lose them both.

He had to make a choice.

A car pulled into the drive then. It would be Celeste returning home from chauffeuring her parents to LaGuardia. He'd suggested a car service, had offered to drive them himself, but his wife had insisted. She knew the way, was comfortable on the freeway. Gabe could stay home and catch up on work. He'd been grateful—three hours in a car filled with Quebecois banter was not his idea of a good time. But it would have been nice to be needed.

Waiting for his wife to enter the house, he chewed his sandwich, thinking about Natalie. She needed him, unlike his wife and daughter, who were both so capable, so independent and strong-willed that he'd become extraneous. Other than the paycheck he brought home, Celeste and Violet were largely ambivalent to his existence. Natalie relied on him financially, too, but also emotionally, physically. His was the first number she called when she was afraid; he was the person she turned to when she was upset, or in trouble. It was his comfort she sought, above all others.

Natalie had few friends, wasn't close to her family, all she had was Gabe. And yet, when she needed him, he left her hurt, alone, damaged. Why? To placate his in-laws, who didn't respect him enough to speak his fucking language? To be there for his daughter, who'd disappeared the moment her grandparents left? Or was it to please his emotionally distant wife, who was indifferent to his presence?

Celeste walked in, looking weary from the long drive. "Hey," she mumbled, barely looking at him. "Where's Violet?"

"She went into the city to see that play, remember? I told her she could stay at the apartment tonight."

"Right." She grabbed a glass and filled it with filtered water. He watched her take a lemon from a porcelain bowl full of them and roll it on the marble surface to soften it. As she was cutting a wedge, Gabe set his sandwich down.

"We need to talk."

Was he really going to do this? Was he going to end his twenty-nine-year marriage to be with his twenty-one-year-old sugar baby? The moment felt fantastical, dreamlike. But it also felt right. Natalie needed him. And he needed her. He needed her love, her devotion, her adoration. He deserved it.

"We do," Celeste agreed. "Let's sit down."

What was happening? He was about to leave his wife, and suddenly she was hijacking the conversation. But he left his sandwich on the counter and followed her to the sofa. Celeste set her water glass on the reclaimed barn door that served as a coffee table in their casual family room and began.

"I was waiting for my parents to leave. For Violet to be out. There's something you should know."

"Okay . . ."

"Violet's been harming herself."

He felt himself go pale. "What?"

"She's been cutting herself. And burning herself with matches."

"Jesus, Celeste . . ." Parenting was his wife's job—her *only* job. "How could you let this happen?"

"She hid it from me. Under her clothes. I think it's the pressure of living up to our expectations . . . And I think she's worried about me." Celeste swallowed. "About us."

"What do you mean?"

"I think she's afraid that once she moves out, we'll split up." His wife's eyes filled with tears. "She worries about my health. If the cancer comes back, and I don't have your support . . ."

"That's not going to happen," Gabe said, but his words sounded hollow and false.

"And she's afraid that, if we separate, she won't see you. I know she doesn't act like it, but deep down, she still adores you." Celeste reached for his hand. "She still needs you, Gabriel. She needs you so much."

His world tilted on its axis. Moments ago, he'd been prepared to walk away from his wife, from his daughter, from all the years they'd invested. But this changed everything. His darling girl was hurting herself, cutting and burning her skin. Because she was afraid she'd lose him. Violet still loved him, adored him, depended on him. . . . He would not abandon her and her mother; he would not be a selfish, narcissistic cliché. When he got back to the city, he would end it with Natalie. He'd be there for his family. In a weird way, Violet's self-harm had saved her parents' marriage.

He took his wife's hands. "I have no intention of leaving you," he said adamantly. "You and Violet are my life."

"I know our marriage hasn't been . . . *complete*," she said. "Since I got sick, since the medication . . . I haven't felt very *sexual*."

"It's okay." He gathered his wife in his arms. "You're all I need, Celeste. You and our daughter."

"Thank you," she murmured into his shoulder, and he felt her tears of love and gratitude wet his collar. After a moment, she pulled away and wiped her eyes. "What did you want to talk about?"

"I was worried about you," he said quickly. "I thought you seemed tense."

"I knew I couldn't hide this from you. You know me so well."

He reached for her hands, took them in his. "Violet will be okay, Celeste. I'll take care of you both."

She smiled, her eyes still shiny with emotion, and collapsed back onto his chest. He kissed her hair and stroked her back. She needed him now. She really needed him. It was what he'd wanted all along.

The Necklace

By the time Nat met Gabe for lunch on Monday, she'd largely recovered from the trauma of Tag a Sugar Baby. While she'd wanted to spend the weekend with her lover, his absence had given her time to process and handle the situation. She'd smoothed things over with a call to her mom, who hadn't really understood the concept of the mean-spirited page anyway. And she'd convinced herself that people her age had short memories. By the time she started third year, everyone would have forgotten. And if they hadn't . . . ?

It was on a solo walk on the High Line that she'd realized her options. She could drop out of school. Her relationship with Gabe hadn't diluted her passion for art, but it had dampened her enthusiasm for higher education. It felt traditional and confining.

With Gabe's support, she could rent a warehouse space and explore art on her own terms. She had two years of lessons under her belt, a solid foundation upon which to develop her skills, to hone her artistic viewpoint, find her signature style. Becoming a children's book illustrator suddenly seemed pedestrian, evidence of her cautious, small-town thinking. She could envision herself as a legitimate artist now, with gallery showings, selling pieces to collectors and celebrities. With Gabe's money and connections, she could thrive as an artist.

They were now seated in a bustling Italian restaurant not far from Gabe's office. He'd been so eager to see her that he'd suggested they meet for lunch, couldn't even wait for their standing dinner date. Happily, she'd agreed. When she'd arrived at the busy eatery, dressed in a formfitting shift dress and wedge heels, he'd planted a chaste kiss on her cheek. He probably had colleagues, even clients in the restaurant. She knew enough to play it cool.

Gabe looked handsome but a little tired as they ordered. He got the pasta with clams. She, the cannelloni. He ordered them a bottle of white wine, even though it was the middle of the day. But the reunion felt celebratory, in a way. Nat's school was finished. Violet would be graduating in a month. It felt like they were poised on the precipice of a new chapter.

"How was the fund-raiser at Violet's school?" she asked, chewing a mouthful of tender cannelloni.

"Good," Gabe said dismissively, taking a sip of wine. "I got you something." He pulled a black velvet box out of his pocket and passed it to her.

Natalie accepted it with trembling hands. Gabe had gotten her gifts before—a book he'd read that he thought she'd like, clothing, or a bottle of prosecco—but this was different. This was jewelry. Expensive jewelry as indicated by the insignia on the box. Tentatively, she opened it.

"Oh my god," she gasped, as she looked at the diamond-and-white-gold necklace nestled in a bed of satin. "It's stunning."

"I'm glad you like it."

She touched the delicate chain, the oval pendant. "I don't know what to say." Her voice was husky with emotion. "No one's ever given me anything this beautiful."

"I wanted you to know how much these past few months have meant to me."

It was the delivery, not the words themselves, that made her stomach plummet: cold, clipped, final. She looked up at Gabe—his tense jaw, his ice-blue eyes. She looked down at the necklace. It was not a gift. It was an omen. She snapped the velvet box closed.

"What's going on?"

"You're an amazing woman, Natalie. You're gorgeous and smart and funny . . ."

"Are you dumping me?" Her voice was shrill, louder than she'd intended. She saw Gabe's jaw clench.

"It's my daughter," he said, leaning toward her. "She's going through a difficult time and she needs me."

Nat's voice trembled. "I've always respected your relationship with her."

"I know you have. But . . . Violet wants to move in with me. Part-time at least. She and her mother aren't getting along. She's emotionally unstable. She's been cutting herself. I—" His voice cracked. "I can't go on seeing you."

This couldn't be happening. Gabe had assured her that what they had was real. He had found her an apartment so she could be close to him. His daughter was growing up, was going traveling or to college. They could finally think about a future.

"Maybe I could meet her?" Nat tried. "She doesn't have to know about *us*. I could be her friend. I could talk to her and help her with her problems." Without a trace of irony, she added, "I remember how hard it is to be her age."

"I think a clean break is for the best."

She was speechless. Blindsided. The room was swirling around her, and she felt sick to her stomach. "No," was all she could say.

"Yes," he said coolly. "We had an *arrangement*. And, now, that arrangement is over."

Who was this man, so heartless and cold? She didn't know him.

"It was more than that," she said, tears pooling in her eyes, "you know it was."

He didn't respond but reached in his pocket, extracted a thick envelope. "I want you to have this."

She looked at the white package next to her plate of cannelloni. He was buying her off. "I don't want it."

"Yes, you do. I'll pay for the apartment until the end of the summer," he continued, taking a sip of wine. "In the fall, you might want to move into campus housing. Or you could take over the rent payments. I'm sure you'll have no trouble finding another man on the website to support you."

It was like he'd punched her. Or spat in her face. "I don't want another man," she said, tears falling from her eyes. "I want you."

"I'm sorry, Natalie," he said, sounding firm, adamant, like a lawyer. "It's over." He stood then and tossed a stack of bills on the table. He was paying for lunch. "My driver will take you back to your apartment."

She watched him stride out of the restaurant.

33

......

The Reason

Nat lay in bed for four days, barely eating, rarely sleeping, crying incessantly. It may have been indulgent, but she had nothing to do, nowhere to be, and no one who cared about her. Her isolation would have been overwhelming, had she cared about her mental health. But she didn't. She couldn't think about pulling herself together, about moving forward. All that mattered to her was Gabe.

Between the wall and her bed, discarded and forgotten after a lovemaking session, she found his tie. It was dark gray, with a dense pattern of leaves, vines, and flowers, reminiscent of Victorian wallpaper. (It was, in fact, a design by the English artist and philosopher William Morris.) Nat kept it draped around her neck, kissed it, dried her tears with it. At one point, she considered hanging herself with it, the symbolism achingly delicious. But who would find her body? A neighbor, likely, when she'd started to decompose and stink up the building. And Gabe would never even be alerted.

Her feelings toward him vacillated wildly. When she woke in the mornings, she pined for his love, sending him desperate texts pleading for him to talk things through, not to give up the beautiful connection they'd shared. By midday, she'd begun to negotiate, suggesting they discuss redefining their relationship, perhaps stepping back, slowing things down. In the evenings, after she'd had some wine or vodka, she'd be consumed by anger and loathing. That's when she'd call him, leaving venomous, slightly slurred messages.

"You can't just tell someone you love them and then buy them off with a fucking necklace!"

"You're a liar! And a monster! I hate you!"

"I'm going to find your daughter and tell her everything. She deserves to know what kind of man her father is."

Gabe did not respond to any of her overtures.

It was remorse that finally got her out of bed and into the shower at five forty-five that morning. Light was peeking through the fog of anger and desperation, and she realized her actions had been melodramatic. Gabe would think she was pathetic. Or psychotic. And his opinion mattered to her. She was still hopeful for a reconciliation. Perhaps when Violet was a little older, had dealt with her issues, had absconded to college or an NGO in South America, Nat and Gabe could be together again.

She had to see him. She had to apologize.

Wearing a bright, flirty dress, she took the subway uptown. The doorman at Gabe's prestigious
building would have orders to block her access, so
she loitered down the street, sipping a paper cup of
coffee she'd picked up on Madison, trying to look
casual, unobtrusive. It was almost seven now. The
town car would be arriving any minute to shuttle
Gabe to his downtown office. Perhaps she should
approach Oleg first? The driver liked her, even
understood her. He could be an ally in her quest to
access Gabe. On the other hand, Oleg was the hired
help. He may have been asked to be a gatekeeper,
even a bodyguard. No, she would wait until her
former lover emerged and go to him directly. Tentatively. Carefully.

She had been standing there for over an hour
when she suddenly realized it was Saturday. Fuck.
In her fug of grief and alcohol, she had lost track of
the days. Gabe might have gone away for the weekend. If he was in his apartment, he could be inside
for hours, might not emerge all day. And what if he
exited with Violet? Could Nat approach the pair
without seeming like a deranged stalker? Gabe
would never engage with her in front of his daughter. She decided to give up and go home, return
on Monday. But after the large cup of coffee she'd
been nursing, she would have to pee first.

The coffee shop where she'd so recently purchased a latte refused to let her use their restroom
without a purchase. Annoyed, she left and went to
a vegetarian breakfast place next door. She hadn't
eaten more than toast and crackers for days, and she
was suddenly famished. Ordering a tofu scramble

and gluten-free toast, she used the facilities and then returned to the booth. But when the plate arrived, her stomach revolted. The crumbled tofu was a poor substitute for eggs, but she wouldn't have been able to ingest the genuine article, either. She was still too desolate, too disappointed, too destroyed to keep food down. Still, she sat there, nibbling some toast (if you could call this sawdusty item toast) and sipping a bitter cup of coffee. Her studio apartment, once her haven, now felt sad and lonely. Returning home would mean more crying, more drinking, more wallowing.

And that's when the girl walked in.

Nat recognized her right away. The dark hair, the pierced septum, the striking bone structure. What Nat hadn't expected was her demeanor. A girl with Violet's looks, money, and pedigree should walk with confidence, with the air of someone who had the world at her feet. But Violet's energy was dark and heavy; somehow hostile and vulnerable at the same time. Gabe hadn't lied. His daughter was troubled.

She was accompanied by a pale girl, a little heavy, with artfully shaved blond hair, a prominent lip and eyebrow ring. Nat watched the pair slide into a booth just ahead and across from her. Moving her tofu around on the plate, Nat watched Gabe's child peruse the menu. When their young waitress approached, Violet and her friend asked a lot of questions about the food. Their words were not discernible, but Nat assumed they were inquiring into the ethical harvesting of the soybeans, the use of chemical fertilizers on the tomato plants, the wages paid to the fruit pickers. Nat ordered another cup of coffee and watched the girls drink green tea, embroiled in a deep, serious conversation. When their food arrived, they ate heartily. Clearly, this restaurant passed muster with their dietary requirements.

The fair girl tossed her napkin onto her near-empty plate and stood. Leaning down, she kissed Violet on the lips and then left. Nat was mildly surprised by the incongruous pairing. Violet was miles out of her blond girlfriend's league; she just didn't know it. Violet was tall and beautiful and radiant. Of course, she was. She was Gabe's daughter.

When Violet signaled for the bill, Nat signaled for her own. As the younger girl paid, Nat dug some bills out of her wallet. Tossing them on the table, she followed Gabe's offspring out of the restaurant.

34
· · · · · ·

The Met

Nat followed Violet Turnmill at a discreet distance for several blocks. The girl was headed uptown, her stride casual but purposeful. Nat wondered if Violet was meeting her father. Her pulse quickened at the thought of seeing Gabe. And at the thought of him seeing her. He would be angry, protective of his daughter. He'd think Nat was obsessed, unhinged, a stalker. She should turn around right now, go back to her apartment. But she couldn't. Violet Turnmill was pulling her along in her force field.

When Violet turned right on Fifth Avenue and crossed toward the park, her destination became evident. The Met. Nat loved the Met, had visited numerous times. Thanks to its donation policy for New York residents, she had been a regular attendee even when she was broke. Experience informed her that she could easily lose Violet inside the massive building, the multitude of exhibits, the sea of weekend visitors. The pretty girl was ascending the steps now, moving toward the doors. Nat scurried up after her.

Violet moved directly to the express entry for members and patrons. Of course she had a membership; the Turnmills were wealthy, cultured, sophisticated. As Nat waited in the short residents' line, she kept her eyes trained on Violet's dark hair. She could not lose her now.

Inside the gallery, it took Nat a moment to locate her mark. Gabe's daughter was moving through the main hallway, headed for the stairwell. She seemed to have a destination in mind, wasn't distracted by any of the other exhibits. Nat trailed behind her until Violet reached the second floor and took a left, entering the impressionists gallery. The pretty girl passed by the paintings on the walls—the Manets, the Monets, the Pissarros—without a glance. Finally, she stopped in front of a sculpture in bronze.

It was *The Little Fourteen-Year-Old Dancer* by Edgar Degas. Nat knew it well. She had studied it at school, visited it often. It was a personal favorite— this simple girl, a street urchin turned ballerina— immortalized by a great man. With a deep breath, Nat moved closer, stopping just a couple of feet from Gabe's daughter. Nat's eyes were fixed on the almost life-size sculpture, but all her attention was focused on the beautiful dark-haired girl beside her.

They were close enough that Nat feared Violet would hear her pounding heart, would sense her taut, nervous energy. But Gabe's only child was enraptured by the statue before her and didn't even notice Nat. She had to say something, to connect with Violet in some way. It was a need, a compulsion. Keeping her voice calm and steady, Nat spoke.

"It wouldn't happen today, would it?"

Violet glanced over, surprised to be addressed by a stranger. "What wouldn't?"

"A grown man spending hour upon hour sketching and sculpting a pubescent girl." Nat kept her eyes on the bronze statue. "It would be considered perverted."

"Uh . . . because it would be perverted," Violet snorted.

"Degas wanted to depict commoners, the real people of France," Nat continued. "Most artists of the time only featured idealized body types. Heroes or goddesses."

"Hmm. . . ." The girl sounded dismissive. Nat upped her game.

"When Degas first displayed this sculpture, critics were really cruel. They said the dancer looked like a monkey, that her face was obviously of *low character*."

Violet looked at her then. "Are you an artist?"

Nat met her light brown eyes, smiled. "I'm an art student. You?"

"No." She turned back to the statue. "I just like her. My dad used to bring me here when I was a kid."

At the casual mention of Violet's father, Nat felt her stomach twist. But she maintained her cool. "And now you come alone?"

"Yeah," the girl said dismissively. "My dad's busy."

But he's spending more time with you. Because you're having emotional problems.

Instead, Nat said, "My dad would never bring me here. He lives in Vegas, for one. And he'd have no idea who Degas was. He'd think he was a rapper. Or maybe a boxer."

Violet chuckled. "Dads suck. Like most men."

"They sure do." They were silent for a beat, and then Nat filled the void. "The little dancer's father died when she was young. Her mother was a laundress. One of her sisters became a prostitute."

Violet said, "You know a lot about her."

"I did a project." Nat smiled. "It's all on Wikipedia."

"I'll have to read up on her."

"Now you don't need to."

Violet smiled, and their eyes connected for a moment. Nat felt an odd sort of pull. She couldn't let Violet go, not now. Before she could chicken out, she said, "I'm going to get a coffee in the café. Want to join me?"

Violet Turnmill's brow crinkled ever so slightly. Was she suspicious? Surprised that a stranger would ask her out for coffee after a two-minute conversation?

And then the younger girl shrugged. "Sure. I could use a coffee."

35

· · · · · ·

The Return

The week after Gabe ended his arrangement with Natalie had been hell. He'd returned to Sagaponack, working from home to be close to his wife and daughter. Violet seemed perplexed by his presence, but he explained that he had a light caseload, so he wanted to spend some time with his "favorite girls." She'd looked at him as if he were speaking Farsi. It would take time to worm his way back into his daughter's affections, but he would get there.

All the while, his phone nearly exploded with angst and vitriol. Natalie's texts veered from pleading to raging, with all stops in between. Locked in the master bathroom, he listened to the voice messages begging him to reconsider, negotiating with him to redefine their relationship, threatening to tell his daughter, to destroy him, kill him even. (He could tell Natalie was drunk.) The girl was a fucking lunatic.

He thought about Emily and the other sugar babies who had so gracefully accepted his payoffs. But he'd known Natalie was different. He'd been drawn to her passion, her authenticity, her lack of sophistication. And the girl had loved him, truly loved him. He should have known she would not go easily.

But then, abruptly, the harassment stopped.

He'd been right to ignore her overtures. Natalie had come to her senses, realized he wasn't going to engage. She'd probably moved on, replaced him with a new sugar daddy. Gabe could relax now, focus on Violet. He no longer had to worry about Natalie showing up at his apartment or his office; about her approaching his daughter. Thank god. It was truly fucked-up that his relief was peppered with disappointment.

Pressing the puree button on the blender, he watched the kale, bananas, blueberries, and chia seeds turn into a pleasing green mush. He needed to keep his energy up, his mind sharp, his focus on his family. It was Sunday; he would go to the gym and then get a massage. Violet had gone into the city for the weekend, but she'd be back for their usual Sunday dinner. And he would be waiting.

Celeste walked into the kitchen then. "Want a smoothie?" he asked. She needed the cancer-fighting antioxidants. His wife was the picture of health since her disease had gone into remission, and he had a vested interest in keeping her that way. Violet couldn't handle another crisis.

"Yes, please." His wife perched on a barstool and

accepted the green concoction. As she brought it to her lips, he leaned in, his elbows on the counter.

"We need to talk to Violet tonight. About Honduras."

Celeste set down the glass. "She's really excited about it."

"Well, she can't go," he stated. "She's too fragile. She's too unstable."

"She's eighteen, Gabe. We can't forbid it."

"We can, and we will," he snapped, righting himself. "I'm not letting my daughter travel to a fucking third-world country while she's cutting and burning her arms and legs."

His wife flinched slightly in the face of his anger. But then she sighed. "You're right . . . But we can't tell her now. It's almost her graduation. We're hosting the pool party."

"After that then," Gabe said. "We'll tell her she can go to Honduras when she's more stable and more mature." He took a drink of his smoothie. "When she's finished her degree."

Celeste's eyes narrowed slightly. Was Gabe really using Violet's mental-health issues to push her into college? He was, but he wasn't about to admit it to his wife. If she called him on it, he was ready. He would inform her that he was in charge now; he had to be, because Celeste had failed as a mother. She was too soft, too indulgent, too weak. Their daughter was a disaster: moody, fragile, directionless. . . . And it was all Celeste's fault.

But his partner simply said, "Okay." She knew better than to take him on. Celeste took her smoothie and padded out of the room.

Gabe downed the rest of his drink and felt a surge of power, of confidence. It wasn't the superfoods coursing through his system; it was the knowledge that he was doing the right thing. It had been a mistake to let Natalie distract him from his pivotal role in his child's life. His own parents had been exhausted and distracted, working themselves into early graves. Gabe had survived their neglect, even thrived because of it. But Violet was different. She was sensitive and emotional. She needed her father's attention, his affection, and his guidance. He was here now, present and engaged. Placing the glass in the sink, he grabbed his car keys and headed to the garage.

Daddy was back. And soon, the little girl he'd adored would be back, too.

36

. . . . . .

The Invitation

Nat sipped a glass of vodka and Coke as she stared at the pretty face filling her computer screen. Violet Turnmill. It had been four days since their introduction at the Met. Nat had spent most of those four days sifting through the younger girl's photos on social media. They'd followed each other on Snapchat and Instagram shortly after their coffee date, had friended each other on Facebook, too. Gabe wasn't on any of these *juvenile* platforms, wouldn't know that his ex-lover and his daughter had struck up a friendship. Possibly even more than a friendship.

Nat had not set out to flirt with Violet, but she couldn't ignore the way the younger girl had looked at her, couldn't deny their chemistry. She knew that Violet was pansexual (as stated in her social media profiles), and she'd seen her kiss the fair-haired girl.

Nat was straight, had never even experimented with a female. But there was something about Violet . . . familiar yet strange. Exotic. Fascinating. Nat took a sip of vodka and looked at a photo of Violet lying by a stunning pool with a menagerie of her unconventional friends. The girl was gorgeous in her bikini, her natural beauty undiminished, even magnified by her unassuming aspect. Nat felt a confounding mixture of attraction, jealousy, and loathing. She drank more vodka.

Their coffee date in The Met's café had been illuminating. Painfully, horribly illuminating. Nat had been nervous, almost trembling from the proximity to Gabe Turnmill's only child. He would kill her if he knew she had approached his daughter, but Nat didn't care. She had to get to know Violet, had to make that connection. Somehow, despite her inner turmoil, Nat had affected an outward appearance of calm.

"Did you grow up in New York?" Nat had casually asked, when they were seated, sipping cappuccinos.

"Mostly. My parents bought a weekend house in Sagaponack when I was little. Eventually, my mom and I moved out there full-time."

"Sounds nice."

"It's a beautiful house. But the Hamptons are boring." She brought her coffee cup to her lips. "Rich. White. Traditional. Where did you grow up?"

"Small town in the Pacific Northwest."

"I thought you said your dad lived in Vegas?"

"He does. I was ten when my parents split." Nat's voice was tight as she asked, "How old were you?"

"They're still together," Violet said. "My dad works in the city, but he comes home to my mom and me every weekend."

Nat absorbed this news without a visible reaction, but inside, her intestines roiled with betrayal. Gabe was married. He had a wife. Everything he'd told her had been a fucking lie.

"He's a workaholic," Violet continued. "He drives all the way home and then spends the entire weekend on his laptop. My mom forces us to have a family meal on Sundays, but she's the only one who enjoys it."

"He sounds like an asshole."

"He's a *corporate lawyer*." Violet spat out the words, like she was saying *pedophile*. "We don't have the same principles. I mean, I have principles. He doesn't."

No, he doesn't.

"You know how you can idolize someone and then you find out who they really are?" Violet's voice had turned tremulous. "My father cares about money and success and power. That's it."

Nat's voice was husky. "And your mom?"

"She's a good person. She had cancer a few years ago, but she's okay now." Violet's eyes were misty. "We've had our issues . . . I was pretty wild when I was younger. But she's always stood by me. She always supports me."

Nat held it together until she got home from the museum, and then she came apart. Hot tears of shame and hatred and guilt poured down her face, sending a sharp pain searing through her head. She'd been deceived, used, played, and the thought made her want to vomit. Gabe had lied to her. Why?

But she knew why.

If Gabe had told her he was married, she would never have gone out with him. Well, that wasn't entirely true. She would have gone for the first drink, the pay-per-meet, and then she would have walked away. She wouldn't have fallen for him, wouldn't have convinced herself that they had something real. And that's what Gabe Turnmill needed: blind devotion. He got off on it. His enormous ego could only be fed by pure adoration. It didn't matter to him that Nat's heart was broken, that his lie had upended her life. He had charmed her, played her, and then dropped her when he got tired of her.

He was a narcissist. A sociopath. A monster. So why did she still miss him? Why did she still love him?

She had to let it go and move on. She had to figure out a way to pay her rent or give up the studio and apply for student housing. She needed to stop day-drinking, had to find a job. But here she was, drunk at two in the afternoon, sifting through Violet Turnmill's Facebook photos, hoping to catch a glimpse of Gabe in the background. Since the girls' museum encounter, they had been texting regularly—friendly chatter, flirtatious banter. Nat knew she shouldn't encourage Violet's interest, should cut off the friendship before it went any further. But she couldn't. The connection to Gabe, however sick and wrong, was irresistible.

Nat's phone vibrated then. It would be her mom; no one else cared about her. Maternal instinct had alerted Allana that all was not well in her distant daughter's life.

Are you okay? Haven't heard from you in
ages. . . .

But Nat had not responded to her mother's texts. What could she say?

I'm not so good. My sugar daddy broke up with me and I just found out he was married all along. I won't be able to afford rent in the fall, but instead of finding a job, I spend my days staring at online photos of his pansexual daughter, who has a crush on me. How's the weather?

But when she retrieved her phone from between the couch cushions, she found a text from Violet.

My parents are having a graduation pool
party for me. Want to come?

She couldn't. She couldn't walk into the home that Gabe shared with his wife and daughter and hang out by the pool like she was just another one of Violet's friends. She couldn't meet Violet's mother, Gabe's wife, and act like she hadn't been having a passionate affair with the woman's husband for months. She couldn't pretend to meet Gabe for the first time, watch him blanch with shock, then squirm with guilt and regret and fear. Or could she?

Her phone *pinged* again.

My friend Mark is coming from the city. He
can pick you up.

And then another text:

> You can stay for the weekend if you want. My parents' house has plenty of room.

Sipping her vodka, Nat pictured herself sleeping in the Turnmills' luxuriant Hamptons home while just down the hall, Gabe lay wide awake next to his wife. He'd be too angry, stressed, and terrified to sleep. Would he come to her? Slip into the guest bedroom and make love to her under his own roof? Or would he sneak down the hallway and press a pillow to her face as she slept? To her surprise, Nat realized she didn't care. Either way, she would be close to him.

Violet texted again.

> If you don't want to, I get it. It probably sounds really juvenile to you.
> But my mom is letting us have some drinks.
> And our pool is beautiful.
> I'd really like it if you came, but only if you want to.

Draining her glass and placing it heavily on the coffee table, Nat put the poor girl out of her misery.

> Hi Violet. I'd love to come to your party

The Encounter

Gabe's wife had insisted on having thirty of Violet's friends over to celebrate her graduation. Their daughter had refused to participate in a traditional prom, labeling it heteronormative, classist, and a Hollywood-constructed experience. Celeste had reasonably felt that the milestone should be marked by some sort of occasion, so she had suggested the pool party. Surprisingly, Violet had agreed.

They had hired a caterer, allowing Gabe and his wife to relax in the family room with a drink, popping out on occasion to ensure the kids were playing nicely. Well, Celeste popped out on occasion. Gabe stayed on the sectional sofa, sipping his Scotch and reading a biography of John Adams. He didn't know his daughter's friends, and he didn't want to. These schlubby kids with their colorful hair, prominent tattoos, and hideous piercings were a phase that she would soon outgrow.

His wife strolled into the family room then, carrying a glass of iced lemon water. Gabe looked up from his book.

"How's it going out there?"

She nestled into the sofa beside him. "I think Violet's having some issues with her girlfriend."

"Our daughter has a girlfriend?"

His wife gave him a faux disapproving glare. "She's been dating Fern for three whole weeks."

"Our daughter's girlfriend's name is *Fern*?"

Celeste suppressed a giggle. "Wait till you see her lip ring."

"Christ."

"She's a nice kid, but I don't think Violet's that into her. She seems to have a crush on a new girl. She's a little older, more conservative."

"Sounds like a step up from Fern."

"Come out and say hi."

He started to make an excuse—one more chapter, one more drink—and then he remembered. . . . He was Violet's father: her engaged, present, hands-on father. He got up off the couch. "Let's go party."

Celeste led the way to the pool, where a gaggle of unappealing misfits congregated around the bar. They were underage, but his wife had, surprisingly, allowed an alcoholic punch to be served. ("It's cranberry juice, ginger ale, and a tiny bit of vodka," Celeste whispered. "Don't tell them how weak it is.") Gabe pasted on a pleasant host-dad smile, but he was afraid it looked like a grimace.

"Violet," Celeste called, "introduce your friends to your dad."

"Everyone, this is my dad," Violet mumbled. "Dad, this is everyone."

There was a chorus of muttered greetings, but Gabe didn't hear them.

Because he'd spotted her. She was standing next to his daughter, sipping a glass of punch, looking gorgeous in a white T-shirt and cutoff jeans. He could see the outline of a red bikini under her top, and the fuck-off necklace he had bought her sparkled at her throat. He felt a surge of anger, fear, and lust. Natalie's eyes met his, reflecting his ambiguity.

I hate you. I want you. I'm going to ruin you.

Why was she here? What the fuck was happening? Gabe felt the weight of sixty odd eyes on him and realized he should respond. "Hi, kids." His voice sounded high-pitched and strained.

Natalie stepped forward then, her smile saccharine. "Thank you for having me in your home," she said sweetly. She turned to Celeste. "Violet said it would be all right if I spent the night."

No. No fucking way.

"Of course," Celeste said, "We've got plenty of room."

Fern, with the lip ring, suddenly marched off toward the house in a huff, and Gabe worked out what was going on. Natalie was the *new girl*, the older girl Violet had a crush on. Natalie was using his daughter to get to him. She had befriended Violet, maybe even kissed her, maybe even more. And now she was here, in his home, planning to spend the night. Rage and fear blurred his vision, but he still clocked Natalie giving his daughter's hand a sympathetic squeeze. His sugar baby was a psycho.

Melody, the crazy paralegal, had accepted a payoff. But Natalie wouldn't. She hadn't gone to these lengths for money. It was never about that for her. Natalie was here to hurt him. To fuck up his daughter. To ruin his marriage. His chest constricted menacingly. If he had a heart attack right then, he would welcome it.

Violet was scurrying toward the house, chasing after the jilted Fern. The horde of weirdos was buzzing about the love triangle in their midst. God, if they only knew it was a quadrangle. Celeste leaned in to his ear. "I'll go in and check on the girls."

"Don't," he said. He didn't want to be left alone with Natalie. "Let them work it out themselves."

But his wife was already jogging toward the house. He'd never been able to control her. A server in Bermuda shorts and a Hawaiian shirt was headed their way with a fresh tray of appetizers. The teens swarmed around the offering—faux chicken drumsticks—leaving him and Natalie standing alone.

"What are you doing here?" he kept his voice soft, his tone casual. The freaks were too busy stuffing their faces with the food he'd paid for to listen in. But just in case . . .

"Violet invited me," she said, matching his frequency. "We've become friends."

"That's quite a coincidence."

"Not really."

He heard the threat in her voice, but he knew how to disarm her.

"I've been worried about you," he whispered. "How have you been?"

"Not good," she said, and her eyes filled with tears. "I'm sorry to show up here. I know it's fucked-up. But . . . why did you lie to me? I just . . . I can't . . ."

She was going to fall apart right here, right now. Maybe he could attribute it to the Fern fiasco, if Natalie would play along. "It's okay," he murmured. "We'll find someplace to talk."

Fern was stalking back toward them now, trailed by Violet and Celeste. The light-haired girl's eyes were red from crying, but she looked calm, almost dazed. She passed by them and headed straight to the bar. Within moments, she had returned, a glass of punch in her hand.

"Fuck you, whore." She threw the red drink in Natalie's face.

"Jesus Christ!" Gabe cried.

"Oh my god!" his daughter shrieked.

The partygoers erupted in horrified delight. But Natalie said nothing. She stood stock-still, cranberry juice, ginger ale, and vodka dripping down her face. Her white T-shirt was stained red, looking uncomfortably like blood. Gabe felt an inappropriate surge of protectiveness toward her, a twisted desire to shove pasty Fern into the pool.

Predictably, Celeste took control of the situation. "Fern, go to my car. I'm taking you home." The girl sniveled but didn't dare talk back to his authoritative wife. Celeste took Violet by the shoulders then. "Don't let her ruin this for you. Stay with your friends, and I'll be back in half an hour." And then, Celeste turned to Gabe.

"Get Natalie cleaned up," she said into his ear. "She can borrow some of Violet's clothes. And then get her out of here."

His wife hurried after Fern, and for a moment, he watched her go. His daughter was being consoled by her alternative friends, but Natalie stood alone. She hadn't moved, was still dripping red punch, and crying. She was so pathetic, he almost felt sorry for her. But she was malicious and deranged, had come here to wreck his marriage, to fuck up his relationship with his daughter. She did not deserve his sympathy. But he couldn't leave her standing there like Carrie on prom night.

Grabbing her hand, he led the tearful girl toward the house.

The T-Shirt

It was the word thrown in Nat's face, not the drink, that rattled her. Fern could not have known that Nat had been paid for sex, could never have guessed that it was Violet's father who'd compensated her. But somehow, the younger girl had selected the precise word that would undo Natalie. *Whore.*

She'd stood in shock as Gabe swore, Violet shrieked, and the other kids squealed and gossiped. Violet's mother, Celeste, had taken control, insisted Fern had to leave, had driven her home. Nat had remained frozen with humiliation and shame, red liquid dripping from her face. And then Gabe had taken her hand, gently but firmly, and led her to the house.

Without a word, he'd escorted her up the stairs,

to the second floor, where the family slept. It felt private and intimate and inappropriate for her to be there. But it felt so good to be alone with him. She had always loved how he'd taken control, taken care of her. If it was over between them, why had he rescued her? Why hadn't he comforted Violet or driven Fern home? As she stood dripping juice and soda and vodka on the hardwood floor, Gabe dug through a linen closet.

"Dry yourself off," he said, handing her a slate-gray towel.

She complied, wiping the sticky liquid from her face and neck. Her makeup came off on the towel, and she knew she looked a smeared, smudged, tear-streaked mess. Gabe would find her repulsive. Crazy, obsessive, and hideous.

"You have to leave," he said, his blue eyes cold like they were the day he'd ended it.

"I need to talk to you."

"If my wife and daughter found out about us, it would destroy them."

Fresh tears sprang to Nat's eyes. Violet was a good kid. Her mother had been warm and welcoming. Nat hated herself for what she'd done to them. But it was not her fault. It was Gabe's fault. He had lied to her. He had cheated on his wife.

"Why didn't you tell me you were married?"

"I fucked up," he said softly. "I didn't think things would get so intense between us."

It was the first time he'd admitted that they'd had something powerful. She grabbed on to that. "We can work this out, Gabe. We just need to communicate."

"It has to be over between us. I'm sorry."

"I don't care that you're married!" Her voice was shrill, louder. "I still love you!"

He grabbed her roughly by the arm and led her into a bedroom. She took in the muddle of pale blue sheets and pillows, the mound of a matching duvet. On the wall: a poster for a school play, a rainbow flag, a signed photograph of Gloria Steinem. They were in Violet's room.

Gabe went to his daughter's dresser, yanked open a drawer, and grabbed a black T-shirt. "Get changed," he snapped, tossing the shirt to her. "I'll drive you to the bus station."

She hated him. He was dismissing her. He was looking out for himself.

She loved him. He was taking care of her. He was getting her out of this mess.

Their eyes locked then: love, lust, hatred, intermingling in a sick challenge. She pulled the stained T-shirt over her head and dropped it on the floor. She was in her bikini top, perfectly respectable, but the look in Gabe's eyes was not. He wanted her. A surge of triumph, of power coursed through her, and she smiled. Reaching behind her, she undid the clasp on her tiny top, let it fall to the floor.

He was on her then, his lips bruising hers, his hands rough on her breasts. He turned her around, pushed her up against the wall, and fumbled with the button of her shorts. Nat had never had rough sex, had never thought she would enjoy it, but she was aroused, almost rapturous. She reached back for him, groping for his belt. She wanted him so badly, didn't care that they were in his wife's house, in his daughter's bedroom. But suddenly, he jumped away from her like she was on fire.

She heard it then: feet climbing the staircase. Turning, she saw the terror in Gabe's eyes. She could destroy him right now, ruin his relationship with his daughter forever. Or . . . she could save him. Nat pulled the black T-shirt over her head, slipped her arms through the holes, just as Violet entered the room. The girl's pretty brown eyes landed on Nat first, and then her father, standing near the dresser, hands clasped in front of his crotch. What did the girl see? What did the scene look like?

"Is it okay if Natalie borrows that shirt?" Gabe said. He was so quick, so smooth.

"Sure," Violet said, assuming nothing inappropriate. She smiled at Nat. "It looks good on you."

"Thanks."

"I'll be downstairs." Gabe scooped up Nat's T-shirt and bikini top, shot her a quick, warning look, then he was gone.

Violet waited until she heard the rumble of her father's descending feet before she spoke. "I'm sorry about Fern. She's insecure and jealous. She has a bad temper."

"I noticed."

"She thinks there's something between us," Violet said, her eyes soft. "I was just wondering . . . Is there? Something between us?"

Nat looked at Gabe's daughter: young, vulnerable, hopeful. Nat should say no. She should tell this girl to work things out with Fern. Or to focus on her graduation, or her trip to Honduras. But Violet was her conduit into Gabe's world. He could not dismiss Nat if she had a hold on his daughter. Nat could not set Violet Turnmill free.

"I feel something," Nat said. "But we have to take it slow."

Violet moved closer. "I don't want to take it slow. I've never felt like this before."

"You're just a kid."

"I'm eighteen. I'm an adult."

"You have to deal with Fern. You're about to graduate. You're leaving soon . . ."

"I don't have to leave." Violet moved closer still. "I was only going to Honduras to piss off my dad."

Mission accomplished.

"I could move into the city for the summer," the younger girl suggested, tentatively touching the pendant on Nat's chest. "We could hang out. Get to know each other better."

"Maybe." Nat pulled the necklace away, dropped it into her T-shirt. "I have to go."

"Stay . . . Please."

"I can't. You should be with your friends."

"I'll tell them to leave. I want to be with you." And then, Violet leaned in and, gently, timidly, kissed Nat on the lips.

The girl tasted like weak cranberry punch and smelled like sunscreen. Her lips were full and soft, and Nat felt a stir of arousal. But she didn't respond, didn't kiss Violet back. Her lips were still sore from Gabe's hungry mouth on hers. Moments ago, he'd had her pressed up against the wall, about to roughly take her from behind. And now, his daughter was kissing her, so softly, so tenderly. It was weird and sick and depraved. How had Nat's life gotten so fucked-up?

Violet pulled back, and Nat seized the opportunity. "I'll text you," she said, moving toward the door.

"Promise me I'll see you again."

Nat paused. "Of course. I've got your shirt."

She raced down the stairs to find Gabe.

The Luxury Liner

Gabe drove Natalie to Bridgehampton, where she could catch the Luxury Liner back to Manhattan. He had to speed to make the last departure at four forty-five. The Jitney had later shuttles, but that would necessitate a drive to Montauk. He didn't want to be stuck in a car with Natalie for more than ten minutes. He didn't trust himself around her. If he spent too much time alone with the crazy bitch, he would either fuck her or kill her.

Celeste had still not returned from delivering the distraught Fern when he'd stuffed Nat's sodden shirt and bikini top into a plastic bag, bundled Natalie into his Mercedes, and hit the road. Violet had stood in the driveway, watching Natalie leave like a lovesick puppy. He'd rolled down his window and yelled, "Get back to your party! Get back to your guests!" The girl glared at him but strolled back toward the pool.

His eyes were firmly on the road when he said, "Promise me you'll stop seeing Violet."

"Promise me you'll stop ignoring my calls and texts."

He could have pointed out that there was no reason for him to respond to her. It was over. Finished. Kaput. But now he knew what Nat was capable of. He had to manage her carefully.

"I promise," he said, glancing over at her. She looked terrible—sticky, sloppy, disheveled—but he was still attracted to her. "We can talk next week, when I'm back in the city."

"Okay," she acquiesced. "I'll blow Violet off."

"Do you need more money?" he asked hopefully. "If I wasn't generous enough when we met for lunch, I can give you more."

"This isn't about the money," she said, and he could hear the pain in her voice. "This is about us."

It had been worth a try.

The Bridgehampton Community House with its two-story portico was visible now. The luxury bus was already there, loading a handful of unfortunate passengers who had to head back to the city on a Saturday afternoon. He'd purchased Natalie a ticket on his phone while she'd said goodbye to Violet. They were just going to make it. Stomping on the gas pedal, Gabe squealed onto the street, pulled the Mercedes up a few yards away from the massive idling cruiser.

"I'll be back in the city on Monday," he said, turning to his sniveling passenger. "We can talk properly then."

"You promise?"

"I promise," he said, hiding his exasperation as well as he could. "You have to get on the bus now."

She took a deep breath, her nostrils flaring slightly, her chest rising. But she didn't move. Was she going to defy him? Refuse to get out of the car? He would drag her by the hair onto that bus, if he had to. He'd do anything to get her out of here, away from Violet, away from Celeste. Exasperation and panic fluttered in his chest and throat. He was about to plead with her when she lunged.

Her mouth came down hard on his, her tongue forcing its way between his lips. She had vaulted the console, was almost straddling him. Her breasts, under his daughter's T-shirt, pressed into his chest. He didn't want to respond, didn't want her to know how hot she made him, but when her hand reached down to his crotch, his dick betrayed him. She stopped then, gave him a bleary, self-satisfied smile.

"I'll see you in the city," she said. She got out of the car, grabbed her overnight bag from the back seat, and strolled to the bus.

He tore out of there like a bat out of hell, but within a couple of minutes, he realized he had to pull over. Gabe's heart was beating erratically, and for the second time that day, he worried he was about to have a heart attack. On the side of the road, he attempted to breathe slowly, deeply, but it felt like there was a giant rock pressing down on his chest. This feeling was strange, unfamiliar. He was sweating and vibrating, a lump of emotion lodged in his throat. He hadn't cried in decades, hadn't cried at his own parents' funerals, but he was going to now.

Gabe led a complicated life. He had a high-pressure career, shady business dealings, two homes, a wife with health issues, a difficult daughter, and a string of mistresses. Until now, he'd kept all the balls in the air with finesse and aplomb. But everything was spinning out of control. Celeste could find out about his affair, find out who it was with, and she would hate him. His first and only real love would hate him. Violet would hate him more, hate him longer. She would lose all remnants of adoration, admiration, and respect when she found out her dad had cheated on her mom with Violet's own girlfriend. She would never speak to him again. Their community would find out and turn on him. He would be alone, a pervert, a monster, a laughingstock.

When that obsessed paralegal had shown up on his Sagaponack doorstep, he'd considered hiring someone to get rid of her, permanently. There were professionals who could make it look like a break-in, or a random mugging gone wrong, make sure it would never be traced back to him. He knew people, men who made problems go away. Like that kid, Cole Doberinsky. The boy had been beaten and traumatized, and he had disappeared. But it would take more than that to get rid of Natalie. If Gabe asked, and if he paid, he could have his sugar baby erased. All it would take was a phone call.

He had to do it. He had no choice. Digging in his glove box, he found a napkin and wiped the tears from his face, blew his nose into the crisp paper. With trembling hands, he placed the call.

40

· · · · · ·

Double Vodka Cranberry

It was 8:30 P.M. when Nat finally arrived in Midtown. A passenger had been sick on the bus, necessitating an unscheduled stop and an ad hoc cleaning crew, turning the two-and-a-half-hour journey into almost four. She was walking toward the subway that would take her back downtown to Chelsea, when she decided to go for a drink. The events of the day had taken a toll, and she needed to relax. And going back to her empty apartment was not appealing. She knew she looked a mess, but there were plenty of venues that would be indifferent to her bedraggled appearance. She located one quickly and found a seat at the bar.

The bartender inspected her ID, then asked, "What can I get you?"

"Double vodka and cranberry," she said, a nod to

the day's events. There had been about a teaspoon of vodka in that punch. Violet's mom had tricked those silly kids into thinking they were having a boozy party. Nat had had five glasses at least and felt completely sober. Of course, she was a more seasoned drinker than a bunch of high school kids. Maybe Violet and her friends had gotten a buzz? Perhaps that's why Violet had been brave enough to kiss her?

She reflected on the intimate moment in Violet's bedroom. The girl's lips had been so soft, gentle, tentative. Before today, Nat had not been attracted to girls, and she still wasn't. But she was attracted to *Violet*. The girl was vulnerable, beautiful, and sexy. And she was Gabe's daughter.

The drink arrived, and she downed half of it in one long swallow. As the vodka soothed her tension, relaxed her muscles, and muddled her thoughts, she considered a relationship with Violet Turnmill. Maybe she and the pretty girl could have something real? Nat would be close to Gabe in a different way. She would have a role in his life as Violet's partner. They'd spend weekends at the Hamptons house, eating breakfast together, swimming in the pool. At night, they'd have dinner, drink wine, talk and laugh. Maybe that would be enough?

But it wouldn't be. Because at the end of that perfect day, Gabe would go to bed with Celeste, and it would tear Nat apart.

Violet was not the answer. Nat had to fix her relationship with Gabe. They had made a deal: she would stay away from Violet and he would open the lines of communication between them. Finishing her drink and ordering another, she decided to put their agreement to the test. It had been only a few hours since she left him, but she sent him a text.

Made it back to the city

She waited for his response. He'd be with his family now. Celeste would be home, they'd be discussing the disastrous party over a bottle of wine. Gabe preferred Scotch, though. Did his wife drink spirits with him like Nat had? Nat had never really liked Scotch, but she'd liked sharing it with him. Violet would be locked in her room, thinking about Natalie, maybe even touching herself as she did. The thought gave Nat a perverse thrill.

If Gabe planned on honoring their deal, he'd have his phone on hand. It would be safe in his pocket, away from Celeste's prying eyes. He'd have it set on vibrate so he'd know when she summoned him but wouldn't alert his wife. He'd have to excuse himself—go to the bathroom, or for a walk or a drive. And then he'd write back.

I'm glad you're home safe.

It was good to see you.

See you Monday!

She smirked as she took a sip of her second drink. He wouldn't mean it, of course, but he would say something along those lines. Gabe had to appease her, had to play along, or she would take his daughter away from him. She'd arrange to meet the girl in the city, where they'd talk, flirt, maybe even more. Gabe would never risk it. Nat had the power now.

But when the second drink was gone, and Gabe still hadn't replied, she felt a combination of panic and anger. He was breaking their deal, going back on his promise. Why was she surprised? He was a liar and an adulterer and a heartless piece of shit. Her inhibitions lowered by the alcohol, she texted him again.

> We had an agreement
> Answer me, or I'll text Violet

She gave him a chance to respond as she paid the bill and left a generous tip. She didn't even look at her phone until she was outside on the sidewalk. When she did, there was a text. But it wasn't from Gabe. It was from Violet.

> I need to see you

The girl missed her, cared about her. It was a crush, of course, an infatuation, but it was better than the utter disregard, even disdain, with which Gabe treated her. Nat could respond to Violet if she wanted to. And she did. She wanted to keep the girl on the line in case she needed her.

Nat was about to reply when the phone vibrated again. It was Gabe, his timing impeccable.

> See you Monday.

It was not what she'd hoped for, but it was something. It was enough. She blocked Violet's calls and messages, removing the temptation to engage. She was not ready to betray Gabe. Not yet, anyway. Shoving the phone into the pocket of her shorts, she stumbled toward the subway.

The Footprint

As Nat emerged from the underground station and shambled toward her apartment, exhaustion threatened to overtake her. She had traveled to Sagaponack and back in a day. She'd met Gabe's wife, kissed his daughter, and nearly had sex with him . . . twice. She'd had a drink and the word *whore* thrown in her face. And she'd had several cocktails—even if most of them were ridiculously weak. Her eyes were heavy as she let herself into her building, squinting in the bright lights of the lobby.

She rode the tiny elevator up to her second-floor apartment and unlocked the door. Flicking on the lamp, she went straight to the freezer. One more slug of vodka would ensure a deep, dreamless sleep. The bottle was alarmingly low, and she'd forgotten to fill the ice cube tray. But she poured a couple of inches of liquor into a glass and added a splash of orange juice. She had just swallowed the first mouthful, when she noticed something wasn't right.

Nat's apartment was a mess, but it was *her* mess. She knew the stack of unopened mail (mostly bills), the paper coffee cups, the empty take-out containers, and the packaging from a new mascara that littered her coffee table. The dresser with its drawers perpetually ajar, the sofa with its jumble of pillows and jackets and blankets, those were all familiar to her. In fact, it was a new sense of order that shook her. Someone had tidied the throw pillows. Someone had closed the dresser drawers and her laptop. It hadn't been her.

She took another drink and moved into the tiny living area. Nothing else seemed amiss. Gabe's patterned tie was still on her bed, next to her pillow. The window was open a crack, just as she'd left it. There was a flimsy locking mechanism meant to block further access. It wasn't the most secure system, but the apartment was on the second floor. A thief would have to be pretty determined to scale the fire escape and break into her studio. And for what? Her laptop was still sitting on her desk, the diamond pendant was still around her neck.

Her double bed was pressed up against the window, and she looked down at the covers pulled back to reveal the fitted sheet. And there it was, in the center of the pink cotton. Faint, but there. A footprint.

It was from a sneaker, not a huge foot but much larger than Nat's. A man had come through her window, had stepped on her bed, and riffled through her belongings. What was he searching for? Nat spun around, cataloging her possessions. Everything seemed to be present and accounted for. And then she remembered the gun.

The weapon was stored in the back of her wardrobe, wrapped in a T-shirt, and concealed in an old purse. Oleg had never asked for it back, and Nat had never offered. Setting down her vodka and orange juice, Nat dived into the closet, rummaging for the bag and its dangerous contents. She found the large, fake-leather purse and stuck her hand inside. It was empty.

Maybe she'd moved the nine-millimeter? She wasn't sure she could trust her memory after all the emotional turmoil she'd experienced. Nat scoured the closet and came up empty. Moving to her dresser, she tore through its contents and found no weapon. Panic rising, she looked under her bed, under the sofa, behind the flat-screen TV, through the kitchen cupboards. And then she remembered the hall closet. On the top shelf she had three shoeboxes filled with knickknacks and trinkets. She pulled one down and opened it. The pistol was there, still wrapped in a plain white T-shirt.

She stared at the weapon with fresh eyes. Oleg had given it to her months ago, when she was weak and frightened and helpless. She was different now. Gabe's betrayal had changed her, hardened her. Nat had experienced rage and hatred and it had blackened her core. Once, she'd been unsure if she could even point a gun at Cole. Now, she knew she could fire it. If she needed to, she could insert the magazine, rack the slide, and pull the trigger.

Putting the gun back on the shelf, she polished off the vodka and orange juice, contemplating the possibilities. Someone had been in her apartment; she knew it. A random break-in was implausible. A thief would have taken the electronics and the gun. But the footprint was there on the bed, the pillows were tidied, the drawers closed. Who would gain entry to her home only to tidy up? What did they want? Just to rummage through her belongings? Just to be in her space? And then a culprit occurred to her. . . .

Cole.

Grabbing her phone, she called her mom. It was still early on the West Coast, and Allana answered after the first ring.

"Natalie. Finally. I've been trying you for weeks."

Nat ignored the irritation in her mom's voice. "Is Cole in Blaine?"

"I think so. Why?"

"I think he's here. In New York. I think he's been in my apartment."

"What makes you say that?" She heard her mom's skepticism.

"Because someone broke in and went through my stuff."

"Is anything missing?"

Nat couldn't tell her mom the truth. Allana would think her daughter was delusional. And maybe Nat was? So she lied. "My laptop's gone."

"Why would Cole want your laptop?" her mom asked. And then, "Have you been drinking?"

"I was at a party. I had a few drinks," Nat snapped.

"I can send you some money to help replace it," her mom offered, sounding scolded. "I just sold a little house in Birch Bay. My commission will clear next week."

"Don't worry about it. Just call Trish and find out where Cole is." Nat hung up.

Moving to the freezer, she dumped the remains of the vodka bottle into her glass, splashed in some more orange juice. Passing out was her only hope of sleeping tonight. How could she rest knowing someone had been in her apartment? That he could come back at any time?

And then an idea struck her. The break-in could be used to her advantage. She would contact Gabe, tell him how frightened she was, how vulnerable. Gabe would probably be in bed, snuggled up with his age-appropriate wife. But she had to reach out to him. She texted:

Someone broke in. I'm scared.

She waited, drinking her cocktail, anticipating the three shivering dots that prefaced his response. Nothing. She could call and wake him up. But his phone would be silenced for the night. She could text Violet, tell her to go get her father, to have him call Nat immediately. It would alert the girl and her mother to Nat and Gabe's connection. It would require a creative explanation. But Gabe was sharp and articulate; he was a lawyer. He'd be able to concoct an excuse. This was an emergency. She was reaching for her phone when it dinged.

Is anything missing?

Just knowing he was there sent relief coursing through her. Relief and adoration and love. Nat's thumbs stumbled over the letters as she typed another lie. She was getting used to this.

He took the necklace you gave me

He didn't respond right away, and she wondered if he remembered the pendant sparkling at her throat when she'd removed her wet T-shirt before him. But men didn't notice things like that, and his gaze had been locked on her breasts. And she could have come home, removed the pendant, and then gone out again. She sent another text.

I think it was Cole
Should I call the police?

His response came promptly.

No. Lock the windows and the door. I'll come tomorrow. Try to get some sleep.

The words were like a warm blanket, comforting, reassuring. Swallowing the remnants of her drink, she fell on the bed, on top of the intruder's footprint. She hated lying to Gabe, but it had worked. Tomorrow, he would come and make everything right.

She slept.

42
. . . . . .

The Zoo

It was almost 11:00 A.M. by the time Gabe was on the highway back into the city. He'd wanted to leave earlier, but Celeste needed him to move the folding tables from the pool area back into the garage. And then she'd insisted on packing several plastic containers of leftover party food into a cooler bag for him to eat during the week. He'd stood by impatiently, anxious to leave. He'd told his wife he had a desperate client, an urgent Sunday meeting. It wasn't entirely a lie. This meeting would save his marriage, his daughter, his life. It would take care of Natalie Murphy, for good.

She had already texted him this morning.

When are you coming?

He'd apologized for his tardiness, blamed traffic, though he hadn't even left, suggested they could have dinner and talk.

Dinner? I was hoping for lunch.

He would see what he could do, he'd promised, depositing his weekend bag and a cooler full of hummus and marinated tofu into the trunk of the Mercedes. As he was climbing into the front seat, his phone buzzed with her response.

What if Violet texts me? What should I say?

His daughter had left last night, gone to stay with a friend—Sarah? Or Sonja? Gabe couldn't recall. When he'd returned from dropping Natalie at the bus, all the guests were gone. And so was his daughter.

"Violet's upset," his wife explained, her voice weary, her face haggard. "This was supposed to be a celebration, and it turned into a fiasco."

Was there something pointed in his spouse's tone? A hint of accusation, perhaps? No, he was being paranoid. There was no way Celeste could know that Violet's girl-crush had been Gabe's lover. Because, if Celeste had known, there would be no subtle jab, no annoyed insinuation. His wife would have exploded. She would have confronted him, raged at him, and then divorced him. She could never find out.

"She's gone to Sonja's," Celeste continued. "I

wanted her to stay home, to talk about how she's feeling, but she said she wanted to be with her friends."

"It's normal," Gabe assured her, "they get off on drama at this age."

He, too, would have preferred his daughter remain under the same roof, so he could keep an eye on her. And on her phone. He had no way of knowing if Violet had reached out to Natalie. But Natalie's recent text asking his advice on how to respond to a potential message from Violet indicated that his lover had not heard from the younger girl. Not yet, anyway. So he responded to her:

> Tell Violet you're sick, tell her you need space,
> tell her you're not interested.
> I'm coming.

And then he hopped in his car and sped off.

Near Bridgehampton, he pulled over to get gas. As he filled the tank, he scanned his phone, saw a slew of texts from Natalie.

> Where are you?
> You must be driving. Drive safe
> Can't wait to see you xoxoxo

God, the girl was so needy, so clingy, so obsessed. Hopping back in the Mercedes, he muted his phone and dropped it into the console. Soon, he merged onto the Long Island Expressway and hurtled toward the Bronx Zoo. He was meeting the man, the handler of problems, there at two thirty.

The location had been Gabe's idea. It was easily accessible off his route to the Upper East Side and, on the slim chance that he was spotted, he could blame his presence on nostalgia. He and Celeste had taken Violet to the zoo when she was little, when they'd all lived together in the city. Now, his girl was graduating, launching into her adult life. It was completely normal for a father to revisit the childhood haunt.

Gabe had a mind for such details. His personal and professional life had long been a study in discretion. In his line of work, it was de rigueur to cover one's tracks, to erase the paper trail. The firm had an IT department that would wipe the phones of lawyers upon request. Every few months, Gabe would have his e-mails, his texts, and his phone calls permanently deleted. He wasn't exactly a Luddite, but he preferred to leave such matters to the professionals. He'd hand the device over as soon as Natalie was dealt with.

Shortly after their breakup in the Italian restaurant, Gabe had deleted his sugar-dating profile. He had chosen the site because of its privacy guarantees. When a member deactivated his account, his record was immediately and irrevocably expunged. No one would ever see Gabe's impressive profile or read the flirtatious messages he'd exchanged with several women. And there would be no trace of his connection to Natalie Murphy. So no one would suspect him.

The night before, as he lay next to his sleeping wife, he'd come up with a plan. A break-in gone wrong would cover all the bases. It would get rid of

Natalie, along with her laptop, phone, the necklace (he was pretty sure she was lying about the break-in), and any other traces of Gabe's presence in her life. He had not been present when she signed the lease on the apartment, so the landlord could not ID him. And the real estate agent, Calvin, would never betray him. Gabe had always given Natalie envelopes of cash to cover rent and expenses. He had not made love to her in her bed for over two weeks. Hopefully, the girl had washed her sheets since then.

His mind flitted to the last time he'd been with her in that double bed pressed against the window in the cramped studio. She'd made them screwdrivers and they'd frolicked between the sheets like tipsy teenagers. Natalie had been fun and refreshing, had made him feel young, sexy, and invincible. He hated that it had to end this way, but she wouldn't suffer. Quick and painless. He'd been adamant about that. A stab of regret constricted his heart muscle.

But this was her fault, he reminded himself. Natalie had broken their arrangement, had come after his daughter, his family. She was crazy and drunk and could not be reasoned with. An overhead sign announced the exit that would take him to the Bronx Zoo. If he took it, he would be sealing Natalie's fate. And his. If he drove on, he'd be allowing Natalie to destroy his family, his reputation, his life.

He took the exit.

43

·····

The High Line

Nat waited all day for Gabe to contact her. She tidied the apartment a bit, gathering the empty take-out containers and placing the empty vodka and wine bottles near the door to be taken out to the recycling bins. But she was too distracted, too lacking in motivation to do a thorough clean. The footprint was still on her bed, though she'd slept on top of it. It was faint, but it was there. The only evidence she had that Cole Doberinsky had invaded her space.

Her mom had e-mailed her confirming that Cole was MIA once again. "That doesn't mean he's in New York," Allana said, "but be extra careful, just in case."

Cole *was* in New York; Nat could feel his presence. She may have lied to Gabe about the necklace going missing, but she had not lied about her fear and unease. Cole was still obsessed, still angry. Once Gabe knew that Cole had resurfaced and was practically stalking Nat, he would protect her. He would keep her safe.

To kill time, she went to the liquor store and replaced her empty bottle of vodka and bought some Scotch for Gabe. She'd invite him over for a drink before dinner, or a nightcap after. Either one would lead to sex; she knew that. The fact that he still wanted her was made abundantly clear in Violet's bedroom, and later, in his car at the bus stop. The attraction between them could not be denied, no matter how difficult their circumstances.

When she still hadn't heard from him at three, she sent him a text.

Where r u?

He didn't respond.

She tamped down the panic building in her chest and made herself a drink. Just one, but a strong one to settle her nerves, and climbed into the shower. She had a head full of lather when she heard her phone ping, alerting her to a new message. Reaching out to grab the device next to the sink, she read Gabe's missive.

Sorry. Got held up. How about a walk on the High Line?

The suggestion was sweet and romantic, something a real couple would do. A real couple who needed to talk things through. She dried her hands on the towel hanging on the back of the door and responded.

Come over for a drink first?

He replied instantly.

We can walk up to Hell's Kitchen, grab one there.

He didn't want to be alone with her. He couldn't resist her. It was both flattering and concerning. If they were rekindling things, why did he *want* to resist her? But they needed to talk, to discuss a way to move forward in their relationship. If they fell into bed together, it would distract them from that necessary task. She texted back.

Meet at the stairs on 20th in an hour

It was almost seven, still humid and warm, as Nat walked down her street toward the High Line. The elevated pathway with its perennials, grasses, and shrubs was popular with both tourists and locals for scenic strolls. Nat, in a floral spring dress, the diamond pendant glinting at her throat, felt optimistic about this reunion with Gabe. The scene in Sagaponack had been truly fucked-up, but it was behind them. She had done what was necessary to get Gabe to talk to her, to see her, to remedy things. As she neared their rendezvous point she stopped, remembering that her necklace had supposedly been stolen. Releasing the clasp, she removed the jewelry and dropped it into her skirt pocket.

Gabe was waiting at the bottom of the steep stairwell, as agreed. He was wearing a ball cap and aviator sunglasses. The accessories made him look young and cool. She couldn't see his eyes, couldn't tell if he was watching her approach, but as she got closer, his lips softened into a smile.

"You look pretty," he said, and she heard the warmth in his voice.

"You look good, too. I like the shades."

"I didn't sleep well last night," he said, by way of explanation.

"Neither did I."

They stared at each other for a moment, neither one expressing the thoughts that had kept them awake. Nat had, technically, passed out drunk. But if she hadn't, she'd have been thinking about Gabe and how they could fix things. She'd have thought about Cole and the break-in and what he planned to do to her. She'd have thought about Violet and how the girl felt about her.

"Shall we go up?" Gabe gestured toward the stairs. Nat climbed up first, feeling her lover on her heels. His presence behind her was both familiar and new, comfortable and awkward. So much had happened in the two weeks since Gabe had ended it but being with him still felt right.

When they reached the reclaimed rail line, they strolled uptown in silence. The path was busy on such a pleasant evening, but the other guests were ensconced in their own conversations, or enraptured by the view of the Hudson, the art installations, the late-spring greenery. Nat didn't know how to start the conversation they needed to have. With their sudden breakup? With Violet? With Nat's arrival at Gabe's Hamptons home? But her partner spoke first.

"So someone broke into your apartment."

"Yes," she said, grateful for his interest. He still cared about her, still wanted to protect her. "It has to be Cole. The footprint looks about his size. He's not in Blaine. And the necklace is gone."

"Nothing else was taken?"

"I don't think so."

"Are you sure you didn't misplace it? Have you looked everywhere?"

"Yes," she said, guilt making her voice shake. "I looked everywhere."

"And the footprint," he said calmly. "Have you had any guests who might have put it there?"

"I haven't had any guests," she cried, "not since you." It sounded shrill and desperate, but she was offended by the suggestion. "Only my friends Keltie and Ivan from art school, but that was weeks ago."

"Could Ivan have stepped on the bed?" Gabe's voice was calm, regulated. He was in lawyer mode.

"No." But her friends' last visit drifted into her mind. She remembered them drinking, playing music, dancing around the studio. It felt like years ago that she had been so light, so carefree. Could Ivan have jumped on the bed during their dance session? When had she last washed her sheets? Household chores had fallen by the wayside since she'd been outed at school, since Gabe had dumped her. The glass of vodka she'd had was muddling her thoughts. Self-doubt was creeping through the fog. But she said, "He didn't."

Gabe left it there, didn't push the subject any further. They walked without talking until Nat took the opportunity to shift the conversation. "I need to explain. About Violet."

"You don't need to explain," he said, still lawyerly. "Just promise me you won't see her again."

"I promise," Nat said. "If that's what it takes for us to get back together."

"It does."

They were the words she'd been pining for, the assurance she'd craved. But the delivery was monotone, perfunctory. It set her nerves on edge.

"So we're getting back together?" she clarified, glancing over at him as they moved steadily forward.

"Yes," he said, eyes concealed behind the reflective glasses. "But I have to go away for a while."

"Where are you going?"

"To France. For business."

"I could come?" she bravely suggested. "I'm not working right now. I've never been to France. Or anywhere in Europe."

"I'd love that," he said, and he almost sounded genuine. *Almost.* "But I'll be working all the time. And Celeste's sister and brother-in-law live there. They'll want to spend time with me, so you'd be left on your own."

"But I'll be left on my own here," she said, her voice tinged with annoyance. "I want to be with you."

"And you will be," he said. "When I get back."

They'd reached the end of the High Line by

then, and Nat was relieved. The vodka was wearing off, leaving her feeling antsy and wound-up. Gabe had promised a drink after their walk. She was sure more alcohol would ease the tension, smooth things over. They walked down the sloping ramp in heavy silence, continued along Thirty-Fourth Street.

"Shall we get a drink somewhere?" she suggested, glancing over at him. She wanted to sit facing him, wanted him to remove his glasses. He wouldn't be so glib with her then, when there was eye contact.

"I wish I could," he said, moving past the Hudson Yards subway station, "but I've got an early flight tomorrow. I have to pack."

"A quick one then? Or I could come to your place and help you get ready."

"I don't think so."

He was blowing her off, trying to get rid of her. She stopped walking.

"What's going on, Gabe?"

"Nothing." He gave her arm a conciliatory squeeze, but it felt cool, impersonal. "When I get back from my trip, we'll be together."

"But you can't give me an hour of your time now?"

She saw the tension in his jaw, and she knew his eyes, behind his glasses, would be like ice. "This is an important business trip and I need to focus," he said, condescension dripping from his voice. "You know my business and my family come first. That hasn't changed."

Suddenly, it became clear. He wasn't reconciling with her; he was buying time. There was no business trip to France. Gabe just wanted a couple of weeks to strategize a way to tell Celeste and Violet about the affair. Or, more likely, he'd make up a story, label Nat a crazy, obsessive stalker, portray himself as completely innocent. He might cop to a one-night stand gone wrong, might even admit to the financial arrangement, lamenting his lonely life in the city. But he would convince his wife and daughter that he was the victim, that Natalie was dangerous, the enemy. And maybe she was?

"Fine"—she forced a smile that made her face want to crack—"we'll be together when you get back."

"I'm glad you understand." Relief softened his tone. "I'm going to walk up to Tenth and grab a cab."

"Okay."

"I'll try to text, but I've got a packed schedule."

"I'd love to hear from you, if you have time."

"Goodbye, Natalie."

"Bye."

He leaned in and gave her a chaste kiss on the lips. For the first time, she felt no pull, no desire, nothing but animosity, nothing but the sting of betrayal. He turned and left her then, walking toward bustling Tenth Avenue. She watched him stride away, her heart pounding in her chest, her throat, her ears. And then she called after him.

"You don't mind if I hang out with Violet for the next couple of weeks, do you?"

The words halted him. He whirled around. "What?"

She closed the distance between them. "Once we're together, I'll stop. But . . . I'll be all alone here. I don't really have any friends, and I really like your daughter." Her words were pointed. "I like her *a lot*."

His handsome face darkened with rage. "You fucking cunt," he growled. "Stay away from Violet or I'll . . ."

"Or you'll what?"

"I'll kill you," he said quietly. "Don't think I won't."

"You're going to kill me?" she repeated, her voice loud and shrill. "You're threatening my life right now?" Passersby were glancing over, alerted to the dramatic scene. What did they see? A distinguished older man vibrating with anger. A girl in a floral dress shrieking at him like an angry shrew. Did Nat look unstable? Insane? She felt it. Her self-control was slipping away, her last shred of decorum dissipating. But she was too full of rage and hate to stop.

"Fuck you, Gabe!" she spat, the momentum of her outburst building. "I'm not going away. Violet wants me, and she hates you. I'll take your family away from you! I'll bring you to your fucking knees!"

Gabe's face was pale and bloodless. The loathing in his eyes was obscured by his glasses, but she could feel it coming off him, tangible waves of hate. For a moment, she thought he would grab her by the throat and choke her to death right there in broad daylight. But he didn't. He just turned to go.

She caught his wrist, her nails digging into his flesh. It felt good to hurt him. "Don't you fucking walk away from me," she growled.

But Gabe didn't flinch, though she could feel his skin breaking under her talons. He wrenched his arm from her grasp and quickly but calmly walked away.

"I hate you!" she screamed after him, her composure abandoning her completely. Tears and snot streamed down her face, spit flew from her lips. She was a monster, a horrid, frothing, monster. But still . . . she couldn't stop. "I'll destroy you, you selfish prick! I'll fucking kill you!"

He kept walking, never turning back, like he was impervious to her words. But she knew how to hurt him. Her hands were shaking so hard she feared she'd drop her phone on the sidewalk. But somehow, she managed to send the text to Violet.

I miss you. Want to hang out soon?

Violet would, of course. The girl was infatuated with Nat, wanted to date her, wanted to build something with her. And now, Nat wanted that, too. She would unblock the younger girl from her phone. When she responded, Nat would arrange to see her, to kiss her, to make love to her. In the end, it would be a disaster. Violet would be crushed; Celeste would be pained. But Gabe would be totally and utterly destroyed. And bringing him down was all that mattered now.

44
· · · · · ·

Smooth Jazz

Jesus Christ. The bitch was even crazier than Gabe had thought. At his rendezvous at the zoo, he'd told the man to handle the situation in the next week or so. But her outburst, her threats, her obvious mental illness changed everything. Natalie had to be disposed of now, before she had a chance to talk to Violet, before she could contact Celeste. When he'd put several blocks between himself and the outraged girl, he dug his cell from his pocket.

"Take care of it," he growled into the phone. "To-night. I'll give you an extra five grand."

He hadn't wanted to pay more, but the matter needed to be expedited. And the guy, the *handler*, was a professional; money was his language. The man was going to break into Natalie's apartment and be waiting when the girl came home. She was small and weak. She'd probably be drunk (she was always drunk lately). The man would take her out easily, take her phone, her laptop, and any other evidence of Gabe's existence. Another break-in gone wrong. And that would be the end. Gabe would likely never even hear about it.

He couldn't go home to his apartment or downtown to his office. He couldn't go anywhere where Natalie might find him. When he'd spotted her standing by his pool with his daughter, he had felt panic and fear. But this was different—more visceral, even mortal. She had threatened to kill him, and he believed she would. The girl was a deranged alcoholic consumed by rage. If she got her hands on a weapon, she would murder him in a second.

After a few more blocks, his heart rate began to slow, and his head began to clear. He'd been overwrought, panicking. Natalie wasn't going to try to *murder* him. She didn't have a gun or a knife. And she was just a kid. An angry, obsessive kid, but that was because she loved him, because she wanted him back. Killing him would negate the possibility of a reunion. Sticking out his arm, he hailed a cab and instructed the driver to take him to his apartment uptown. As he sat in the back, he checked his phone. There was a text from his wife.

> Have you heard from Violet? She's not answering my texts.

Of course, he hadn't. Despite his recent efforts, his daughter was still cool and distant with him. She wouldn't reach out in her time of romantic turmoil. He wrote back to his wife.

No.

Celeste's response was instant.

Should I call Sonja's mother? Make sure Violet's okay?

Celeste was overreacting, as usual. She was too protective of their daughter, overly doting, even cloying. No wonder Violet was such a mess, always upset or pissed off about something. But he had to soothe his wife.

She's with her friends. She probably has her phone off. She'll be fine.

He sensed the relief in Celeste's reply.

You're probably right. If you hear from her, let me know.

The cab pulled up on Park and Gabe paid the driver. The door was opened by his obsequious doorman. "Good evening, Mr. Turnmill."

"No guests," Gabe instructed curtly, hurrying through the lobby to the waiting elevator.

In his apartment, he poured two fingers of Scotch and swallowed it without ice. The alcohol burned in his chest, made his eyes water, but soon, he felt its relaxing effect. He fixed another drink, with ice this time, and sat on the sofa. Flicking on the TV, he roamed through the channels, but he was still antsy, still on edge. He kept hearing noises, muting the volume, moving to the door to listen intently. Logically, he knew he was safe. Natalie wouldn't get past the doorman. But the gatekeeper could be tricked, manipulated, paid off.

His phone was buzzing. It would be Natalie attacking/disparaging/threatening him. It could be his wife, assuring him that Violet had checked in, that she was fine. But no, he knew it was his former girlfriend, spewing her venom and bile. The sound set his teeth on edge. He ignored it, drank more Scotch.

Fuck it. He was too wound up to stay here. There was a jazz bar on East Eighty-Ninth. Music always relaxed him when he was embroiled in a tough case and would do the same for him now. He could walk there, find a dark corner table, let the music and the booze work their magic. And then, when he was calmer, he'd walk home and sleep.

When he woke in the morning, Natalie would be dead.

Green Eyes

Nat should have gone home, should have washed the streaks of makeup from her face or taken a cold shower. She should have scrubbed Gabe's blood from under her fingernails, eaten something, or called her mother. But she did none of those things. The anger vibrating through her being was arousing, almost sexual. It felt good to hate Gabe, to plot his destruction. It made her feel connected to him, in some fucked-up way. She wasn't ready to let it go.

A block from where her lover had abandoned her crying and shrieking on the street was Ninth Avenue. Nat walked to it, headed toward Hell's Kitchen and its array of bars and restaurants. She'd wiped away the smudges of mascara, blush, and bronzer with a tissue, leaving her face devoid of makeup.

She no longer looked like the perfect, phony doll Gabe had fallen for; she looked like herself.

The venue she selected was an odd mix of old-timey saloon, hip eatery, and sports bar with mounted TVs airing MMA fights and baseball. But it would serve the purpose. She found a lone stool at the crowded bar and ordered a rusty nail and a shot of vodka. The tattooed bartender didn't bat an eye at her strong order and didn't ask for ID. Nat liked this place already.

"Cheers," she said, when he slid the small glass of vodka toward her. She downed it easily and waited for Gabe's favorite cocktail. Setting her phone on the bar, Nat checked her text messages. Nothing from Violet. It was confounding. Had the girl reconciled with Fern? Or had Gabe come clean to his wife and daughter already? No, not yet. He would fall on his sword in person. Or more likely, spin his web of lies. If Nat could get to Violet before Gabe got back to the Hamptons, she would still have a chance to wound him. She texted Violet again.

Would love to see you

The rusty nail materialized, and she took a large swallow. It tasted like a brew of gasoline and paint thinner. How had she convinced herself she liked these? But the burning liquid stoked the flame of hatred in her belly, so Nat downed it and ordered another. Next to her, a couple of tourists, middle-aged women from Nebraska in town for a "girls' weekend," drank white wine. They attempted to spark up a conversation with her but soon abandoned their efforts. Nat gave off an aura of drunken hostility.

She was on her fourth drink (fifth if she counted the vodka shot) when she felt the man's gaze upon her. He was at the end of the L-shaped bar, drinking alone. He was in his late thirties, a swarthy, pockmarked face beneath a shaved head. He was unremarkable, except for his light green eyes, and the way they darted away when she looked at him. Like most young women, Nat was accustomed to unwanted attention, to leering looks and lascivious smiles. But this man wasn't flirting with her. If he had been, he would have met her stare. A bristling sensation crawled up the back of her neck. She waved for the bill.

It was after eleven when she stumbled onto the street; too early to go home, but she had to get out of that place, away from the shady man sitting at the end of the bar. Glancing over her shoulder, she ensured he hadn't followed her outside. He hadn't. Perhaps she'd imagined his nefarious interest? Gazing down the street, she weighed her options. There were more bars, more restaurants. She could slip inside, find another stool, order another glass of poison. And then, on the next block, she noticed a velvet rope, a huge bouncer in head-to-toe black. A nightclub.

She hadn't gone dancing since she met Gabe. He was conservative, older, would have been out of place in the hot, hedonistic club scene. But Nat would fit right in. She lurched toward the doorway, eager to lose herself in its cavernous anonymity. The big man standing sentry gave her a quick once-over and unclipped the rope. She paid the twenty-dollar cover and was ushered into the sanctified space.

The club was humid and dark, loud and over-stimulating. It was packed with partiers, though it was Sunday. This crowd didn't hold down nine-to-five jobs. They were students and servers, cooks and creatives. This was where a girl her age should spend her nights, not at jazz clubs or French bistros, not in bed with a man older than her father. These were her peers, her people. Nat pushed her way toward the bar and ordered another vodka shot, and a vodka cooler. Downing the shot, she took the bottle and hurtled to the dance floor.

She was not a huge fan of EDM, but it was working for her tonight. She was losing herself in the frenetic rhythm, melding into the mass of gyrating bodies. She danced for twenty minutes or two hours, she didn't know. There were hands on her waist, but she was okay with it. Many of the clubgoers were high on ecstasy or molly, the drug-induced serotonin surge making them touchy-feely. It was harmless. She brought the bottle to her lips, swallowed the last drops of the sickly sweet beverage.

A woman in a silver shift dress with dark skin and white teeth was dancing with her, smiling at her. Nat smiled back, feeling flattered, warm, wel-come. The woman made her think of Violet, tall and pretty, the desirous look in her eyes. The lights were strobing to the beat, blinding Nat, blurring the faces around her. Only the silver woman and her bright smile were distinguishable. The hands on her waist (were there just two, or were there more?) were roaming now, touching her in places she didn't want to be touched. She drank more, tried to relax, to go with it, but she couldn't. The air was thick with perfume and sweat and suddenly, she couldn't breathe. Panic was pressing down on her chest, the wall of bodies closing in on her, drowning her. And then, a flash of green eyes.

She pushed through the revelers, fleeing the dance floor. She needed to leave, urgently. Where was the door? Her heart was skittering and racing, her lungs screaming for air. She couldn't see, was struggling to walk. She was drunk, too drunk. But something else was wrong, making her tremble and vibrate. Had she been drugged? But why? By whom? Was she the random victim of some club pervert? Or had the man with the green eyes followed her here, targeted her? The faint red glow of the exit sign entered her field of vision, and she lunged toward it, finally, gratefully, bursting out into the night.

The street was quieter now, belying the bedlam behind the double doors. Nat stumbled down Ninth Avenue, away from the club. Her heart continued to flutter, her lungs gulping in the moist night air. The area felt unfamiliar, strange and foggy, like she was viewing it through a greasy lens. Her legs were weakening, and she wouldn't be able to walk much farther. She needed help. She needed Gabe.

She wanted him to come, to wrap his strong arms around her, to tell her she was safe. She wanted to climb into his big town car, wanted Oleg to chauffeur them uptown to Gabe's apartment. There, Gabe would make her tea and tuck her into his comfortable bed. She would call him, and he would rescue her. He had always been there when she needed him. Her small purse dangled from her shoulder, her phone inside it. Her fingers fumbled with the zipper. And then she remembered.

Gabe didn't love her anymore. He had abruptly ended their relationship—without kindness or explanation. He'd faked a reunion, lied to her, manipulated her, even threatened her life. The hatred came rushing back like a tsunami. Despite her muddled brain, her heart muscle remembered.

Fuck him. Fuck Gabe.

She hated him so much she could kill him. If she went home and got her gun, she could find him, and shoot him. She could blow his fucking head off. And she would enjoy it.

A yellow taxi was moving slowly down the street, looking for patrons in need of a ride home. She raised her arm, but the weak appendage would barely move past her shoulder before flopping back down, dead and useless. But the cab had spotted her, was slowing down. She staggered toward it, her limbs as awkward as a baby fawn's. But she made it. She got into the back seat and closed the door behind her.

"Take me to the West Twenties first," she slurred, giving the driver her address. "And then take me uptown."

Blood

Nat woke up in a strange room. But it wasn't a strange room; it was her apartment. It took her a moment to acclimate to the familiar surroundings from an unfamiliar vantage point. She was on the floor in the entryway, still in the cute spring dress she'd put on to meet Gabe. There was a small puddle of sick beside her, and streaks of blood on the hardwood floor. Her hands and her knees smarted. Her head pounded. Her stomach churned.

She tried to stand, but she was weak and dizzy. But she needed to get away from the vomit and the blood, their pungent and metallic scents. Half sitting, she dragged herself on one elbow and one hip, toward the bathroom. There, she turned on the shower, tore the slip of a dress from her sticky body, and climbed into the tub.

The water pelted her huddled form as she sat on the cool porcelain. If she tried to stand, she would fall, but she needed to wash away the filth and grime of the night before. What had happened to her? How had she gotten home? She felt battered and numb; she knew something very bad had taken place the night before. But what? She remembered the fight with Gabe at the end of the High Line, drinks at a bar, a man with green eyes. She remembered stumbling into a nightclub, ordering a drink and then . . . ? And then a frightening void.

Blood was swirling in the water, circling the drain. Her hands and knees were raw and scraped, her chin, too. But there was so much blood. Too much blood. Had she gotten her period? She was too weak to check. Despite the warm water, she was shivering uncontrollably, her head still throbbing. Someone had drugged her, had slipped something into her drink. And then what? A sob shuddered its way out of her throat, a tortured, guttural sound. She had been hurt and abused, and she had no one to help her.

With tremendous effort, she turned off the water and climbed out of the tub. Her hair was matted and wet, unwashed, dripping in her face. She pulled a towel off the rack and patted at her bruised body. She tried to wrap the soft cotton around her slick form, but it required too much coordination and strength. Naked, she dragged herself out of the bathroom.

All she wanted was to reach the bed, to go back to sleep for days, weeks, months. Her purse was tossed on the floor, close to where her inert body had lain, next to the vomit and blood. Inside was her phone, her lifeline. She wanted to call Gabe. Or her mother. Even the police. She wanted to check her text messages to see if Gabe had reached out. She wanted to apologize to him, to make everything better. She wanted to find out who had done this to her and why. But she couldn't. Her inflamed and poisoned body craved sleep above all else.

Crawling up on her bed, naked and wet, she slept.

The Knock

When she woke, it was still light. Or was it light again? She didn't know how long she'd been asleep—a couple of hours? A day? Longer? Her wet hair had dried into an unintentional beehive, her bloody hands and knees had crusted over. Her throat screamed for water, and her bladder was full to bursting. But the pounding in her head had not receded. If anything, it was louder and more tangible. Because it wasn't in her head. It was at her door.

The words became audible then, a female voice.

"New York Police Department. Open up, Ms. Murphy."

Her first instinct was relief: the police knew what had happened to her the other night, were here to get her statement. They would arrest the bastard who had drugged her; they would make him pay for what he had done to her. But how did they know?

"Coming!" she cried, but her parched throat would not cooperate. The pounding continued.

She found her robe in a pile of clothes at the end of her bed and wrapped it around her naked body. Her head was still aching, throbbing in unison with the fist on her door. She had to let them in, had to make the noise stop. Side-stepping the puddle of bodily fluids coagulating in the entryway, she opened the door.

"Natalie Murphy?" It was a woman, in a blazer and pants, sensible shoes. She had dark hair and dark eyes that emanated both strength and weariness. Behind her was a big man, his chubby red face blooming like a rose from a too-tight collar, and a younger man in uniform.

It hurt Nat's throat to articulate the word. "Yes."

"We'd like to talk to you about the death of Gabriel Turnmill."

The words did not compute, Nat's drug-addled brain could not make sense of them. Because Gabe wasn't dead. She had just seen him the day before. Or the day before that. Or was it two days ago? They had argued, yes, but he had stormed off, very much alive. And then she had gone drinking and clubbing and then . . . And then what? What had she done?

She stepped back, tried to shut the door in the cops' faces, but they were faster and stronger. The woman muscled her way inside, the men on her heels. Nat scrambled backward, stepping in the puke and blood, losing her balance, falling to the floor. Her bladder released then, hot urine soaking her robe.

The officers surveyed the apartment, taking in the filth, the chaos, the smell.

"Jesus Christ," the fat guy muttered.

The female detective snapped, "Get dressed." Then she turned to a uniformed officer, said something about a warrant and evidence, but Nat didn't take it in. She was scrambling through the mess for some clothes, tears streaming down her cheeks. This couldn't be real. Gabe couldn't be dead. She couldn't have anything to do with it. It didn't make sense, none of it did. She needed to remember.

The men left the room, allowing Nat to dress. The female cop tossed her a tea towel, and Nat dried the pee off her legs, her humiliation extreme. She pulled on a bra, a pair of sweats, and a T-shirt. The clothes smelled funky, the pants had food on them, pizza sauce by the look of it, but it didn't matter. As Nat dressed, the woman with the dark eyes introduced herself as Detective Correa. Her tone had softened with her colleagues out in the hall.

"I know you're upset, and I know this is scary," she said, "but we'll go to the station and have a little chat. I'm sure we can get this all sorted out."

Nat nodded tearfully, but Gabe was dead. How could they sort that out?

The Tenth Precinct was just a couple of blocks from Nat's apartment. She had strolled by the Italian Renaissance–inspired building so many times, the officers congregating outside its doors nodding hello, wishing her a good night. She'd found them intimidating, attractive, fascinating—big-city cops like in all the TV shows. Despite the proximity, she was put in the back of a squad car. It would have been humiliating to march her through the streets like a criminal. Because she was innocent. She had to be.

Inside the Chelsea station, it was bright and bustling, full of officers in uniform and not. There were other people, too. . . . Attorneys? Or suspects? Or loved ones of the accused? Nat didn't know. How could she know? She'd never been inside a police station in her life, had certainly never been taken in for questioning. But here she was, Detective Correa's proprietary hand on Nat's upper arm, steering her through the desks, toward a destination at the back.

It was almost a relief when the woman led Nat into an airless room and closed the door on the cacophony outside. "Have a seat," she said, indicating a table with a notepad and pen, a paper cup of water. Nat chose the chair against the wall, facing the door. She guzzled the water, soothing her scorched throat but making her stomach churn. When had she last eaten? What day was it? She noticed the one-way glass embedded on the wall as she sat and knew she was being watched, likely recorded. But that was okay because she had nothing to hide. Did she?

"What happened to Gabe?" she blurted, tears filling her eyes. "Is he really . . . dead?"

Correa sat across from her, gave her a maternal smile. "Let's start at the beginning, shall we?" She picked up the pen, slid the notepad closer to her. "Tell me about your relationship with Mr. Turnmill."

"We're friends."

"How did you meet?"

Nat's heart rabbited in her throat. She didn't want to admit the origins of their relationship. It sounded debauched and sleazy, possibly even illegal. The detective sensed her hesitation.

"I know this is rough, Natalie, but we want the same thing here. We want to find out what happened to Gabe. It'll really help us if you're honest."

It was an interrogation tactic, possibly even a trap. But Nat didn't know how to protect herself because she didn't know what she had done. Gabe was dead; she needed to know how, and why. And she wanted to talk to this strong woman with the soft eyes, wanted Detective Correa to help her. She swallowed.

"I met him through a website."

"What's the name of the website?"

Nat told her. The detective jotted it down. "Does this site match up wealthy men with girls who want to make some extra money?"

"Yes."

"So is that the relationship you had with Gabriel Turnmill? Sugar daddy and sugar baby?" She was matter-of-fact, no judgment.

"At first," Nat said. "But then we fell in love."

Correa kept writing, didn't look up. "Did you know he was married?"

"No," Nat said, tears slipping from her eyes. "I found out later."

"That must have made you angry."

Nat was not that naive, not that stupid. "It hurt me," she retorted.

The detective met her eyes, sizing her up. Then she smiled. "Did you know he had a daughter?"

"Yes."

"And did you get to know his daughter?"

It was the intonation of the question that revealed the detective's hand. Correa knew everything. The police had talked to Violet and Celeste. They knew Nat had visited the Sagaponack home, knew she had befriended Violet. They had found Gabe's phone and read the angry missives Nat had sent him, listened to the voice messages where she'd threatened to kill him. They weren't questioning her as a witness; she was a suspect. She was in big trouble.

"I think I need a lawyer."

"Sure," the detective said casually. "One of my colleagues will call a public defender for you." She nodded toward the one-way glass. "I'd like to keep chatting, if you're up for it."

A lawyer would advise Nat to shut up. She knew this from all the Shonda Rhimes shows she'd watched with her mother. But she had to know.

"What happened to Gabe?"

"He was found dead at the bottom of a stairwell on East Eighty-Eighth, early in the morning of May twentieth." The detective's voice was calm, her eyes appraising Nat's every reaction. "He'd been shot once, in the face."

A horrified sob found its way through Nat's clenched lips.

"There was a necklace found on the stairs near the victim's body," Correa said, opening a manila file folder. She slid a photograph toward Nat. "Do you recognize it."

Nat's hand threatened to fly to her throat, but she held it in her lap. She remembered taking the pendant off, putting it in the pocket of her dress before she met Gabe at the High Line. But there it was, in the image before her.

"Your social media accounts show you wearing this necklace."

"I had one like it," Nat said. "There was a break-in at my apartment. Last Saturday. They took the necklace." She was lying to the police now. This wasn't going to end well.

"Did you report it?"

"No. Gabe told me not to."

"Why would he tell you not to?"

"I—I don't know."

"A gun was found wrapped in a woman's T-shirt, in a nearby dumpster. Do you own a gun, Ms. Murphy?"

She couldn't deny it. They were going to get a warrant to search her apartment. If the gun was still there, she'd be caught in a lie. "I got it for protection. I was being harassed by an old boyfriend. Cole Doberinsky. You should find him and talk to him."

Correa jotted down Cole's name.

"Gabe paid to have Cole beaten up," Nat offered. "Cole hates him. He could have killed him."

"We'll talk to Mr. Doberinsky."

"I think it was Cole who broke into my apartment. He probably took the necklace and the gun."

"So you think ballistics will show that your gun killed Gabe Turnmill?"

"No. I—I don't know." She was getting confused; she should stop talking. "But if it does, then Cole probably took it."

"Do you have a permit for the weapon? Did you register it with the state?"

"I got it secondhand. At a pawn shop." The lies were piling up, threatening an avalanche that would bury her, but she wouldn't bring Oleg into this. He had been kind to her, protective of her . . . she owed him.

"Where were you on Monday morning, around one thirty A.M.?"

"At home. I'd been at a club, but someone put something in my drink. I felt sick, so I went home. I'm not sure what time it was. Maybe around midnight."

"Where was the club?"

"Hell's Kitchen."

"Can anyone corroborate that you were at home between one and five A.M.?"

"No. I didn't see anyone."

"A witness saw a woman matching your description on the Upper East Side, not far from the crime scene."

It was impossible. Nat had gone home after the club. Unless she hadn't.

There was a knock at the door, and Correa got up to answer it. Nat could see the fat detective but couldn't hear his muttered words. Her interrogator nodded and returned to Natalie.

"Natalie Murphy. I'm arresting you for the murder of Gabriel Turnmill."

"No." It came out a sob.

"You have the right to remain silent. Anything you say can and will be used against you in a court of law. . . ."

The detective was Mirandizing her, just like on TV. But Nat was not on a detective procedural. This was real. This was happening. But those TV shows had taught her a few things.

"Can I make a phone call?" she said tearfully. "Isn't that my right?"

The detective's eyes softened slightly. "Who do you want to contact?"

Gabe. He was the only person who would know how to get her out of this mess. He was a lawyer; he had money. But Gabe was dead. And the police thought Nat had killed him.

She would have to call her mom, though the news would devastate her. Allana would not be able to help her daughter financially, would not be able to fly across the country to come to her aid. Her mother had Nat's young siblings to care for. But there *was* someone else she could try.

"I'd like to call my dad," she said.

48
. . . . . .

Holding

After Nat spoke to her father, she was "processed." A fresh-faced male officer recorded her biographical details, swabbed her cheek for DNA, and took her photograph. With her hair dried into a crazy helmet, her puffy face, a scrape on her chin, she looked like a lunatic. *Criminally insane.* She had to hand over her phone, her apartment keys, even a receipt she'd found in the pocket of her rumpled sweatpants. Her fingernails were cut and collected, her hands tested for gunshot residue before she was digitally fingerprinted. Not once did the young officer look at her like she was a person. She was simply a project.

After what could have been two, three, or four hours—Nat had lost all sense of time—she was cuffed and taken out to a van. It was dark as she and two other females were led to the vehicle that would shuttle them to central booking. The late hour did not bode well for a short stay. They would have to spend the night, would be arraigned the next day, if they were lucky.

Her dad had said he'd come. Despite their distant and strained relationship, he would help her through this, would not let her go down for a murder she didn't commit.

"Did you do it?" he'd asked her, point-blank.

"No." But her voice had wobbled, relaying her doubt. Because Gabe was dead. And she couldn't remember what she had done that night. But still . . . "I could never kill anyone," she said, as adamantly as she could.

At central booking, Nat and her cohorts were led through a maze of dimly lit, concrete corridors to a windowless holding cell. Outside, it was night, but in there, it was broad daylight. Brighter than broad daylight. Eleven women sat on hard metal benches pressed up against the light green walls. A short partition hid a toilet and a sink that Nat resolved not to use. (The smell emanating from the general area was not inviting.) She and the other recent arrivals were given a sandwich and a carton of milk, and then the heavy bars to their enclosure were slammed shut. A large woman with a tattoo snaking out of her shirt got up from the bench. "Are you going to drink that?"

Nat glanced at her carton of milk. Without hesitation she handed it over.

It was not just the light that kept Nat awake and alert. It was fear of the present and the future;

confusion about the past. She sat on the cold floor, nibbling the bland cheese sandwich, willing herself to remember. What had she done after she left that nightclub? She remembered stumbling toward a cab. And then . . . nothing. Blank. Somehow, she had gotten home, had passed out on her apartment floor. But what had she done in between?

Eventually, her cellmates succumbed to exhaustion, lying on the bench, curling up on the floor—no pillows or blankets were offered. But Nat had been in a heavy, drugged sleep for days. She would not join them, could not relax. The words she had told her father rang in her head: *I could never kill anyone.* It was true. She had never been violent before. But she'd never experienced the intense feelings she had for Gabe. Love and hate were two sides of the same coin. She had been willing to use Gabe's daughter to destroy his family. Was shooting him that much worse?

Without the sun, a watch, or her phone, the only indication she had that it was morning was when the guards arrived with small boxes of cornflakes, more cartons of milk, and bananas. The inmates were not given spoons, so Nat filled her mouth with the crunchy flakes and took a drink of milk. She forced down the banana, though it was bruised and overripe. She didn't know when the next meal would come, undoubtedly another dry sandwich. Still, she had not used the toilet or sink.

Her companions were being taken out, one by one. Nat waited. Hours passed, though she didn't know how many. A sandwich arrived, and she surmised it must be around noon (she had no way of knowing that her breakfast had been served at 4:00 A.M.). Two women came in to mop the cell, but they ignored the filthy bathroom area. Sometime later, a second sandwich, a *dinner* sandwich arrived, and Nat began to panic. How long could they keep her here? If this were a TV program, some ridiculously attractive lawyer would be advocating for her release right now. But this was not TV. Nat had no one to fight for her.

She had just finished her peanut butter and jelly when a guard came to the bars. "Natalie Murphy!" She jumped up, put her hands behind her back as she'd seen her cellmates do, let the stocky guard cuff her. Nat was led back through the concrete maze and deposited in yet another cell. But this one had a small window and no bathroom. That meant a short-term stay. It had only two other women in it. One of them was crying softly; the other sat stoic, hard, jaded. She had been there before.

Nat took a bench. Turning her head, she could see out the window, a glimpse of darkening sky. In the previous dank, windowless cell, she'd felt fear, panic, confusion. But seeing that slash of night brought a painful realization. Outside that window, life was going on as normal. People were living their lives: working, buying groceries, meeting friends for dinner. Nat might never do any of those things again. She might never be free. For the first time since she'd been booked, tears rolled down her cheeks.

A man, small and bird-boned, dwarfed by his gray suit, approached the cell. He had unruly curly hair that he'd attempted to control with heavy product. If not for the silver threads running through his coif, he would have looked about twenty-five. Nat judged him to be in his early forties.

"Natalie Murphy?"

Nat swiped at her tears, hurried toward him. "That's me."

"My name is Matthew Hawley. Your father hired me to represent you."

Her heart swelled. Her dad, who'd abandoned her as a little girl, had come through for her now. A lump of gratitude, perhaps even love, clogged her throat.

"Your father arrived this morning. He's waiting in the courtroom. Your mother is on her way. Your parents believe in you and support you."

Nat had thought she was completely alone. She wasn't. She swiped at a fresh batch of tears.

"You're about to be arraigned for the second-degree murder of Gabriel Turnmill," Matthew Hawley said, unfazed by her emotions. "The DA's case is circumstantial, but from what I can see, the evidence is damaging."

A pain twisted Nat's intestines, and she felt she might throw up. This couldn't be happening. It all felt so surreal. But her whole life, since she'd started seeing Gabe, since he'd abruptly ended it, had felt surreal. This was part of her new, fucked-up reality.

Her lawyer kept talking. "When we go before the judge today, we'll plead not guilty. When I've had time to examine the evidence and do some investigation, we can discuss a defense. If the DA offers a plea, it would be wise to consider it."

"I didn't do it," Nat said, hands gripping the

bars of her cell. "I can't remember the night, but I couldn't kill someone. Especially not Gabe."

But if she could have killed anyone, it would have been Gabe. She'd hated him that much.

A vein twitched in her lawyer's temple. "Let's focus on getting you bail. You'll be called up soon."

Through the bars, Nat watched the diminutive man hurry away.

The Arraignment

Perhaps an hour after Matthew Hawley left her,
a bailiff led Nat into court. The room had high
ceilings and dark wood wainscoting; an intimidating space filled with intimidating people. Not all
of them were there for her. The press occupied
several seats, alert for a sensational case worthy of
their attention. There were numerous lawyers in
suits, waiting for clients. The seating area was filled
with wives and mothers, husbands and fathers—of
the victims and the accused. All were waiting for
the defendants to be brought before the judge.
Many of the women, and a few of the men, were
crying.

Scanning the crowd, Nat found her dad. He had
not changed much during their years of estrangement; a little heavier, the lines around his mouth

more pronounced. Their eyes met, and her own fear and pain reflected back at her. She'd been angry with him for so long, had blamed him for so many of her issues. But now she saw him for what he was: a troubled man, fighting his own demons, trying to do right by his child.

A court officer called her docket number. "The people against Natalie Doris Murphy." The bailiff led her to the center of the room, where Matthew Hawley and his large gray suit joined her. A Korean-American woman, petite and feminine despite her power suit, stood to their right. She didn't look much older than Nat, but she emanated an air of formidable capability. On the bench, looming above them, was the judge, an imposing figure with dark skin juxtaposed against thick white eyebrows. He was completely bald, his pate shiny like it had been buffed and polished. His name plate read: JUDGE GORDON BELL.

Judge Bell briefly scanned the file in front of him before he spoke. His voice was commanding but perfunctory. (Nat knew from television shows that judges like him might process as many as a hundred arraignments per day.)

"The prosecution will bring forward notices."

The tiny woman, evidently the assistant district attorney, moved forward, submitting various papers to the judge, while announcing their corresponding numbers. Matthew Hawley was invited to do the same, and he approached the bench with more forms. Nat stood by, forlorn and confused. She heard her lawyer plead *not guilty* on her behalf, but the rest of the process was a confounding blur of paperwork and legal jargon. When the judge brought up bail, Nat's focus became intense.

"Natalie Murphy is charged with felony murder," the petite prosecutor began. "She has no ties to the community. No job, no property, no family in New York. The people request remand."

The judge allowed Hawley to counter.

"The defendant's father has flown across the country to be in court today, and he's able to post bail. Her mother is on a plane as we speak. The defendant has no criminal history and no warrants against her." He paused, then, his voice softening. "The defendant is a young, naive woman from a small town. This experience has already caused her extreme emotional distress. Sending her to Riker's could cause severe damage to her mental health."

"May I remind the court," the prosecutor sniped, "that this *young, naive woman from a small town* is accused of shooting her sugar daddy in the face."

The spectators burst into scandalized whispers. Matthew Hawley erupted, defending his client against the prejudicial remarks. But Nat couldn't take in any of it. Her ears were ringing, her cheeks burning, the room swimming before her eyes. The charges against her, articulated in such a crude fashion, were so salacious, so degrading, so mortifying. She knew how they would sound to her father, to the judge, to the onlookers. Nat had sold herself to a rich man, and when he no longer wanted her, she had killed him. Her knees shook as shame and self-hatred threatened to overwhelm her.

She felt the judge's heavy gaze on her then. For

the first time, he was looking at her, not as another arraignment to process, but as a person. The mess of a girl trembling before him must have stirred his sympathy. Or perhaps, he just saw how weak, how pathetic, how harmless she was.

"Bail is set at five hundred thousand dollars."

It was an astronomical sum, a faint hope, but it was hope. Nat looked toward her father. He was standing, his expression tense and troubled. Did Andrew Murphy have half a million dollars to secure his daughter's release? Could he afford to get her out of jail and still pay for her defense lawyer? She knew little about her dad's career in Las Vegas, knew nothing of his net worth or finances. But his slight nod, his hint of a smile informed her that he would get her out. For now, at least. Her chin trembled with gratitude and emotion.

The bailiff took her arm and led her back toward the door from whence she'd entered. She would return to the cells until the paperwork was filed, her bail posted. As she approached the door, she turned back to the courtroom, longing to connect with her father's eyes, to ensure he was still there, that he wouldn't walk out on her again. And that's when she spotted them.

Behind the prosecution, three rows back, sat Gabe's wife. She wore a casual dress and no makeup, her face ashen with grief. Her dark eyes on Nat were soft and wet. Celeste was flanked by an older couple, their hands on her, protective and supportive. The resemblance was undeniable: they were Celeste's parents. Violet was not with her mother and grandparents, of course she wasn't. Celeste would not subject her daughter to this ugliness and trauma.

Nat felt a tug at her elbow. With some relief, she let the bailiff escort her back to her cell.

50

. . . . . .

Freedom

By the time Natalie's bail was processed (her father had contracted a bail bondsman who would charge him 15 percent on the half million), her mother had arrived from Blaine. As Nat walked away from the holding cells ("the pens" she heard them called), she spotted her parents waiting anxiously in the bustling corridor. They were talking intently, her father's hand rubbing her mother's arm in a comforting way. It had been years since Nat had seen her parents together. It had been even longer since she had seen them act civilly, even kindly toward each other. When her mom spotted her bedraggled eldest child emerging from captivity, she burst into tears.

"I'm okay, Mom," Nat assured, as her mother held her and wept into Nat's hair. Her dad stood by awkwardly, unsure of his place in their former family unit. Andrew Murphy had been dark and mean, and then he had abandoned them. His desertion had damaged his daughter, contributed to her terrible choices. If Nat wanted, she could hold on to her anger, even blame her dad for her toxic relationship with an older man. But her father had come when she called him. He was there, trying to help her, trying to save her life.

Gently, Nat extricated herself from her mom's embrace and moved to her dad. He opened his arms, and she fell into them, the years of resentment melting away, replaced by unfamiliar sensations: comfort and warmth. Andrew stroked her hair, murmured assurances into her ear. It was there, in her daddy's arms, that Nat fell apart.

Their emotional moment was interrupted by a male voice. "Excuse me?"

Natalie and her parents turned toward the speaker. He was slim, boyishly handsome, holding a small recording device toward Nat's face. "Anything you'd like to say about your involvement in Gabe Turnmill's murder?"

Gabe had been a powerful attorney, New York society, a one-percenter. And he had been a sugar daddy. His murder was a scandal.

"No comment," Nat's dad snapped. The small family hurried from the courthouse.

The conditions of Natalie's bail included surrendering her passport, wearing a monitored ankle bracelet to ensure she did not leave the court's jurisdiction or approach Gabe's family, and house arrest between the hours of 8:00 P.M. and 8:00 A.M. Her mom would stay with her in the studio apartment; her dad was renting a cheap—at least by New York standards—hotel room in Midtown. When a taxi dropped them off in Chelsea, Nat unlocked the front door (her keys had been returned to her, but her phone was now evidence) and ushered her mom into the building.

"For God's sake," Allana muttered, when they entered the small suite, "did the police really need to tear the place apart?"

Nat didn't admit that the state of her apartment had more to do with her own slovenly habits than the police's search for evidence. The vomit and blood were still on the floor, dried to a putrid crust. The air was fetid and close, but still an improvement from the atmosphere in the basement cell Nat had so recently occupied.

Allana opened the window and let the night filter into the studio. Even though it was after 11:00 P.M., her mom set about cleaning the apartment, while Nat went to shower. She wasn't sure when she had last slept (shock and exhaustion had muddled her thoughts, messed with her perception of time), but she needed to rinse away the filth and stink of the holding cells first. The hot water softened the scabs on her knees and hands, allowing blood to ooze from the wounds. She watched it run down her shins and swirl down the drain. And then, a flash of remembrance.

She saw Gabe's face, pale and terrified. He was saying something inaudible, pleading for his life probably. And then a bang, a gunshot, rang through her head, rattled her brain. She staggered in the shower, gripping the edge of the tub before she collapsed. Her memory was returning, and it was horrifying. She didn't want to remember murdering the man she'd loved.

When she got out of the shower, she found her mom putting clean sheets on the bed. She turned as Nat entered in her towel. "Are you okay? You're pale and you're shaking."

She couldn't tell her mom the image that had revisited her. "I'm just tired."

"You need to sleep. Do you want to eat something first?"

Nat shook her head, suddenly overcome by exhaustion. Tears brimmed in her eyes, and a ragged sob shuddered through her chest. Her mom took control, finding a nightie in the overstuffed dresser drawers and pulling it over Nat's head. She helped her daughter climb into the fresh sheets, still smelling of lavender-scented laundry soap despite weeks in the closet. Allana kissed Nat's cheeks, like she had done when Nat was a little girl.

"You sleep," her mom said gently. "I'm here."

It was two or three hours later when Natalie awoke drenched in sweat, disoriented and panicked. It took her a moment to distinguish her surroundings, to remember that she was home, for now. The apartment was dark except for the light slipping from under the bathroom door. Her mom was in there, talking softly on the phone. She must have called home to chat with Derek, to check on Astrid and Oliver. Allana was still on Pacific time. It was not as late for her. Quietly, Nat got up to change her soaked nightie, her mom's voice just audible in the still space.

"She's doing okay, all things considered," her mom said. There was a long silence, followed by a muffled response that Nat couldn't make out. And then: "I don't know, Derek. But she's my daughter. I'll stand by her no matter what."

Natalie pulled a cool, dry T-shirt over her head as she absorbed her mom's words. Her own mother thought she was capable of murder. Had Allana seen a darkness in her even when she was a little girl? Was there something in her childhood that had foreshadowed her ability to take a life? Or was it only now, since Nat had moved to New York, since she had sold her body to a rich man, that the evil act seemed within her bailiwick?

And yet, Allana was here. She had left her young children to support her eldest. And Nat's dad was here, too. She crawled into bed, exhaustion softening her angst. Soon, she had fallen back to sleep.

The weekend passed in an anxious, monotonous blur. Nat's mom had visited New York only once before, when she was a teen, so Nat played tour guide. But there was no joy in it. The city that had once had her so enamored, now felt cold and harsh. Her dad joined them on a few outings, but it was tense and forced. After the weekend, he flew back to Vegas.

"I've got some business to take care of," he told her, "and then I'll come back."

Nat nodded, but her ingrained mistrust of her father's word was hard to overcome. Even if Andrew didn't return, *never* returned, he had done enough. He had bailed her out of jail; he had hired her a defense attorney; he was paying her legal bills. Andrew Murphy had been her dad when she needed him to be.

And Nat was a murderer. She had no right to ask for more.

51
. . . . . .

The Lawyers

Natalie and her mom met with Matthew Hawley at his office in Midtown. The lawyer had offered to come to them, but assuming his hourly rate, they didn't want him to incur travel time. Nat and Allana took the subway uptown to the intimidating tower that housed the Blacklock Law Firm. A polished receptionist led them into a meeting room, where they were soon joined by Mr. Hawley. In his rumpled suit two sizes too big for his slight frame, the attorney stood in stark contrast to his cold, sleek environment. Accompanying him were two attractive associates—a white female, a black male—who fit the decor so precisely they seemed almost ornamental.

They took seats around a custom concrete conference table. Hawley pulled out a moleskin journal and a pen while his colleagues set up laptops. "Start at the beginning," he urged Nat, his smile avuncular. "You can be honest in this room."

Nat was glad of her lawyer's accessible nature. Ignoring his intimidating sidekicks, she told Hawley about her relationship with Gabe, how she'd met him through the sugar website, how their relationship had morphed into something meaningful. "We loved each other," she assured her attorney, and vicariously, his two associates and her mother. "It was real, before it all went wrong."

She recounted Gabe's abrupt breakup, her shock, pain, and confusion. Nat explained how she'd followed Violet Turnmill to the Met, how the girl had quickly developed a crush on her, how Nat had accepted the invitation to her graduation pool party. "I shouldn't have gone," she admitted, "but I just wanted to see Gabe. To talk to him."

Hawley met her eyes. "Did Gabe's wife and daughter have any idea about your relationship with their husband and father?"

"No," Nat answered truthfully. "They were completely clueless." She heard her mother exhale heavily. Her daughter's moral lapses were a source of disappointment. Or was it disgust?

Finally, Nat told her defense counsel about her walk with Gabe on the High Line, about their horrible fight on Thirty-Fourth Street, how she'd clawed his wrist, his blood and skin getting under her nails. She relayed her visit to the saloon/sports bar, the creepy man with the green eyes who had scared her out of there, how she'd ended up at a club.

"Someone must have roofied me or something. I

remember walking out onto the street and then . . . that's it." She omitted the flash of memory in the shower: Gabe's frightened face, his desperate plea, the sound of the gunshot. "It's all a blank until I woke up on the floor of my apartment."

The typing stopped. The pen was set down on the table. Matthew Hawley leaned back in his chair.

"We've submitted our demand to produce to the prosecution. When they hand over discovery, we'll review it, do some investigations of our own, and strategize a defense."

Nat's mom spoke in a tight voice. "How long will all this take?"

"The prosecutor has six months to indict."

"Six months?" Allana could not mask her panic. Six months away from her job, her husband, her young children. Six months of sleeping on Nat's hard sofa, of wandering around an inhospitable city, of supporting a daughter who had killed a man.

"We can negotiate pre-indictment," Hawley assured her. "Often, an expeditious plea bargain is the best course of action."

A *plea bargain*.

Nat didn't know what that meant, exactly, but she was too afraid to ask.

Discovery

So Natalie and her mother waited. Days and then weeks passed. On occasion, a photographer would snap Nat's photo as she and her mom went to buy coffees or groceries, but otherwise, they were left alone. Nat's mom and Derek paid the rent on the studio for another month. Allana's calls home became tense and fraught. "Yes, I know I have three children, Derek. But only one of them is fighting for her life right now." Nat could feel the strain she was causing her mother's marriage through the closed bathroom door.

Her father called regularly. He spoke to Nat and to her mom. Her parents agreed that Andrew would relieve Allana for four days, so she could go home to her family—her *good* family, not her screwed-up disaster family in New York. Sharing the small space with her dad was awkward, intense, but ultimately therapeutic. And getting to know her father again proved a good distraction from the fact that she'd been charged with murder. But her alleged crime was always there, hanging over all of them.

And then, just over three weeks after their initial meeting at the law firm, Natalie and Allana were summoned again. In a different boardroom, with the same decorative associates, Hawley began his spiel.

"We've gone through the prosecution's discovery, and we now have the details of their case against you."

Nat heard her mother's intake of breath, felt her grip Nat's hand.

Matthew opened the file on the concrete table, began to read from it. "Ballistics tests confirm that the nine-millimeter Beretta they found near the scene is the murder weapon. Your prints are on it, and it was wrapped in a T-shirt they've established to be yours through DNA and hair samples."

Fuck.

"A necklace belonging to you was found at the scene. A witness saw a young woman matching your description in the vicinity, the night of the murder. The bartender at the sports bar remembers you, but no one at the nightclub can verify you were there. We've checked with the cab companies but none of the drivers can recall taking you home. Unfortunately, you have no alibi for the time of the murder."

Allana's hand was crushing Nat's, their palms getting sweaty and clammy. But Nat couldn't let go.

She felt she was holding on to her mother for dear life. If Allana released her, Nat would drift away, fall, tumble into a deep, dark void from which she would never return.

Hawley wasn't done. "Phone records show hundreds of calls and texts to Gabe Turnmill's phone." He looked up from the file briefly. "You threatened to kill him several times."

"I was upset," tears of fear, regret, and hopelessness, welled up in Nat's eyes. "I didn't mean it."

"We have a few things on our side." The man's prominent nose was back in the file. "The witness who saw you on the Upper East Side is a shut-in in his eighties, probably not reliable. There was no GSR on your hands, and we can explain Turnmill's DNA under your fingernails due to the fight you had near the High Line." He looked up at her then. "And the rookie cop who found your T-shirt with the gun thought it was covered in blood. Turns out, it was cranberry juice."

"What?"

"The lab tested it. The red stains were from cranberry juice."

Nat's pulse hammered so loudly in her ears that she could barely hear her own words. "It's the wrong shirt," she said. "I kept the gun wrapped in a plain white T-shirt, hidden in a shoe box. The juice stains came from Violet's graduation party. Her girlfriend was jealous. She threw a drink at me."

No one spoke, but their eyes relayed their confusion.

Nat tried to remain calm as she recounted the day of the pool party. After Fern had doused Nat with her drink, Gabe had taken her upstairs where she had removed her wet top and donned a shirt of Violet's. (She left out the fact that she and Gabe had been about to have sex in Violet's room when the younger girl entered, professed her romantic feelings, and kissed Nat on the lips.) Nat explained that Gabe had put her wet shirt and bikini top into a plastic bag. She recalled him handing it to her before he drove her to catch the bus back to the city.

"I distinctly remember the logo on the bag," she said. "It was from a specialty deli. It had an over-flowing cornucopia on it."

Hawley said, "So how did this T-shirt end up in an Upper East Side dumpster with the murder weapon?"

"When I got back to the city, I went to a bar," she said excitedly. "Maybe I left the stained shirt there? Or I could have left it on the subway on the way home."

"And, someone found it and planted it at the crime scene?" The attorney's tone was understandably skeptical.

"No. . . ." Nat was flustered. "Maybe I took the shirt home and it got lost in the clutter? Someone broke into my apartment. He could have taken the shirt and planted it at the scene."

"But you didn't report the break-in to police."

"No, because nothing was taken." She glanced sheepishly at her mom. Nat had already admitted that she'd fabricated the laptop theft.

The female attorney looked up from her papers. "You told Detective Correa that your pendant was stolen during the break-in."

"I—I was confused," Nat stammered, her face burning. "But there was a footprint on my bed. A bigger shoe than mine. The police must have photographed it."

"There's nothing in the reports about a break-in or a strange footprint," the male associate contributed.

Her mom added, "I changed Natalie's sheets when I first arrived. I didn't notice a footprint on the soiled ones when I took them to the laundry."

Panic gripped her. The window of hope was closing. "Did anyone talk to Cole Doberinsky? He was here. He was stalking me."

The sleek blond lawyer looked at her file. "Cole Doberinsky was located in Portland, Oregon," she said. "He has a solid alibi for the time of the murder."

But someone *had* been in her apartment. Nat had been distraught, drinking heavily, but she had not fantasized the break-in to get Gabe's attention. The footprint was not simply a figment of her imagination. Was it?

The female associate continued. "Mr. Doberinsky says you arranged to have him badly beaten, leaving him with permanent damage to his right eye. He also submitted a Facebook message into evidence. You threatened to kill him."

They didn't believe her. And she couldn't blame them. It all sounded so far-fetched, a desperate grab at innocence. She'd told so many lies, kept so many secrets . . . she didn't know what was true anymore. And suddenly, she realized it didn't matter what was true. It only mattered if she could prove it.

Her rumpled lawyer articulated her concerns. "It would be extremely difficult to make a case that you were framed, Natalie."

No one spoke for a moment, but she clocked the glances exchanged between her legal team and her mother. Then Matthew Hawley's watery brown eyes found hers.

"The prosecution has offered a plea deal, and we advise you to accept."

"What kind of plea deal?" Her mom asked.

"We can waive the indictment and plead guilty by way of superior court information. The DA won't budge on second-degree murder. This case has caught the media's attention, and prosecutors don't like to go easy on defendants when the public is watching. But the DA is open to sentence bargaining." Hawley turned his attention from Allana to Nat.

"We'll get you as little time behind bars as possible, Natalie. With your clean record and the dysfunctional nature of your relationship with the victim, I think we can get you five years in custody, the remainder served on probation."

Blood rushed through her ears, her vision blurred. She couldn't spend five years of her life in jail. She wouldn't survive it. Through the fog, she heard her mother's shrill voice. "Five years? She's just a kid!"

"If we took this to trial, she could get fifteen to life," Hawley said. "Natalie has motive. She has no alibi. And the circumstantial evidence is damning."

It was. Even as laymen, Nat and her mother could see that.

"And we don't like your chances with a jury. The

fact that you were in a paid, sexual relationship with the victim casts you in a negative light. The jury, especially the women, will consider you a person of low moral character."

"That doesn't mean she's a murderer," Allana said, her indignation colored by doubt. Would a jury be able to distinguish between a girl who would sleep with an older man for money and one who would kill him when it all turned sour?

"You'll have to allocute," Hawley continued. "That means you'll plead guilty to second-degree murder in front of the judge, the press, and Gabriel Turnmill's loved ones."

A bubble of sick rose into Nat's throat. She would have to admit to murder. In front of her parents, the media, Gabe's wife, maybe even his daughter. Please, not Violet. It would be too perverse. "Go home and think about it," Hawley instructed, gathering his files. "Give us a call when you've made a decision."

"We'll sleep on it," Allana said as they all stood. But it was a platitude only. Everyone in the room knew that Nat would accept the deal.

She had no choice.

53

• • • • • •

The Revelation

They slept in the same bed that night, Natalie and her mom, cuddled together like they had when Nat was little, after her father had left. It was nostalgic and comforting and Nat was able to sleep, despite the decision hanging over her. She woke in the wee hours of the morning to her mom's muffled sobs, Allana's body shaking with contained emotion. Her mother was crying with loss and, possibly, relief. Her daughter would spend five years behind bars. But Allana would get her life back.

In the morning, they rose, showered, and dressed, neither of them mentioning the call they would soon make. The call that would have Natalie stand before a judge and confess to a murder she couldn't be sure she committed. A call that would send her to prison.

"Shall I get us coffees?" Allana offered.

"I'll come with you." Buying a coffee at the corner deli would soon be a freedom Nat could not enjoy. She was slipping into her shoes when her cell phone rang. It was her lawyer.

"I need to see you," he said, his tone clipped and agitated. "It's urgent."

Forgoing the caffeine, Natalie and her mom rode the subway to Midtown. They were hustled into another conference room where they were soon joined by Hawley and his attractive team.

"Some new evidence has come to light." The unkempt lawyer was businesslike, but his cohorts looked almost gleeful. "It changes things."

"What is it?" Nat asked, her throat dry, voice scratchy.

"Gabe Turnmill had hired someone to kill you."

"Oh my god!" It was her mom's voice. Nat was mute with shock. A tornado of emotions whirled inside her: confusion, hatred, and anger—at Gabe and at herself. Gabe Turnmill had wanted her dead. He had never loved her. She had meant nothing to him. She'd been so stupid.

"Mr. Turnmill's personal driver has come forward." Matthew looked at his journal, "A Mr. Oleg Ryback."

Oleg. He had liked Natalie. He had been kind to her, hadn't judged her, understood her even.

"According to Mr. Ryback, Gabriel Turnmill asked him to arrange a hit on you."

A professional hit. So cold, so cowardly.

"The driver set up a meeting between Mr. Turnmill and Ryback's cousin." The lawyer's eyes were on his notes. "Five thousand dollars was exchanged. Ryback's cousin had no intention of harming you, but Mr. Ryback felt he had to play along or Mr. Turnmill would hire someone else to do the job."

Oleg had protected her.

Hawley looked up. "As I said, this changes things."

Nat's voice was little more than a croak. "How?"

"In light of this evidence, the DA has offered a new deal. Second-degree manslaughter. She'll recommend two years in jail, five years probation, with mandatory psychological counseling."

When Nat was first arrested, she'd been locked up for less than two days. It had been hell. Could she survive two years? But it was better than five.

"You'll still have to allocute. And you'll still have a criminal record, which could have long-lasting repercussions."

Her mom asked, "What kind of repercussions?"

The handsome male associate elaborated. "It can make it hard to get a job, or go back to school, or qualify for housing."

"My god," Allana muttered.

"There is another option . . . ," Matthew Hawley said. "We could go to trial. With this new information, we might have a chance at an acquittal on the grounds of self-defense."

Nat felt her heart lighten in her chest. It was hope, that fleeting, ephemeral feeling.

"We'd have to prove you knew your life was in imminent danger when you shot Gabe Turnmill. I know you have no memory of that night, but we might be able to build a case for it."

Might.

"But if the jury doesn't buy it, you'll be convicted of second-degree murder. That means a minimum of fifteen years."

No one spoke for a moment, allowing Nat to process the information. If she went to trial and won, she'd be a free woman. She could pick up where her life had left off—with school and friends and dreams for the future—before Gabe Turnmill destroyed everything. Or she could start over, do something completely new, in a new city where no one knew her sordid history.

But if she lost, she'd be behind bars until she was nearly forty.

Her attorney continued. "The prosecution will come down hard on you at trial. Your paid arrangement with the deceased will be dragged into court."

"There will be a lot more media interest, too," the female associate added. "You and your family will be put under the microscope."

"And trials take time," Hawley continued. "They take money. We'll need months to build a case. It could be a year until we go to court. It could be more."

The strangled noise that came from Allana's throat was barely audible, but Nat heard it. And she sensed her mother's inner turmoil. Her mom would be weighing her daughter's chances of acquittal against the damage her long absence would do to her marriage, her young children, her bank account.

Nat couldn't make her mother put her life on hold any longer. It was too selfish, too damaging for her young siblings. She couldn't take any more of her father's money. Because the revelation that

Gabe had hired someone to kill her had clarified things. Gabe had hated her enough to want her dead, and she him. They had loved and loathed each other with the same ferocious passion. Despite the stained T-shirt she couldn't explain, despite her clouded memory, she knew that she was capable of shooting Gabe in the face. And she knew that he deserved it.

"I'll take the deal," she said. "I'll confess to manslaughter."

The Return

When Celeste first heard that her husband's murderer had accepted a plea deal, she was in France. She and Violet had flown to Nice to visit Celeste's sister. After a few days there, they'd moved to an old, stone house in a medieval mountain village in the Alpes Maritimes. It was less than a two-hour winding drive from the Côte d'Azur, but they rarely returned to the bustling tourist area. They stayed in their cliffside community, shopping at the weekend farmers' market, where they bought ripe tomatoes and oily tapenade and chewy *fougasse*. Celeste cooked for them, simple, wholesome comfort food. They read, swam in the nearby river, napped, and talked.

Violet had been despondent when they'd first arrived. Her father's death, in such a gruesome, violent manner, was distressing. Learning about Gabe's affair with Natalie, the girl Violet had fallen for, was disgusting. Celeste's only child was struggling to process Gabe's murder *and* his betrayal. It would take time. But Celeste was confident that—with love, support and therapy—her daughter would be okay.

The ADA had called Celeste's cell phone, interrupting an idyllic afternoon of rosé and cards with Violet. The defense had learned that Gabe had hired someone to kill his sugar baby. Celeste's husband was not only adulterous and duplicitous; he was capable of murder to cover his tracks. With this new information, the prosecution felt that amending the plea deal was the safest choice. Natalie Murphy would plead guilty to second-degree manslaughter.

If the case had gone to trial, Celeste knew it would have turned into a media frenzy. "The Sugar Daddy Murder," they'd have called it, splashing the gory and salacious details across websites, newspapers, even television shows. Violet already knew that her father had been shot down in the street, that the woman he'd paid to be his girlfriend had been charged with the crime, that the very same girlfriend had been fostering a relationship with Violet. But there would be more . . . intimate, personal, *sexual* details that would tear her daughter apart. The plea deal was a relief.

Celeste was tempted to stay away permanently, to hide away with her daughter and forget about their life in America. But now, she was on a plane bound for JFK. Her husband's killer was going to be sentenced, and Celeste had to be there. In two days, she would stand up in court and she would read her victim-impact statement. She knew the power that crime victims held in sentencing hearings. The DA could recommend a punishment, but it was ultimately up to the judge to impose a prison term. If Celeste's words were powerful enough, her pain well articulated, she could influence what happened to Natalie Murphy.

Judge Amanda Wollner was presiding over the case. Celeste knew the petite septuagenarian professionally from her time serving the court. Wollner was tough, a feminist. Celeste wasn't sure how that lens might color the judge's view of Natalie Murphy, if it would impact the judge's sentencing decision. But Celeste was a passionate and convincing orator. She'd had to be, as defense counsel for the racially profiled, the unjustly accused. Her words would affect the punishment doled out to Gabe's murderer. She was sure of it.

Celeste had been loath to leave Violet alone as she traveled. Luckily, her sister, Claudette, and her brother-in-law, Pierre, had offered to stay with Violet in the old stone house. Celeste's daughter would be doted on, fussed over; she didn't need to worry about her. And this trip to New York would allow Celeste to handle some financial issues and meet with a real estate agent. She was going to sell Gabe's city apartment. Though her husband had been murdered blocks from his Upper East Side pied-à-terre, the place had an evil, toxic energy. Had Gabe entertained Natalie there? Made love to her in the bed Celeste sometimes shared with him? How many other women—*girls*—had he serviced in that apartment? She'd keep the farmhouse, for now. It had been a happy home for Celeste and her daughter, punctuated by her husband's tense weekend visits. If Violet wanted to start over, somewhere else, they would . . . France or Switzerland or back to Quebec. They could go west, to California or British Columbia. They could move to Iceland or Denmark. Celeste would go to the ends of the earth to heal her daughter.

The pilot's voice came over the PA system. "We're beginning our descent into JFK," he said. "Expect some turbulence."

Celeste did. She fastened her seat belt.

The Sentence

Natalie stood before the judge, a dark-haired woman of about seventy with sharp, aquiline features. Judge Wollner was tiny but imposing as she asked Nat to confirm that she understood the nature of her guilty plea, that she freely admitted to committing manslaughter, thus causing the death of Gabriel William Turnmill.

"Yes," Nat replied, in a voice that sounded unfamiliar and faraway.

"And are you currently under the influence of any substance that would affect your ability to enter this plea?" the petite magistrate continued.

Nat responded, "I'm not." But she felt high, disconnected from her body. It was not she who was standing in the crowded courtroom, admitting to murdering Gabe. It was another girl, a stranger, who would soon learn if the judge would accept the sentence recommendation, if she would spend the next two years behind bars for killing her lover.

"And are you entering this plea after full consultation with your attorney?"

"I am."

"You may be seated, Ms. Murphy."

Obediently, Nat returned to her seat next to her lawyer. Hawley gave her a slight nod of approval. Her job was done. Now, she just had to sit and wait as Hawley and the prosecutor addressed the judge, discussing their sentence recommendations in legal terms. A presentence report was submitted by the parole officer who had interviewed Natalie, a heavyset, jowly man who'd asked her about her family, her work history, her emotional well-being, her use of alcohol.

And then the judge made an announcement. "I will now invite victim-impact statements."

Natalie's stomach lurched. This was the moment she'd been dreading above all others. Gabe's loved ones would stand up and vilify her for what she had done. They would articulate their horror, pain, and loss. It was their right. Natalie would have to sit there and take it, while regret and self-loathing withered her soul.

When she'd entered the courtroom, Nat had briefly scanned the spectators, spotting her parents seated together, their faces pale, expressions grim. On the opposite side of the aisle, she had clocked Celeste. Gabe's wife was seated alone; no parents, no Violet, no friends to comfort her. But she didn't appear tearful and distressed this time. She looked calm, aloof, determined.

It was Violet's statement that Nat had truly feared. She was haunted by the memory of their flirtatious banter, the girl's adoring eyes on her, that sweet, tentative kiss . . . She regretted that fledgling relationship almost as much as she did the relationship with Gabe. It had been cruel and wrong to toy with the girl's emotions, to use her to upset Gabe. Natalie deserved whatever vitriol was aimed at her now.

But the girl's mother would speak for her. Celeste was moving toward the microphone mounted on the podium, so calm, so composed. She would not subject her only child to this painful process. The woman had been an attorney. Her words would be carefully chosen, thoughtful, impactful. Nat didn't look at Gabe's wife; she kept her eyes on the table before her.

"Thank you for coming today," the judge said, her tone distinctly warmer than it had been when addressing Nat or her counsel. "Please state your name for the court."

"My name is Celeste Bernier." She spelled it for the court reporter.

The judge said, "You may read your statement, when you're ready."

Celeste began.

"On May twentieth, I lost my husband of twenty-nine years, and my daughter lost her father. Our lives will not be the same without him, and we may never fully recover from the violence that was perpetrated on our family. Gabe Turnmill was my partner, my provider, my coparent. But I now believe he was also a sociopath."

Nat's head jerked up. Had she heard Celeste correctly?

"The man I married twenty-nine years ago ceased to exist. I'm not sure when or why, but at some point, Gabriel Turnmill stopped being a loving husband, a caring father, and a kind, honest man. He became adulterous, duplicitous, and cruel."

Incredulous murmurs rippled through the courtroom. Nat didn't move, didn't turn her head, barely breathed. If she did, reality might come crashing into this dream.

"My husband paid Natalie Murphy a significant allowance for a romantic and sexual relationship. He made her believe that he was single and available; that he truly cared for her. And then, he abruptly cut her off: physically, emotionally, and financially.

"When Ms. Murphy learned about her lover's betrayal, I don't believe she had the emotional or mental maturity to handle it appropriately. She lashed out in a childish, obsessive manner. She became a nuisance, a threat to Gabe Turnmill's reputation, his relationship with his daughter, and, indeed, our marriage. So my husband hired someone to kill her. But it was he who ended up dead."

Celeste paused then—for breath or effect—then continued.

"I don't know Natalie Murphy, but she appears to be insecure, naive, and emotionally fragile. I suspect a personality disorder and alcohol abuse. While I abhor violence in any form, and do not condone her actions, I feel that Ms. Murphy's greatest crime was falling in love with a manipulative, narcissistic man thirty years her senior. In a way, she is a victim here, too."

Natalie's emotions churned: shame, incredulity, and a glimmer of optimism. Celeste was trying to save her.

"My daughter and I do not believe that Ms. Murphy should be incarcerated for her actions. We feel that justice would be better served by offering this defendant the psychological counseling and support she needs, so she can heal and go on to be a functional, contributing member of society."

The tall, confident woman folded her papers and then leaned into the microphone. "I thank the court for its time."

And with that, Celeste left the room.

56
• • • • • •

The Gift

Natalie Murphy was sentenced to a year in jail plus three years of probation, during which she would be prohibited from drinking alcohol and receive mandatory weekly psychological counseling. Despite the recommendations of the prosecution and parole board, Judge Amanda Wollner suspended the sentence. This meant that Nat was free. If she followed the rules and stayed out of trouble, she would remain so.

Her probation had been transferred to Blaine, allowing Natalie to live with her mom, Derek, Astrid, and Ollie. The town that had once felt so stifling and confining was now her refuge. But in a way, Nat was still imprisoned—by gossip and judgment; shame and ridicule. She endured the sneers and whispers . . . even the abuse (Cole's cousin, a girl of seventeen, had spat in her face at the grocery store). Nat could handle a lot now. And being the town pariah was far preferable to actual jail time.

Nat's "job," as it were, was to look after her younger siblings. Her legal battle had been costly for both her parents. While her dad had paid Matthew Hawley's bills, her mom had spent money on flights, on groceries in New York, had missed months of work. Free childcare was a way for Natalie to attempt to repay her mom and Derek for their steadfast support. Besides, it would be virtually impossible for Nat to find regular employment in a town that knew who she was and what she had done.

She was enjoying bonding with Astrid and Oliver. Nat no longer resented their blond perfection; she loved their purity, their innocence. They adored their big sister unconditionally; even if they had known what she had done, it would not have impacted their affections. Each morning, Nat got up and made them breakfast. (Astrid favored cereal, while Ollie was partial to cheese toast.) After she dropped them off at school, Nat spent her days cleaning, grocery shopping, or meeting with her parole officer or psychiatrist. She would collect her charges after school and shuttle them to their various activities. When she got home, she'd start dinner so that her mom and Derek could return from work to a cooked meal. After the first tense weeks, even Derek seemed to appreciate Nat's contribution to the running of their household.

Natalie had not sketched or painted since she'd returned to Blaine. Her dreams of an art career now seemed foolish, pie in the sky. After what she'd endured, she wanted simpler things from her life . . . peace, serenity, security. One day, she hoped to get a job, something low-stress, even monotonous. With a criminal record, the most she could hope for would be some sort of manual labor, factory work, or cleaning perhaps. She might pick up a brush again at some point, but her creativity had been squelched by the ugliness, hatred, and violence she'd experienced.

Other than her court-appointed visits, Nat's days were largely solitary. Her dad had made two visits to see her in the nine months since her release. Their relationship was solid now, resentment of his past abandonment nullified by gratitude for his recent support. But the friends she'd so readily ditched after high school weren't about to welcome her with open arms upon her disgraced return. Abbey had come to visit her a couple of times, but their reunions had been awkward. Her old pal couldn't relate to the things Nat had done, the person she'd become. Even Cole Doberinsky, once so obsessed, would not come near her now.

But today would not be another day spent on her own. Today, she was having a visitor. An important one. Gabe's widow, Celeste, had contacted Nat through e-mail. The woman had been spending a few days at a meditation retreat on Galiano Island, would be flying home via Sea-Tac. Celeste wanted to stop in to see Natalie en route to the airport. Nat was nervous, unsure what the encounter would bring about. But she couldn't deny the woman's request. Nat had already taken so much from her. And Celeste had secured Nat's freedom.

"Should I stay home from work?" her mom asked, when Nat told her about the rendezvous.

"No," Nat assured her. "It'll be fine." But her confidence was forced. She had no idea why Celeste wanted to see her, what she would say. All Nat knew was that she'd have to take it.

The woman was arriving at 9:30 A.M., allowing Natalie time to drop her younger brother and sister at school and come home to get ready. She changed out of her uniform of sweats into a pair of dark jeans and a striped blouse. It was as formal as she got these days. Boiling the kettle, she made tea in her maternal grandmother's pot, set out the matching milk jug and sugar bowl. As the tea steeped, she sat down to await Celeste's arrival.

A rental car pulled into the driveway at precisely 9:33. Nat watched from the window as Celeste emerged from the silver Toyota Camry. She was wearing a short trench with a belted waist to protect her from the April drizzle, yoga pants and running shoes. Her presence was calm, even Zen, in contrast to Nat's own tense affect. The older woman must have come directly from her meditation retreat.

Natalie opened the door before her visitor could knock.

"Hi," Nat said. Should they shake hands? Hug? Nat had slept with this woman's husband, had admitted to killing him. But Celeste had kept Nat out of prison. What was the etiquette?

"Thanks for seeing me." Gabe's widow was cool, composed.

"Of course." Nat ushered her inside. "Can I take your coat?"

"I can't stay," Celeste said, eyeing the tea set on the table. "I just wanted to see how you're doing."

"I'm fine. Everything's . . . fine."

"Are you seeing your psychiatrist?"

"Every week. I think it's helping. I'm on a low-dose antidepressant, too. Just to take the edge off."

"I'm glad." But she didn't smile. "Are you working?"

"I'm babysitting my little brother and sister. It's a way to repay my family. I've put them through a lot."

Celeste nodded in agreement, her eyes darting around the house once more. Nat could sense that the woman had gotten what she came for, was eager to leave. But Nat had more to say.

"Thank you for what you said in court," she said quickly. "It kept me out of jail."

"I meant what I said," the older woman responded. "Gabe used you. He lied to you, and he hurt you. Like he did to so many of us."

Nat had to ask. "How's Violet?"

Celeste's expression hardened. "This has been hard on her, but she's starting to heal. She's been spending a lot of time in Europe. She's trying to move forward."

"I-I'm sorry," Nat said, unable to articulate what she'd done with Violet: befriending her, flirting with her, kissing her.

"I can forgive you for your relationship with my husband," Celeste retorted, "but I'll never forgive you for going after my daughter."

Tears clouded Nat's vision. "I hate myself for everything I've done to you and to Violet." Shame and self-loathing clogged her throat, making her voice hoarse and froggy. "I lost my way. I did horrible things, things I never thought I could do."

Celeste said nothing, just watched as Nat groveled and sniveled. Her dark eyes were blank, unreadable. Did she hate Nat? Pity her? Both?

"I—I don't remember pulling the trigger." A sob shuddered through Nat's chest. "I knew I wasn't a good person, but I didn't think I was a *murderer*."

She was falling apart now, blubbering like a toddler. Nat was ashamed of her lack of composure but was powerless to contain her emotions. And still, Celeste stood, cool and impassive, observing Nat's emotional breakdown.

And then, the woman's hand shot out and grabbed Natalie's. It felt smooth and cool and strong.

"You're not a murderer."

She squeezed Nat's fingers hard and then she left. Nat couldn't move, couldn't speak, couldn't breathe. All she could do was stand in the doorway and watch Gabe's widow walk calmly through the cool spring rain to her car. Nat stood mute and still as Violet's mother backed out of the driveway and sped off. Back to New York. Or Europe. Back to her daughter. When the car was out of sight, Nat finally, gently, closed the door.

She moved to the kitchen table on legs rubbery with shock and disbelief. Spots swam before her eyes, making her grope blindly for a chair. Lowering herself into it, she reached for the teapot, but her hands were trembling, rattling the delicate china so hard she feared it would break. She set the pot back down, pressed her hands to her sides.

You're not a murderer.

But Nat remembered Gabe's bloodless face pleading for his life. She recalled the loud bang of the gun. And she had hated him. God, how she'd hated him. Enough to kill him. But . . . what if she hadn't? What if the images in her mind weren't memories, but simply . . . fantasies?

And yet, Gabe was dead. Someone had killed him. If not Nat, then who? Who else had hated him enough to take his life? And who had hated Nat enough to send her down for his murder? Celeste was a lawyer. She would know how to frame someone. But was the striking matriarch capable of killing her husband? Of planting evidence at the scene? How would Celeste have gotten Nat's gun? Her T-shirt? Her necklace? And why, if Celeste wanted Nat to pay for Gabe's murder, had she stood up for Nat in court?

You're not a murderer.

The shock was wearing off now, realization seeping into Nat's consciousness. She hadn't done it. At the center of her being, she'd known that she wasn't capable of murder. And now, Celeste had verified it. Nat should have been angry, outraged even. She should have called Matthew Hawley and professed her innocence. But Nat had given up her right to an appeal when she'd accepted the plea deal. She could have phoned her mom at work, her dad in Vegas. She could have taken out an ad in the local paper, rented a billboard, screamed it from the rooftops. She was innocent! And yet, Nat sat, strangely, eerily still. Because who would believe her? And who would care? She was still a sugar baby with a dead sugar daddy.

Nat may have been disgraced, humiliated, labeled a killer, but she was not in jail. She was free. And Gabe was dead. Nat had not killed him, but she'd wanted to. Just because she hadn't pulled the trigger herself, didn't mean she hadn't yearned for the bastard's demise with every fiber of her being. Gabe had hurt, manipulated, and betrayed one too many people. And that person had killed him. It didn't matter who it was.

With a steadier hand, she was able to pour herself a cup of tea, add milk and sugar. She took a sip of the sweet, creamy concoction, felt it warm her throat, her chest, her belly. But it was not just the liquid that was heating her from within. It was the knowledge of her innocence. Despite her horrible choices and moral foibles, she had not committed murder. Nat was not a killer. Even if she and Gabe's wife were the only two people who knew it.

A giddy bubble of mirth tickled her chest. It was not quite joy but a jubilant sort of relief. Nat could forgive herself now. She could go on to rebuild her life; she could allow herself to be happy. One day, she would draw and paint again; her creativity had permission to return. Celeste Bernier had come to Blaine, and she had given Nat that gift.

She sipped more tea and listened to the soft spring rain tap against the windowpanes.

The Truth

When Celeste landed at JFK it was after 9:00 P.M., her evening evaporating due to the three-hour time change. Oleg was waiting for her in the town car. He gave her a quick hug of greeting, put her bags in the trunk, then navigated the big vehicle away from the frenetic airport. After they exchanged small talk about her trip, the traffic, the weather, Celeste lay her head back against the leather seat, tired from her cross-country journey. The meditation retreat, led by a guru she'd been following for some time, had been calming and centering. But all her Zen had flown out the window as soon as she'd arrived in Blaine, Washington. The meeting with Natalie Murphy had been edifying, but it had not gone as planned.

Celeste hadn't expected to tell the girl the truth

about Gabe's murder. And she hadn't, not really. But she'd had to say something to assuage Natalie's guilt. The young woman had looked so shattered, so pathetic. Remorse over what she'd done was gnawing away at the girl's confidence and vitality. Her tearful outburst had twisted Celeste's innards, provoking a distinctly maternal response. The words were out before she could censor them.

You're not a murderer.

What did Natalie Murphy think? It didn't matter. Celeste knew the young woman had no legal recourse. She'd forfeited her right to appeal when she'd taken the plea deal. Natalie would logically suppose that it was Celeste who had shot Gabe. He'd lied to and betrayed his wife—just like he had Natalie. And he'd been doing it to Celeste for years. She had an abundance of reasons to want him dead.

The first inkling Celeste had had that her husband was a lying, cheating, duplicitous bastard was about seven years ago. A pretty blond paralegal had brought a brief to their Hamptons house. Gabe had tried to brush it off as an overzealous colleague eager to please, but Celeste knew there was more to it. She read it in her husband's panic, in the woman's desperate expression, in their tense but familiar body language.

She'd planned to confront Gabe when Violet was away at her summer wilderness camp. (Her daughter couldn't know about her father's indiscretions, her parents' marital discord. She'd already shown signs of rebellious behavior.) Celeste would give Gabe an ultimatum: fidelity or divorce. She wanted the marriage to work—they shared a history, they had a child together—but she would not be a cuckold. Gabe would deny the affair; her husband's significant ego would prevent him falling on his sword. But she'd suggest counseling, where they could discuss the distance between them, get their relationship back on track.

And then Celeste had gotten sick, and all her energy and focus had gone into surviving. She had assumed that her husband would stop his philandering in the face of his wife's diagnosis. And Gabe had, for a time. But when Celeste went into remission, his affairs had resumed. It was Suze Weintraub who'd elucidated Celeste's fears when she invited her for coffee.

"I hate to be the bearer of bad news," Suze said, after pleasantries and chit chat, "but Michael and I were at a show the other night. We saw Gabe there."

Celeste nodded. She knew what was coming.

"He was sitting with a young woman—a pretty brunette, barely out of her teens. They were *together* . . . whispering in each other's ears, holding hands, I saw them kiss."

The coffee turned to acid in Celeste's stomach, burning her chest and her throat.

"Michael and I bumped into him in the lobby at intermission. He played it cool, but I know what I saw. I even took a photo."

The svelte woman passed her phone to Celeste for perusal. In profile, Celeste saw a dark-haired girl, barely older than Violet, with fair skin and delicate features. She was staring adoringly at Gabe, who looked handsome, confident, and happy basking in the girl's obvious veneration. She could see the sparkle in his blue eyes.

Thanking Suze for her frankness, Celeste had handed the device back, hurried to the restroom, and vomited.

Oleg's deep voice floated through the darkened car, disrupting her reverie. "There's an accident on the parkway," he said. "I'll take Sunrise Highway."

"Whatever you think is best," Celeste said. "You know I trust you."

His eyes in the rearview mirror smiled back at her.

Oleg and Celeste had become friends about four years ago, when he'd shuttled her home from a charity dinner. She'd been in remission by then but hadn't quite regained her previous stamina. Gabe had wanted to stay late, drinking Scotch and schmoozing, so he'd summoned his driver to take Celeste back to the apartment. Oleg was from Moldova, a country Celeste had studied in an Eastern European history class during college. They'd had a lively discourse about his homeland's complicated past. When they reached the Upper East Side apartment, she found she wanted to continue their conversation.

She was afforded the opportunity less than a month later, when Celeste needed a ride back to the Hamptons after a luncheon. Gabe had agreed to spare his driver for the five-hour round trip. Their Moldova discussion had segued into Oleg's recently immigrated cousin's legal dilemma. The man had been arrested after a fight outside a nightclub (where he'd been defending a female patron's honor, according to Oleg) and was at risk of being deported. Celeste had offered her expert advice, had even called an old colleague who was still practicing to represent Oleg's relative. The cousin, a man with a stocky build and startling green eyes, had had the charges dropped, in the end.

Oleg owed her. And he was her friend. She could count on him to verify Suze Weintraub's claims. They met in Battery Park and walked the Hudson River Greenway. It pained the big European to tell Celeste about the women her husband had been seeing. The dark-haired Natalie was the latest of many. Gabe had provided his most recent paramour with a Chelsea apartment, a trip to Vermont, and monthly envelopes stuffed with cash.

The money, the apartment, the gifts were more upsetting than the infidelity. *Sugar daddy*. People could dress it up in flowery language, but Gabe was a john. And he had turned this girl, this Natalie, into a prostitute.

The marriage was over; it had to be. But Celeste was smart enough to know that she was in a vulnerable position. When she left Gabe, she would damage his enormous ego and he would strike back. Her husband could be cruel, ruthless . . . a shark. Celeste no longer had her own income, and she had a daughter to protect. She would consult an attorney, would get her financial ducks in a row first. In the meantime, she needed Gabe to stop seeing that girl, to stop paying Natalie for sex and companionship. She needed him to stop making a fool of Celeste, and their marriage, and their life.

Using Violet's self-harm had felt exploitive,

but she could think of no other way to have Gabe cease his affair. (She had kept the cutting from him, knowing he'd blow up, knowing he'd seize control, knowing he would make it worse.) But Violet was his kryptonite. While his narcissism prevented true parental love, he viewed his child as a reflection of himself. If she was depressed, unstable, hurting herself, it made Gabe look bad.

And it had worked. Oleg had confirmed that he'd driven the sniveling Natalie home after she'd been unceremoniously dumped over a pasta lunch in the financial district. Gabe had come home then, had tried to connect with his daughter, but Violet was skeptical after his years of emotional abandonment. She wasn't about to jump into her daddy's welcoming arms.

And then, Natalie Murphy had turned up at Violet's graduation party.

Celeste had recognized her instantly, but it had taken her longer to work out the reason for the girl's presence in their home. But Violet's flirtatious giggles and smitten expression soon made it clear. Natalie had fostered a relationship with Violet to get to Gabe. The girl was sick, obsessed, a stalker. She was a problem, and Celeste did not know how to handle her.

Fern had done what Celeste could not. She'd thrown a drink in Natalie's face and called her a whore. It was as if Fern knew the truth when she couldn't have. Gabe had whisked his dripping lover away, and Celeste had shuttled Fern home, her mind spinning, reeling, racing. It was a miracle they hadn't crashed. When she returned, the party guests had been dispatched. Gabe was still delivering his girlfriend to the bus. Violet was alone.

"You can't date that girl," Celeste said, her voice wavering. "Promise me you won't."

"Why not?"

"You just can't."

"You sound like a dictator. You sound like dad."

Celeste had been close to tears when she spat: "I am nothing like your father."

Somehow, it had come out. In her desperation to keep Violet away from the toxic, troubled Natalie, Celeste had told her daughter about her father's affair. Violet's face, when she learned the truth, still haunted Celeste; the pain, the hate and betrayal twisting her innocent features. If Celeste could do it all over again, she would not have told Violet. She would not have let her daughter run to her car and race into the city. But Celeste couldn't have known what would happen.

She couldn't have known that Violet would drive directly to Natalie's apartment, prepared to confront her. When Natalie didn't answer the buzzer, didn't respond to Violet's text, the athletic girl had shimmied up the fire escape and climbed through the studio's window. She had been looking for validation that her mother's accusations were true, and she found it. There, on Natalie's pillow, Violet saw her father's tie. It was a William Morris design, purchased from the Metropolitan Museum of Art's gift shop by Violet, when she was sixteen. It had been a Father's Day gift, lovingly selected. And he had left it at his lover's apartment like it meant nothing.

Celeste could not have known that this evidence

would send her daughter into a spiral of booze, drugs, and rage. She could never have guessed that Violet would reconnect with her old friends that night, the spoiled entitled kids who had round-the-clock parties with alcohol and cocaine and hand-guns tossed casually into drawers. Violet had gone on a bender, drinking and doing drugs, not sleeping for more than twenty-four hours. And then, the next night, still high, messed-up, and angry, she had texted her father.

Hey. R U at the apartment?

So breezy, so casual. Gabe had responded.

I'm at a jazz club on 89th. What's up?
Nothing. Staying with friends tonite. Might come by tomorrow.
OK

The conversation had raised no red flags when the police examined Gabe's phone. With the multitude of venomous missives from Natalie, Gabe's daughter just "checking in" had seemed innocuous. But it was the call that woke Celeste from a fitful sleep at 1:13 A.M., that was damning.

"Mom . . ." Her daughter's voice was small, trembling, broken. "I've done something terrible."

Somehow, Celeste had remained calm, instructing her daughter to return to her friend's party, to wipe down the gun she had liberated from a bedside table, and put it back. She'd told Violet to take a shower, to try to get some sleep, to act like everything was normal. The revelers were all wasted; they didn't keep track of the guests' comings and goings. Violet could slip seamlessly back into the debauchery, her alibi set. And then, Celeste formulated her plan.

The weight of the memory pressed on her chest and she took a deep breath. Oleg, alerted by the sound, met her eyes in the rearview mirror.

"You okay?"

"I'm fine," she said, smiling at her friend, her confidant, her accomplice. "Thank you."

Framing Natalie Murphy for Gabe Turnmill's murder had seemed the best solution. As a former defense attorney, Celeste knew the system, knew how investigations worked. With Natalie's harassing calls and threats on Gabe's phone, she would be the logical suspect. But Celeste also knew that physical evidence would need to be planted, and it would take her over two hours to reach the scene of the crime. So she had called the only person she could trust, the only person who might be able to help her.

She hadn't been sure that Oleg would cooperate; he seemed to pity Nat as a troubled, small-town girl caught up in a rich man's web. But Celeste had convinced him. Natalie was sick, unstable, and, according to Oleg, armed. She needed help—medication, therapy, and lots of it. She would get it while incarcerated. And Violet had to be protected. She was an innocent child driven to commit a horrific crime by her father's unforgivable behavior. Celeste could live without her husband; but she would not survive without her daughter.

The fact that Gabe had asked Oleg to arrange a hit on Natalie Murphy (God, Celeste's husband had *no* scruples) proved an unexpected advantage. Oleg had introduced Gabe to a "handler of problems," a "hit man." It was his cousin Max, the man with the light green eyes, the man who had beaten Cole Doberinsky at Gabe's behest. Max had never intended to hurt Natalie. In fact, he had been following her that night to ensure her safety. Gabe wanted the girl dead, and Oleg wanted her protected. Max had trailed Nat to a bar and then to a nightclub. When he'd gotten the call from his cousin, he'd known what to do.

Max had arranged to have a sedative slipped into Natalie's drink. The girl was already heavily intoxicated. She would be comatose by the time she reached her Chelsea apartment. Max had followed her there, had played the concerned boyfriend for the indifferent cabbie's sake. She had fallen out of the back seat, skinning her knees, hands, and chin. He'd picked Natalie up, retrieved her keys from her purse and helped the girl inside. She'd come to, slurring belligerently, but he'd gotten her inside, unceremoniously dumping her in the entryway. The pendant had conveniently fallen from her pocket, so he scooped it up. Then he rummaged through drawers, cupboards, and closets until he found the gun. Then he had left, caught the subway uptown to meet his cousin at the scene of the crime.

Oleg had told Celeste to stay in the Hamptons to avoid incriminating herself, but she couldn't. Her daughter had just shot her husband in the face. She couldn't pop an Ambien and go back to sleep like everything was normal. Gabe had been shot outside a parking garage at Eighty-Eighth and Lex. Oleg had agreed to conceal the corpse in a stairwell, buying her some time. Celeste had hurriedly dressed, slipped out to her car, and driven through the night. She had to see Gabe's lifeless body to believe he was dead. And she had to collect Violet, to take her home, sober her up, and coach her through what would come next.

Celeste met Oleg and Max on East Eighty-Eighth Street, where her spouse lay in a crumpled heap at the bottom of the concrete stairwell. She didn't need to see the damage the bullet had done to Gabe's handsome features to know he was deceased. Her powerful, vigorous, arrogant husband was reduced to a pile of skin and bone, a bloody, lifeless rag doll. It was discombobulating to see a man, once so confident and robust, now so . . . dead.

Max had tossed Natalie's pendant (ironically, a goodbye gift from Gabe) onto the body in the alcove. And then, he'd prepared to hide Nat's gun.

"Wait," Celeste had said. "I have something."

The T-shirt. She'd found it on the passenger seat floor of her husband's Mercedes that Sunday morning. It was in a plastic bag from Celeste's favorite specialty food shop. She'd grabbed it, afraid Gabe had forgotten some groceries in the car that might spoil. But it was Natalie's red stained shirt and tiny bikini top. She'd put them in the trunk of her car (she hadn't wanted Gabe to use them as an excuse to see Natalie again). Celeste had planned to dump the garments in a public trash can, but now, she was grateful she hadn't. Retrieving the bag from her car, she handed the spattered shirt to Max. He wrapped Natalie's gun in it and dropped the items into a nearby dumpster.

The gun had been the greatest obstacle Celeste had had to contend with. Gabe had been killed by a nine-millimeter Glock. Natalie's pistol was a Beretta. Luckily, Celeste had a friend in the NYPD crime lab. Manny Dosanjh was the firearms examiner. The two had grown close when Celeste was a public defender, having lunch on occasion, even after-work drinks. Manny would have taken it further, had Celeste ever given him an opening, but she hadn't. She'd been loyal to Gabe. Blindly loyal.

Manny had never liked Gabe, had always found him superior and condescending. Even at their recent dinner party, he'd muttered, "You still deserve better," when Celeste had hugged him goodbye.

She knew that now.

It had been a huge favor to ask, but she'd asked it. Manny, assuming it was Celeste who had pulled the trigger, whose life and freedom were at stake, had complied. He had doctored his report to say that Gabe had been killed by a nine-millimeter Beretta, the same gun owned by Natalie Murphy. The sugar baby would go down for her daddy's murder. It was just. It was karma.

But Celeste's anger at Natalie Murphy had dissipated—time, distance, and guilt softening the hate, blurring its edges. When Oleg had made a stopover in France (Celeste had bought the driver and his cousin plane tickets to Europe; it was the least she could do), they'd spent several evenings talking over wine, soft cheese, and crusty bread. Oleg, so kind, so good-hearted, had conveyed Nat's troubled childhood, her lack of a father figure, her alcohol abuse. So Celeste had flown back to New York and made her victim-impact statement. She'd set the girl free.

And now, she had given Natalie the ultimate gift. The knowledge of her innocence.

Oleg cleared his throat and then spoke. "How long will you stay, Celeste?"

"I'm not sure," she replied honestly.

"Will Violet be joining you?"

"No. She's studying. She's applying to the Université Paris Descartes for the fall semester."

"She's doing so much better. I'm glad to hear it."

"Me, too." Her daughter's progress had given Celeste a new lease on life. She leaned forward then. "You don't have to drive back tonight, do you?" Her pulse quickened, and she felt suddenly shy. "It's so late. We could have a drink. And I have so many spare rooms. . . ."

She didn't want to be alone in the big farmhouse she'd shared with her husband and daughter, where they'd pretended to be perfect, happy, normal. And she wanted to spend more time with Oleg, to explore the intense bond they shared. The big man had been there for her like no one ever had. Could a romance blossom from a murder cover-up? From shared secrets and lies? She wasn't sure, but she wanted to find out. And that made her hopeful.

Gabe Turnmill had damaged them all: Celeste, Violet, and Natalie. But he had not destroyed them.

"I can stay," Oleg said, meeting her eyes in the mirror.

"Great." She smiled back. "I'm happy."

And, in that moment, despite it all, she was.

Acknowledgments

I have long been fascinated by sugar arrangements. I'd see young women out with much older men and wonder about the dynamics of their relationships. I remember being young and broke. How easy was it for these girls to slip into this lifestyle? How did it make them feel? And what were the myriad ways it could go wrong? I decided to write a novel about this world. I read articles and interviews. I watched some reality programs. Armed with this cursory knowledge, I began to write.

A few weeks later, I had dinner with Felicia Quon and Nita Pronovost of Simon & Schuster Canada. They encouraged me to set up an online account on a sugar dating site, and to interview some real sugar babies. I was nervous, shy, downright terrified . . . but I did it. And the insights I gleaned were invaluable! I learned who gets into the sugar bowl and why. What they gain from it, and what they lose. I learned about the genuine side, the dark side, the kinky side. About the money and the lingo (salty and Splenda). Thank you to the sugar babies who were so open and honest with me. Thank you, Felicia and Nita, for pushing me to go deeper, and making this book much more authentic.

Also, huge and heartfelt thanks to my passionate, cool, and wise editor, Jackie Cantor. To the inimitable Jennifer Bergstrom and her incredible team at Scout Press: Meagan Harris, Aimée Bell, Sara Quaranta, Jennifer Long, Liz Psaltis, Abby Zidle, Diana Velasquez, and all the salespeople, designers, and everyone behind the scenes.

To my always supportive agent, Joe Veltre, and Tori Eskue, Hannah Vaughn and the team at Gersh.

To the powerhouse team at S&S Canada: Nita, FQ, Catherine Whiteside, Adria Iwasutiak, Rita Silva, Rebecca Snodden, Sarah St. Pierre, Mackenzie Croft, Kevin Hanson and company.

To Kirsty Noffke, Fiona Henderson, Michelle Swainson, Anthea Bariamis, and everyone at Simon & Schuster Australia, and the team at Simon & Schuster UK.

To my friend Shawn Felker. Thank you for all the New York intel! You answered all my questioning phone calls and responded to all my confused texts. You have toured me around New York on numerous occasions, and without you, I wouldn't love it so much.

To all the librarians and booksellers, to all the bloggers, bookstagrammers, and Facebook book groups who do so much to spread the word about books. To name but a few: @Gareindeedreads,

@Jenny_Oregan, @thepagesinbetween, @the_reading_beauty, @jordys.book.club, @Shereadswithcats, @read_read_repeat, @girlwellread, @one.chapteratatime, @givemeallthebooks, @Jennieshaw, @scaredstraightreads, @the_grateful_read @morethanthepages, @agalandherbook, @thegreeneyedreader, @brettlikesbooks, @fully.booked, @book.happy, @outofthebex, @reading.between.wines, @bibliotaph_bean, @deebibliophilia, @erinreadit, @booksandchinooks, @novelteahappyme, @jessicamap, @booksandlala, @jprglisa, @readingbetweenthe_wies, @readingwithsam, @downtogetthefiction, @sweet_books_o_mine, @lifeinlit, @wherethereadergrows, @offtheshelfofficial, @Libbeylazarus, @my_novelsque_life, @beauty_andthebook_, @drink.read.repeat @bookwormmommyof3, @Cindy Bokma, @readwithdogs, @booksonthebookshelf, @lalalifebookclub, @wrenn_bongo_and_books @kate rocklitchick, @cluesandreviews, @nerdoutwithmybookout, @nerdoutwithmybookout, @meet_me_at_the_library, @jenspageturners.

Also: A Novel Bee, Bookworms Anonymous, Chick Lit Central, Bitter Is the New Book Club, BluePoint Press, The Book Whisperer, Linda's Book Obsession, Suzy Approved Book Reviews, The Book Whisperer, Frean Bean's Book Trove, The Girly Book Club . . .

If I failed to mention you by name, please know that I still appreciate you!

To my author friends: We have such a kind and supportive community, and I'm so grateful for all the connections I've made.

To my friends and family, who continue to support me by buying my books, spreading the word, shouting me out on social media, and coming to my launch parties (or even hosting them in the case of Amanda Ross and Neal McLennan!). You are all so appreciated.

To John, Ethan, Tegan, and Ozzie. All my love.

the
arrangement

ROBYN HARDING

Introduction

· · · · · ·

Natalie, a young art student in New York City, is struggling to pay her bills when her friend makes a suggestion: Why not go online and find a sugar daddy—a wealthy, older man who will pay her for dates, and even give her a monthly allowance? Lots of girls do it, Nat learns. All that's required is to look pretty and hang on his every word. Sexual favors are optional.

Though more than thirty years her senior, Gabe, a handsome corporate finance attorney, seems like the perfect candidate, and within a month, they are madly in love. At least, Nat is. . . . Gabe already has a family, whom he has no intention of leaving.

So when he abruptly ends things, Nat can't let go. She begins drinking heavily and stalking him: watching him at work, spying on his wife, even befriending his daughter, who is not much younger than she is. But Gabe's not about to let his sugar baby destroy his perfect life. What was supposed to be a mutually beneficial arrangement devolves into a nightmare of deception, obsession, and, when a body is found near Gabe's posh Upper East Side apartment, murder.

Topics and Questions for Discussion

· · · · · ·

1. When Ava first admits she is a sugar baby, Nat is shocked and slightly appalled, but she ultimately changes her mind. Why do you think it was so easy for her to be swayed? How does she justify her decision? Would her rationale persuade you or even convince you into joining the Sugar Bowl?

2. Nat is quick to avoid a relationship with Miguel and quick to pursue one with Gabe. Why do you think that is? Compare and contrast Miguel and Gabe and what they can offer Nat.

3. Nat has a complicated life back in Washington. How do her experiences there inform the decisions she makes in New York? Do you think she would have turned to the sugar baby lifestyle if she had a more "traditional" upbringing? Why or why not?

4. How does Cole's story foreshadow what happens between Nat and Gabe?

5. When Oleg gives Nat the gun, she feels like she might finally be able to protect herself and stop being a victim. Discuss how this is an ironic notion.

6. Gabe's perfectly compartmentalized life starts to unravel as soon as he begins to lose control with Nat. How does this loss

of power, which he has never experienced before, impact the decisions he makes with Nat and with his family?

7. Describe Nat's relationship with Violet. Do you think her affection for Violet was real? Why or why not?

8. When Nat becomes a threat to Gabe, he turns to violence as a way out. What other options did he have? Why do you think he acted the way he did?

9. Had Gabe not ended up murdered, do you think he would have ultimately left Celeste for another woman, or do you think he would have quit being a sugar daddy after such a tumultuous relationship with Nat? Do you think Celeste would have ultimately left Gabe if not for Violet's actions?

10. Nat believed she had committed a crime. Why? Do you think she would be capable of killing Gabe? If presented with the same evidence as Nat, would you think you were capable of murder?

11. Describe Nat's change of heart at the end of the book. How do her feelings about her family change? How do her feelings about herself change?

12. Why does Celeste decide to visit Nat in Washington? Do you think she made the right decision? Would you have done the same in her place?

Enhance Your Book Club

. . . . . .

1. Like Nat, most college students take on a job to help cover their expenses while in school. Discuss the working experiences you had once you were no longer supported by your parents. What were your motivations for taking these jobs? Would you have ever considered being a sugar baby?

2. Nat's time as a sugar baby was a pivotal turning point in her life. As a group, share difficult situations you faced as young adults. How did you bounce back and grow? If you could take back these experiences, would you? Or have they positively shaped who you are today?

3. Both Nat and Celeste find some closure at the end of the book. Discuss what you think happens next for these women. Do you think they will be able to put Gabe's death behind them? Do you think they will keep in touch?

4. Invite Robyn Harding to join your book club discussion through her website, www.robyn harding.com, or have each member write one or two questions to send to the author.